WHO IS SHE, REALLY?

Today is my birthday. I was born seventeen years ago today, but I'm the only one who knows.

Goose bumps trail on my arms. I know the date of my *real* birthday, not the one assigned at the hospital when my identity was changed, my past stolen.

My birthday? I probe the concept, but there is nothing else. No cake, no parties or presents; the fact of the date is all there is. Memories that should go with it do not. Yet I sense there is more inside me, more I might find and learn if I probe around.

Some of my recovered memories are like cold facts. As if I've read a file about myself and remember certain bits of it and not others. There is no feeling in it.

I know from the missing children's website that I was Lucy, that I disappeared when I was ten, but I can't remember anything of that life. Then somehow I reappear in my teens with Nico. It is only from then on that memories are stealing back; there is nothing from before.

Nico is the one who might have answers. All I have to do is tell him I remember who he is. But do I really want to know?

OTHER BOOKS YOU MAY ENJOY

As I Wake	Elizabeth Scott
Black City	Elizabeth Richards
Champion	Marie Lu
Crossed	Ally Condie
If I Stay	Gayle Forman
Incarceron	Catherine Fisher
Legend	Marie Lu
The Madness Underneath	Maureen Johnson
Matched	Ally Condie
The Name of the Star	Maureen Johnson
Phoenix	Elizabeth Richards
Prodigy	Marie Lu
Reached	Ally Condie
Shattered	Teri Terry
Slated	Teri Terry
Where She Went	Gayle Forman

FRACTURED

TERI TERRY

speak

An Imprint of Penguin Group (USA)

SPEAK
Published by the Penguin Group
Penguin Group (USA) LLC
375 Hudson Street
New York, New York 10014

USA * Canada * UK * Ireland * Australia
New Zealand * India * South Africa * China

penguin.com
A Penguin Random House Company

First published in the United States of America by Nancy Paulsen Books,
an imprint of Penguin Young Readers Group, 2013
Published by Speak, an imprint of Penguin Group (USA) LLC, 2014

THE LIBRARY OF CONGRESS HAS CATALOGED THE NANCY PAULSEN BOOKS EDITION AS FOLLOWS:
Terry, Teri. Fractured / Teri Terry.
p. cm.—(Slated trilogy ; 2)
Summary: Although Kyla has recovered some of her memories, she is not sure how they all fit
together, whether she was really a terrorist, or why she is able to remember anything at all from
before she was "slated"—but she is determined to find the answers.
1. Memory—Juvenile fiction. 2. Identity (Psychology)—Juvenile fiction. 3. Terrorism—Juvenile
fiction. 4. Dystopias—Juvenile fiction. 5. High schools—Juvenile fiction. 6. England—Juvenile
fiction. [1. Memory—Fiction. 2. Identity—Fiction. 3. Terrorism—Fiction. 4. High schools—
Fiction. 5. Schools—Fiction. 6. England—Fiction. 7. Science fiction.] I. Title.
PZ7.T21815Fr 2013   823.92—dc23   2012044317

Speak ISBN 978-0-14-242504-6

Printed in the United States of America

3 5 7 9 10 8 6 4 2

In memory of my dad

1

Rain has many uses.

Holly and beech trees like those around me need it to live and grow.

It washes away tracks, obscures footprints. Makes trails harder to follow, and that is a good thing today.

But most of all, it washes blood from my skin, my clothes. I stand, shivering, as the heavens open. Hold out my hands and arms, rub them again and again in the freezing rain, traces of scarlet long gone from my skin but I can't stop. Red still stains my mind. That will take longer to cleanse, but I remember how, now. Memories can be parceled up, wrapped in fear and denial, and locked behind a wall. Brick walls, like Wayne built.

Is he dead? Is he dying? I shake, and not just from the cold. Did I leave him suffering? Should I go back, see if I can help him. No matter what he is, or what he has done, does he deserve to lie there alone and in pain?

But if anyone finds out what I've done, I'm finished. I'm not supposed to be able to hurt anyone. Even though Wayne attacked me and all I did was defend myself. Slateds are unable to commit acts of violence, yet I did; Slateds are unable to remember any of their pasts, yet I do. The Lorders would take me. Probably they'd want to dissect my brain to find out what went wrong, why my Levo failed to control my actions. Maybe they'd do it while I still lived.

No one must ever know. I should have made sure he was dead, but it is too late now. I can't risk going back. *You couldn't do it then; what makes you think you can now?* A voice that mocks, inside.

Numbness spreads through skin, into muscle, bone. So cold. I lean against a tree, knees bending, sinking to the ground. Wanting to stop. Just stop, not move. Not think or feel or hurt, ever again.

Until the Lorders come.

Run!

I get up. My feet stumble into a walk, then a jog, and finally they fly through the trees to the path, along the fields. To the road, where a white van marks the place Wayne disappeared, BEST BUILDERS painted down the side. I panic that someone will see me coming out of the woods here, by his van, the place they will eventually look when his absence is noted. But the road is empty under an angry sky, raindrops pounding so hard against the tarmac, they bounce back up again as I run.

Rain. It has some other use, some other meaning, but it trickles and runs through my mind like rivulets down my body. It is gone.

The door opens before I get to it: A worried Mum pulls me inside.

She mustn't know. Just hours ago I wouldn't have been able to hide my feelings; I didn't know how. I school my face, take the panic out of my eyes. Blank like a Slated should be.

"Kyla, you're soaked." A warm hand on my cheek. Concerned eyes. "Are your levels all right?" she says, grabbing my wrist to see my Levo, and I look at it with interest. I should be low, even dangerously so. But things have changed.

6.3. It thinks I'm happy. Huh!

• • •

In the bath I get sent to have, I try again. To think. The water is steaming hot and I ease in, still numb. Still shaking. As the heat begins to soothe my body, my mind is a jumbled mess.

What happened?

Everything before Wayne seems hazy, like looking through smudged glass. As if watching a different person, one who looks the same outside: Kyla, five foot nothing, green eyes, blond hair. Slated. A little different than most, maybe, a bit more aware and with some control issues, but I *was* Slated: Lorders wiped my mind as punishment for crimes I can no longer remember. My memories and past should be gone forever. So what happened?

This afternoon, I went for a walk. That's it. I wanted to think about Ben. Waves of fresh pain roll through with his name, worse than before, so much so that I almost cry out.

Focus. Then what happened?

That lowlife, Wayne: He followed me into the woods. I force myself to think of what he did, what he tried to do, his hands grabbing at me, and the fear and rage rise up again. Somehow he made me angry, so full of insane fury that I lashed out without thought. And something inside *changed.* Shifted, fell, realigned. His bloody body flashes in my mind, and I flinch: I did *that*? Somehow, a Slated—me—was violent. And it wasn't just that: I could remember things, feelings and images from my past. From before I was Slated. Impossible!

Not impossible. It happened.

Now I'm not just Kyla, the name given me at the hospital when I was Slated, less than a year ago. I am something—someone—else. And I'm not sure I like it.

Rat-a-tat-tat!

I half spin out of the bath, sloshing water on the floor.

"Kyla, is everything all right?"

The door. Someone—Mum—just knocked on the door. That is all. I force my fists to relax.

Calm down.

"Fine," I manage to say.

"You'll turn into a prune if you stay in there any longer. Dinner is ready."

Downstairs, along with Mum, are my sister, Amy, and her boyfriend, Jazz. Amy: Slated and assigned to this family like me, but different in so many ways. Always sunny, full of life and chatter, tall, her skin a warm chocolate where I am small, quiet, a pale shadow. And Jazz is a natural, not Slated. Quite sensible apart from when he stares at gorgeous Amy all moonily. That Dad is away is a relief. I can do without his careful eyes tonight, measuring, assessing, making sure no foot is put wrong.

Sunday roast.

Talk of Amy's coursework, Jazz's new camera. Amy babbles excitedly about getting asked to work after school at the local doctor's office where she interned.

Mum glances at me. "We'll see," she says. And I see something else: She doesn't want me alone after school.

"I don't need a babysitter," I say, though unsure as I say it if it's true.

Gradually the evening fades into night, and I go upstairs. Brush my teeth and stare in the mirror. Green eyes stare back, wide and familiar, but seeing things they didn't before.

Ordinary things, but nothing is ordinary.

● ● ●

Sharp pain in my ankle insists I stop running, demands it. Pursuit is faint in the distance, but soon will be closer. He won't rest.

Hide!

I dive through trees and splash along a freezing creek to cover my steps. Then crawl on my belly deep under brambles, ignoring pulls on my hair, clothes. Sudden pain as one catches my arm.

I must not be found. Not again.

I scrabble at the ground, pulling leaves, cold and rotting, from the forest floor over my arms and legs. Light sweeps through the trees above: I freeze. It drops, lower, right over my hiding place. I only start breathing again when it continues beyond without pause.

Footsteps now. They get closer, then carry on, faint and farther away until they disappear from hearing.

Now, wait. I count out an hour; stiff, damp, cold. With every scurrying creature, every branch moving in the breeze, I start in fright. But the more minutes tick past, the more I start to believe. This time, I might succeed.

The sky is just brightening as I back out, inch by careful inch. Birds begin their morning songs, and my spirits sing along with them as I emerge. Have I finally won Nico's own version of hide-and-seek? Could I be the first?

Light blinds my eyes.

"There you are!" Nico grabs my arm, yanks me to my feet, and I cry out in pain at my ankle, but it doesn't hurt as much as this disappointment, hot and bitter. I failed, again.

He brushes leaves from my clothes. Slips a warm arm around my waist to help me walk back to camp, and his closeness, his presence, resonate through my body despite the fear and pain.

"You know you can never get away, don't you?" he says. He is exultant and disappointed in me, all at once. "I will always find you." Nico leans down and kisses my forehead. A rare gesture of affection that I know will in no way ease whatever punishment he devises.

I can never get away.

He will always find me . . .

2

A DISTANT *RRRRING* CALLS INTO DEEP NOTHINGNESS. IT pulls me to a moment of regret, half awake, half confusion, then a slow drift back to dreams.

The *rrrring* sounds again.

Wrongness!

Awake in an instant, I spring up, but something holds me and I almost scream, wrestle and throw it to the ground and crouch in a fighting stance. Ready for attack. Ready for anything . . .

But not this. Alien, threatening shapes blur and change, become ordinary things. A bed. An alarm clock, still ringing, on top of a dresser. My restraints, blankets; most on the floor now. Carpet under bare feet. Dim light through an open window. And a grumpy, sleepy cat, meowing protests and caught up with blankets on the floor.

Get a grip.

I hit the stop button on the alarm. Force my breathing to slow, *in, out, in out*; try to calm my pounding heart, but still my nerves scream.

Sebastian stares from the floor, fur bristling.

"Do you still know me, cat?" I whisper, reach a hand for him to sniff, then stroke his fur, as much to soothe myself as him. I pull the blankets back into order on the bed and he jumps up, eventually flops down, but keeps his eyes half open. Watching.

When I woke, I thought I was *there*. Half asleep I knew every detail. Makeshift shelters, tents. Damp and cold, wood smoke, the rustle of trees, predawn birds. Quiet voices. But the more awake I become, the more it is gone. Details fall away. A dream, or a real place?

My Levo says mid-happy at 5.8, yet my heart still beats fast. After what just happened my levels should have plummeted. I twist my Levo on my wrist, hard—nothing. It should at least cause pain. Slated criminals can't do violence to self or others, not while a Levo keeps guard of every feeling. Not while it causes blackouts or death if the wearer gets too upset or angry. With what I did yesterday, I should be dead: zapped by the chip they put in my brain when I was Slated.

Echoes of last night's nightmare fill my mind: *I can never get away. He will always find me* . . .

Nico! That is his name. He is not an insubstantial dream. He is real. Pale blue eyes gleam in my mind, eyes that can glint cold or hot in an instant. He'll know what all this means. A living, breathing part of my past that has somehow appeared in this life, as my biology teacher of all things. A strange transformation from . . . from . . . what? Slippery memory falls away. My fists clench in frustration. I'd had him there, clear, who and what he was; and then, nothing.

Nico will know. But should I ask? Whatever he was, or is now, one thing I do know: He is dangerous. Just thinking his name makes my stomach clench, both with fear, and with longing. To be close to him no matter the cost.

He will always find me.

A knock on the door. "Kyla, are you up? You're going to be late for school."

"Your chariot, ladies," Jazz says, and bows. He puts one foot up on the side of the car to yank the door open. I clamber into the backseat,

Amy in the front. And though it has a feeling of ritual about it, every morning the same, it is so *alien*. A safe sameness that rankles.

I stare out the window on the way: farms. Stubbled fields. Cows and sheep stare, chewing and placid as we go past. Herded to school, not questioning the forces that channel us into our prescribed lives. What is the difference?

"Kyla? Earth to Kyla."

Amy has turned in her seat.

"Sorry. Did you say something?"

"I was just asking if you mind if I work after school? It's four days a week, Monday to Thursday. Mum isn't sure you should be alone so much. She said to talk to you about it."

"Truly, it's fine. I don't mind. When do you start?"

"Tomorrow," she says, with a guilty look.

"You already told them you could, didn't you," I say.

"Busted!" Jazz says. "But what about me? What about spending time with me?" And they pretend-argue the rest of the way.

The morning is a fog. Scanning my ID into each lesson, sitting down, pretending to listen. Trying to channel my face into attentive and eager to learn, so no one will have reason to focus any closer. Scanning out again. Lunch, alone; being ignored, as usual, by most of the other students who keep clear of Slateds. Though they mostly liked Ben—me, not so much. Especially now that he has vanished.

Ben, where are you? His smile, the warm certain feel of his hand in mine, the way his eyes light up from inside. It all twists like a knife in my gut, the pain so real I have to wrap my arms tight around myself to try to hold it in.

Some part of me is aware that I can't contain this much longer. It has to come out.

Not here. Not now.

Then, finally, it is time for biology. A queasy unease grows in my stomach on the way to the lab. What if I've gone mental and it isn't Nico at all? Does he even exist?

What if it is him? Then what?

I scan my ID at the door, walk across to the back bench and sit down, all before I dare look: not trusting my feet to still work if my eyes see what they can't stop imagining.

And there he is: Mr. Hatten, biology teacher. I stare, but that's all right, all the girls do. It isn't just that he's too young and good-looking for a teacher; there is something about him. And it's not just those eyes, that wavy, streaked blond hair, longer than you'd expect for a teacher, or that he is so tall and totally fit—it is more than that. Something about the way he holds himself: still, yet poised for attack. Like a cheetah waiting for the moment to pounce. Everything about him says *danger*.

Nico. It really *is* Nico; no question, no doubt. His eyes, unforgettable pale blue with darker rims, sweep across the room. They stop when they reach mine. As I stare back there is a warm touch inside, a recognition, an almost physical shock that makes it *real*. When he finally looks away it is like being dropped from an embrace.

Not my imagination. Right now, across the room, it *is* Nico. No matter that I knew it, from memories of then and now, compared and held up close together. Until I saw him myself, with these eyes that are new with understanding behind them, I didn't *know* it in my gut.

Then I remember that although the girls in his classes may stare, I don't; at least, not so much.

So through the lesson, I try not to, but it is a losing battle. His eyes flick to mine now and then. Do they hold curiosity? Questions? There is some dance of amused interest when they lightly touch mine.

Take care. Until I can work out what he is and what he wants, don't let him know anything has changed. I force my eyes down to the notebook in front of me, to the pen that skips across the page, leaving behind random blue swirls, half-formed sketches where notes should be. Hand on autopilot.

The pen; the hand . . . *left hand.* It is clasped, without thought, in my left hand.

But I'm right-handed. Aren't I?

I *must* be right-handed!

Breath catches in my throat; my gut fills with terror. I start to shake.

Everything goes black.

She holds out her hand. Her right hand. Tears trickle down her face. "Please help me . . ."

She is so young, a child. With such pleading and fear in her eyes, I would do anything to help her, but I can't reach her. The closer I get, the harder I try, the more her hand isn't where it appears. With some optical trick she is always turned to her right. It is always too far away to grasp.

"Please help me . . ."

"Give me your other hand!" I say, and she shakes her head, eyes wide. But I repeat the demand, until finally she raises her left hand from where she held it beside her, out of sight.

The fingers are twisted, bloody. Broken. A sudden vision flashes in my mind: a brick. Fingers smashed with a brick. I gasp.

I can't grasp her hand, not when it is like that.

Her hands drop. She shakes her head, fading. Shimmering until I can see through her like mist.

I lunge for her, but it is too late.

She is gone.

"I'm all right now. I just didn't get enough sleep last night, that's all. I'm fine," I insist. "Can I go to my last class?"

The school nurse doesn't smile. "I'll be the judge of that," she says.

She scans my Levo, frowns. My stomach clenches, afraid what my Levo will show. My levels should have dropped low after what happened; nightmares sometimes even made me black out when it was functioning as it is meant to. But who knows what it is doing now?

"Looks like you just fainted; your levels have been fine. Good, even. Did you have any lunch?"

Give her a reason.

"No. I wasn't hungry," I lie.

She shakes her head. "Kyla, you need to eat." She lectures on blood sugar, feeds me tea and cookies, and, before she disappears out the door, tells me to sit quietly in her office until the final bell.

Alone, I can't stop my thoughts from spinning around. The girl with the broken hand in my nightmare, or vision, or whatever it was . . . I know who she is. I recognize her as a younger version of myself: my eyes, bone structure, everything. *Lucy Connor,* vanished years ago from her school in Keswick, age ten, as reported on MIA. Missing in Action, the highly illegal website I saw just weeks ago at Jazz's cousin's place. She was part of me before I was Slated. Yet even with my new memories, I cannot remember being her, or anything about her life. I can't even think of her as *I* or *me*. She is different, other, separate.

How does Lucy fit in this mess in my brain? I kick the desk, frustrated. Things are there, half understood. I feel I know them, but when I focus on details, they slip away. Indistinct and insubstantial.

And this was all brought on when I realized I was using my left hand. Did Nico see? If he saw I was writing with my left hand, he'll know something has changed. I'm supposed to be right-handed, and it is important, so important . . . but when I try to focus on *why* I am meant to be right-handed, why I was before, why I don't seem to be anymore, I can't work it out. The memory goes all distorted, like fingers smashed with a brick.

3

MUM APPEARS AT THE NURSE'S OFFICE AS THE FINAL BELL
rings. "Hello there."

"Hi. Did they call you?"

"Obviously."

"Sorry. I'm perfectly all right."

"That must be why you passed out in the middle of a lesson and
wound up here."

"Well, I'm fine now."

Mum tracks down Amy and drives us both home. Once through
the door, I head for the stairs.

"Kyla, wait. Come talk to me a minute." Mum smiles, but it is one
of those that is more on the lips than the whole face. "Hot chocolate?"
she asks, and I follow her into the kitchen. She doesn't chatter as she
fills the kettle, makes our drinks. Mum isn't much of a talker unless
she has something to say.

She has something to say. Unease twists in my stomach. Has she
noticed I've changed? Maybe if I tell her, she can help, and . . .

Don't trust her.

After being Slated, I was a blank. It took nine months in the hospital for me to learn to function: to walk, talk, and cope with my Levo.
Then I was assigned to this family. I grew to see her as a friend, someone I can rely on—but how long have I known her, really? Not even

two months. It seemed longer before because it was my whole life out of the hospital, all I could remember. Now that I have a wider frame of reference, I know people should be viewed with suspicion, not trust.

She sets the drinks in front of us on the table, and I wrap my hands around the mug, soaking heat into cold hands.

"What happened?" she asks.

"I guess I fainted."

"Why? The nurse said you hadn't eaten, yet your lunch box is mysteriously empty."

I stay silent, sip my chocolate, focusing on the bitter sweetness. Nothing I can say about it makes much sense, even to me. Writing with my left hand made me *faint*? And that dream, or whatever it was. I shudder inside.

"Kyla, I know how hard things are for you right now. If you ever want to talk, we can, you know. About Ben, or anything. It is all right to wake me up if you can't sleep. I won't mind."

My eyes start to fill with tears at Ben's name, and I blink furiously. If she only knew how hard things *really* are; if she only knew the other half of it. I long to tell her, but how would she look at me if she knew I may have killed someone? Anyhow, she might not mind being woken up, but Dad would.

"When is Dad getting back?" I say, suddenly aware of his continued absence. He always travels for work: installing and maintaining government computers all over the country. But he is usually home a night or two a week at least.

"Well, he may not be home so much for a while."

"Why?" I say, careful to hide the relief I feel inside.

She stands, rinses our mugs.

"You look like you need some sleep, Kyla. Why don't you take a nap before dinner?"

Conversation over.

Late that night I am lost in confused dreams: running, chasing, and being chased all at once. Awake for what must be the tenth time, I punch the pillow and sigh. Then my ears perk up at a slight sound, a crunch, outside. Perhaps I wasn't woken by dreams this time after all?

Crossing the room to the window, I pull the curtains to one side. The wind has picked up, whipping leaves across the garden. The trees seem bare all at once. Yesterday's storm has littered the world: Orange and red spin in whorls through the air and around a dark car pulled out front.

The car door opens, and a woman steps out; long curly hair falls over her face. I gasp. Could it be? She pushes it back with one hand as she shuts the door, enough for me to be sure: It is Mrs. Nix. Ben's mother.

I grip the window ledge tight. Why is she here?

Excitement rushes through my body: Maybe she has news of Ben! But almost as soon as the thought forms, it is gone. Her face, caught in the moonlight, is pinched and white. If she has any sort of news, it is not happy. Footsteps crunch on the shingle below, and there is a light knock on the front door.

Maybe she has come to demand to know what happened to Ben, what I did. Maybe she is going to tell Mum I was there before the Lorders took him away. It flashes painfully in my mind: Ben in agony, the rattle of the door when his mum came in. I'd told her I found him with his Levo cut off, and—

The rattle of the door. She had to unlock the door to get in. I'd told her I found him like that, but she must know I lied. How else could it have been locked when she got there?

The door opens downstairs; there is a faint murmur of voices.

I have to know.

I slip quietly across the room and out to the landing, then take one careful step at a time down the dark stairs. I listen.

There is the faint whistle of the kettle, low voices; they are in the kitchen.

A step closer, another. The kitchen door is part open.

Something touches my leg, and I jump, almost cry out, until I realize it is Sebastian. He winds around my leg, purring.

Please be quiet, I beg silently, bending to scratch behind his ears. But as I do my elbow bumps the hall table.

I hold my breath. Footsteps approach! I duck into the dark office opposite.

"It's just the cat," I hear Mum say, then there is movement, a faint *meow.* Footsteps retreat back to the kitchen; there is a click as she shuts the door. I creep back into the hall to listen.

"I'm so sorry about Ben," Mum says. I hear chairs move. "But you shouldn't have come here."

"Please, you must help."

"I don't understand. How?"

"We've tried everything to find out what happened to him. Everything. They won't tell us a thing. I thought, maybe, you could . . ." And her voice trails away.

Mum has connections. Political ones; her dad was prime minister before he was assassinated, on the Lorder side of the Coalition. Can she help? I listen eagerly.

"I'm so sorry. I've already tried, for Kyla's sake. But it's a blank wall. There is nothing."

"I don't know where else to turn." And there are faint noises, snuffling and hiccupping. She's crying; Ben's mum is crying.

"Listen to me. For your own good, you have to stop asking. At least for now."

And there is no logic, no thought, no control: I can't help it. My eyes fill, my throat closes up tight. Mum tried to find out what happened to Ben. For me. She never told me, because she never found out anything. What a risk she took; asking questions where Lorders are involved is dangerous. Potentially lethal.

What a risk Ben's mum is taking, right now.

When they start saying good-bye, I sneak back up the stairs and into my room. Relief that Ben's mother never told Mum she found me with Ben that day mixes with sorrow. She feels like I do: the loss. Ben was their son for more than three years, since he was Slated. He'd told me they were close. I long to run to her so we can share this pain, together, but don't dare.

I wrap my arms around me tight. Ben. I whisper his name, but he cannot answer. Pain hits me like being crushed. Trampled. Smashed into a million pieces. Before, I had to stop myself from feeling it all or my Levo would make me black out. Now that it's not working, the hurt is so much, I gasp. Like surgery without anesthetic: no dull ache, but the slash of a blade, deep inside.

Ben is gone. My brain is working better now, no matter the messed up memories inside it. He is gone, and he is never coming back. Even if he lived through his Levo being cut off, there is no chance he survived the Lorders. With my memories comes knowledge: Once the Lorders take someone, they never return.

It hurts so, I want to push it away, hide from it. But Ben's memory is one I must keep. This pain is all I have left of him.

His mum comes out of the front door moments later. She sits in her car a few minutes before leaving, hunched over the steering wheel. As she pulls out, a light rain starts to fall.

Once she is gone from sight, I open the window wide, lean out and stretch my arms into the night. Cold drops fall light on my skin, along with hot tears.

Rain. Something about it is important, itches in my memories, then slips away.

4

I LEAN OVER MY SKETCH, FURIOUSLY DRAWING LEAVES, branches, remembering to use my right hand. The new art teacher the school has finally come up with doesn't look dangerous, or inspiring. He doesn't look much of anything. He's nothing like Gianelli, the man he replaces. But so long as I can draw, anything, even just trees as instructed, I don't care how insipid the instructor.

He moves around the room, making bland comments now and then, until he stops at my shoulder. "Hmmm . . . well . . . that's interesting," he says, and moves on.

I look down at my sheet of paper. A whole forest of angry trees I've drawn, and in the shadows underneath, a dark shape with eyes.

What would Gianelli make of this? He'd say, slow down, and take more care, and he'd have a point. But he'd like the wildness just the same.

I start again, soothed by the scratch of charcoal on paper. The trees less angry. This time, Gianelli himself looks back at me from their shadows. No one but me would recognize it as him: I know what happens when you draw the missing, as he did. Instead, I draw him as I imagine he might have been, a young man lost in a sketch. Not the old man the Lorders dragged away.

An hour later, I scan my ID at the door to study hall and step into the classroom. Start to walk to the back . . .

"Kyla?"

I stop. *That* voice: here? I pause, then turn. Nico leans against the desk at the front of the room. He smiles, a slow, lazy smile. "I hope you are feeling better today."

"I'm fine, sir," I say, and manage to turn away, walk to my seat without falling over.

His presence as bored teacher in charge of making sure we study silently shouldn't be that much of a surprise. They change all the time, so it was bound to be Nico sooner or later. Yet I wasn't expecting to be faced with him again, so soon. I have to hold my hands together on my lap for a moment to stop them from shaking.

I open algebra homework, something I can pretend to do without much effort. And I try to stare at the page, pencil carefully in my right hand. Nico has a red pen and papers to grade in front of him at the desk up front. Yet I can tell he is pretending as much as I am, glancing my way all the time.

Of course, I wouldn't know that if I weren't watching *him*. I sigh, and attempt to solve an equation for *x*.

But the numbers swim, won't behave, and my mind wanders as the minutes tick away. I doodle around the borders of the page, then draw vines and leaves around the date I've written as usual at the top. But then the numbers jump into stark focus: 11/03. *It is November the third.*

Almost with an audible *click* inside, a chink of knowledge falls into place.

Today is my birthday. I was born seventeen years ago today, but I'm the only one who knows.

Goose bumps trail on my arms. I know the date of my *real* birthday, not the one assigned at the hospital when my identity was changed, my past stolen.

My birthday? I probe at the concept, but there is nothing else. No cake, no parties or presents; the fact of the date is all there is. Memories that should go with it do not. Yet I sense there is more inside me, more I might find and learn if I probe around.

Some of my recovered memories are like cold facts. As if I've read a file about myself and remember certain bits of it and not others. There is no feeling in it.

I know from the missing children's website that I was Lucy, that I disappeared when I was ten, but I can't remember anything of that life. Then somehow I reappear in my teens with Nico. It is only from then on that memories are stealing back; there is nothing from before.

Nico is the one who might have answers. All I have to do is tell him I remember who he is. But do I really want to know?

When the bell rings, even though I tell myself to bolt out quick and leave this choice, whether to speak to him or not, until I can make sense of it, I dawdle. A shiver—of what, excitement? fear?—tracks down my spine. I walk slowly to the front of the room where Nico stands by the door. The last of the other students have gone. We are alone.

Just go I tell myself, and start walking past him.

"Happy birthday, Rain," he says, voice low.

I turn back. Our eyes meet.

"Rain?" I whisper. Touching and tasting the name, owning it again. *Rain.* Another time and place rush back, vivid and clear: I chose this name for myself three years ago, on my fourteenth birthday: I remember! It is *my* name. Not Lucy, the name given at birth by parents. Not Kyla, the one chosen years later by an indifferent nurse filling in a form at the hospital after I was Slated. Rain is *mine.* And it is as if the sound of my name said out loud, at last, explodes any final resistance or barrier inside.

His eyes widen and flash. He knows me, and more. He knows I know *him*.

Danger.

Adrenaline surges through my body, a burst of energy: fight or flight.

But the look falls from his face as if it never was, and he steps back. "Try to remember your biology homework for tomorrow, Kyla," he says, his eyes glancing over my shoulder.

I turn, and there is Mrs. Ali. Hate flashes through me, and then fear: but it is Kyla's fear. I'm not afraid of her. Rain isn't afraid of anything!

"Try to remember," Nico says again, this time leaving off the meaningless homework reference added for her ears. He disappears up the hall.

Try to remember . . .

"We need to have a little chat," Mrs. Ali says, and smiles. She is at her most dangerous when she smiles.

Two can be so. I smile back. "Of course," I say, and try to still all that sings inside. My name! I am *Rain*.

"I won't be taking you between your classes anymore; you obviously know your way around the school now," she says.

"Well, thanks so much for your help so far," I say as sweetly as I can manage.

Her eyes narrow. "I've heard you've been moping about classes, looking a misery and not paying attention. Yet you seem happy enough today."

"Sorry about that. I'm feeling much better."

"Now, Kyla, you know if anything is ever bothering you, you can talk to me." She smiles again, and a shiver goes down my back.

Be careful. Her official job title may be teaching assistant, but she is so much more than that. She's been watching me for any sign, any deviation. Anything outside rigid, expected Slated behavior—any hint of returning to my criminal ways—and I could be returned to the Lorders. Terminated.

"Everything is fine. Really."

"Well, see that it stays that way. You must try your best in school, at home, and in your community, to—"

"Fulfill my contract. Take advantage of my second chance. Yes, I know! But thank you for reminding me. I'll do my very best." I grin, happy enough with the world to even share my smile with a Lorder spy. That Mrs. Ali won't be in my footsteps at school anymore is an unexpected bonus.

Her features war between confusion and annoyance. Too much?

"See that you do," she says, ice dripping from her voice, the smile gone. She obviously likes it better when I quake in her presence.

Shame that *Rain* doesn't quake.

Red, gold, orange: The oak tree in our front garden has covered the grass with color, and I fetch a rake from the shed.

I have a name.

I attack the leaves with the rake, pulling them into piles, then kick them about and start over.

I have a name! One that *I* chose; it is who *I* wanted to be. The Lorders tried to take that away, but somehow, they failed.

A car pulls in across the street, one I haven't seen before. A boy, about my age or a little older, gets out. Baggy jeans and T-shirt rumpled like he's been driving for hours, or asleep—hopefully not both at the same time—yet the whole "I don't care what I wear" look suits him. He opens the trunk. Takes out a box and carries it into a house. Comes out again, sees me watching and waves. I wave back. Kyla wouldn't; she'd probably blush or something. Rain has nerve. He takes in another box.

On the other side of the car he drops down as if going down a pretend escalator, and looks back to see if I'm watching. I roll my eyes to the sky. He carries on with various other tricks; I bag and cart the leaves around the back of the house, and go inside.

"Thanks for doing the leaves," Mum says. "They were a mess."

"No bother. I felt like doing something."

"Keeping busy?"

I nod, then remind myself to tone down a little, before too many mood swings get her to take me to the hospital for a check. That thought gives me a real sense of disquiet, and the smile falls away.

Mum puts a hand on my shoulder, gives it a squeeze. "We'll have dinner as soon as—"

The door opens. "I'm home!" Amy yells.

Before long we're at the table listening to an in-depth report of her first day as after-school assistant at the doctor's office.

And it turns out that working there is an amazing source of community gossip. Soon we know who is having a baby, who fell down the stairs after too much whisky, and that the new boy across the street is Cameron from up north, come to stay with his aunt and uncle for reasons, as of yet, unknown.

"I love working there. I can't wait until I'm a nurse," Amy says for about the tenth time.

"Did you see any good illnesses?" Mum teases.

"Or injuries?" I add.

"Oh! That reminds me. You'll never guess."

"What?" I say.

"It happened this morning, so I didn't see, but I heard *all* about it."

"Go on and tell us, then," Mum says.

"A man was brought in with the most horrible injuries."

"Oh dear," Mum says. "What happened?"

And I start to get a bad feeling. A twist of unease deep in my gut sort of very bad feeling.

"Nobody knows. He was found in the woods at the end of the village, beaten half to death. Head injuries and hypothermia, out there for days they think. It's a wonder he's alive at all."

"Did he say who did it?" I ask, struggling to control my breathing, to look natural.

"No, and he may never say anything. He's been taken to the hospital in a coma."

"Who is he?" Mum asks, but I already know before Amy says another word.

"Wayne Best. You know, the creepy builder who did the brick walls for the hall."

Mum tells us to stay out of the woods, away from the footpaths. She is worried about some maniac being on the loose.

But I am the maniac.

"Can I be excused?" I say, suddenly feeling ill.

Mum turns to me. "You've gone all pale." She puts a warm hand on my forehead. "You feel clammy."

"I'm a little tired."

"Go on, early to bed. We can wash up."

Amy groans, and I head for the stairs.

I stare at the wall in the dark, Sebastian a welcome band of warmth stretched along my back.

I did that. Put a man in a coma. Or Rain did; she came back at the same time. Or what? Are we the same person, or two in one? Sometimes I feel I am her, as if her memories and who she was take over. Sometimes, like now, she slips away, as if she never were. But who was Rain, really? And somehow Lucy fits in with Rain's past, but how?

The same birthday ties us all together: the third of November. I hug the knowledge, the secret, inside. However these bits of me fit together now, that is the day I started in this world.

My mind drifts, sleep on the way. But then the dates shift into sharp focus, and my eyes snap open.

Seventeen today. I got out of the hospital in September: I'd been there for nine months. Slated, then, less than eleven months ago. I was already sixteen. It is illegal to Slate anyone over the age of sixteen. Lorders may break their own laws now and then if they have a reason, true enough. But why would they in my case?

There are still all these disconnections inside. I feel I almost understand it all, but if I look too closely, it vanishes. Like something I can only see sideways, out of the corner of my eye.

Nico might be able to explain, if he wants to; my past as Rain at least. But what would he want in return?

Perhaps Rain and all she was are best forgotten. I can take now, and tomorrow, and all the days after, make of them what I will. Stay out of trouble and leave Nico behind. Avoid him, pretend it never happened.

Either way, Wayne could spoil it all.

You should have killed him.

5

Next day in biology, there is a surprise: New boy, Cameron, appears at the door.

He spots me and goes straight for the empty stool to the left of mine. Smiles a silly grin as he sits down.

Ben's seat. I fold my arms in on myself, blink hard, don't look at him. The empty space next to me hurt, but having someone sit there feels worse.

Nico turns around to the whiteboard. Every girl has her eyes on him, on the way his clothes hug his body, the movement of muscles under his silky shirt as he raises his arm to write.

He turns back and faces the room, standing next to the board. "What does this mean?" he asks, gesturing to the words he has written: *Survival of the Fittest.*

"Only the strongest survive," one student offers.

"That can be part of it. But you don't have to be the strongest to win, or the dinosaurs would have eaten all our ancestors for lunch." He scans across the room until his eyes fall on me. "To survive, you just have to be . . . the best." His eyes hold mine as he says the words, slowly, drawing them out.

Finally he looks away. Starts going on about evolution and Darwin, and I try to take notes, to pretend I am somewhere else. Or better, some*one* else. Just get through this lesson and get out of here, and—

Something lands on my notebook. A square of paper? I unfold it.

With these words written on it: *And so, we meet again!*

I glance at Cameron. He winks.

I stifle a grin. *We haven't met yet,* I write underneath. Then, pretending to stretch, drop it on his book.

It flies back again moments later. I glance at Nico. No reaction. Still going on about dinosaurs. I unfold it.

Yes, we have: You are She Who Jumps on Leaves. I am He Who Hefts Heavy Boxes from Car. Also known as Cam.

So it is Cam, not Cameron, as Amy heard in community gossip. And he is every bit as mad as he appeared yesterday.

I chew my pencil for a while. Ignore, or—

A pen pokes my arm. Mad, and impatient. Yet I know what it is like to be the new one, to know nobody.

All right. I write on the square: *Leaf Lady, also known as Kyla.*

I fold it up, flick it back across.

"Congratulations!" a voice says to my right. It is Nico: standing next to our table and looking straight at me. Along with every pair of eyes in the room.

"Ah . . ."

"You are the lucky winner of a lunchtime detention. Now try to pay attention for the rest of the class."

Heat creeps up my face, but not from the embarrassment of a room full of eyes. Nico's say, *Gotcha!* The cheetah has pounced. And there isn't a thing I can do about it.

Cam, to his credit, protests that it was his fault, but Nico ignores him. The class continues, and I stare at the clock as the minutes count down, hoping somebody else will get nabbed for some other misdemeanor, that we won't be alone. But there's no chance of that. Not with Nico in charge.

The bell rings, and everyone starts packing up. Cam stands with a stricken look on his face. *Sorry,* he mouths, and follows the last students. The door swings shut behind them.

Alone.

Nico stares, face unreadable. Seconds stretch to more seconds, and inside I am . . . what: scared? But it feels more like something else. Like the fear that comes from something that is both terrifying, and a thrill: ridge walking in a storm, or rappelling down a cliff.

He flicks his head in a gesture that says *follow me.* We leave the lab and go down the hall to a row of offices.

He looks both ways, takes a key out of his pocket, and unlocks one of the office doors.

"Come," he says. No smile, nothing. Cold.

I follow him in, feet dragging; no choice, but dread is pooling inside. He locks the door, then in a sudden movement grabs my arm and twists it tight behind my back, pushing my face into the wall.

"Who are you?" he says, voice low. "Who are you!" Again, louder this time, but controlled. No one would hear.

He pulls my arm tighter. As if the pain in my shoulder is a trigger, *I remember.* And I'm somewhere else. Some other time, place. Where Nico's sudden tests like this could bruise the unwary. But I know how to escape this one! With a flash of joy at memory, I jump up to loosen the arm grip, twist and plant a fist into the hard muscles of his stomach.

He lets go and starts to laugh, rubbing at his stomach. "I had to be sure. I'm sorry. Is your arm all right?"

A smile takes over my face. I shrug my shoulder around in a circle. "Fine. But if you'd really wanted to hold me you would have pulled my arm up higher. That was a test."

"Yes. That maneuver was pure Rain." And he laughs again, delight shining in his eyes. "Rain!" he says again, holding out his arms, and I move closer until they are around me, warm and tight. And I feel a sense of coming back to a place I am meant to be, where I was always meant to be. Where I know who and what I am, because Nico does.

Then he holds me out at arm's length, studies my face, assessing.

"Nico?" I say, uncertain.

He smiles. "You remember me. Good! I always knew you'd survive, my special Rain." He sits me down on a chair, him perched on the desk above. Takes my hand and looks at my Levo. "It worked, didn't it. This thing is just a thing." And he spins it on my wrist: no pain, no nothing. Levels in mid-happy.

I half smile, then it falls away. "It worked? Nico, please. Explain to me. I remember pieces of things, but it's all such a mess. I don't understand what has happened to me."

"Always serious. We should be laughing! Celebrating." And because his smile is so infectious, so alive, mine follows. "You have to tell me: What finally released your memories?"

And I shrink away from thinking of it. If he knows about Wayne, he'll deal with him, like any other threat to one of his own. *His own.* I hug the belonging inside.

"You were close a few times before, I could see it. I thought that whole thing with Ben would have done it."

Ben. His name brings a twist of agony. The hurt must be on my face.

"Lose the pain: It makes you weak. Do you remember how, Rain? You march it to the door in your mind, and lock it up."

I shake my head. I don't want to forget Ben. Do I? And some glimmer of my thoughts last night comes back to me: Nico and his ways are dangerous.

I say out loud the thing that was there all along, hidden in plain sight in my mind, yet unrecognized. "You're with the AGT, the Anti-government Terrorists. Aren't you?"

He raises an eyebrow. "You have been forgetting!" He takes my hands in his. "Don't use the Lorder name for us that way, Rain: We are Free UK. The teeth that Freedom UK was supposed to have in the Central Coalition, but never did. We are the splinter that hurts: I am, and so are you. The Lorders fear us. They'll be on their way out soon, and this great country will be free again. We *will* win!"

A chant from the past echoes in my mind: *Free UK today! Free UK today!*

And I remember Nico filling in what history lessons left out. After the UK pulled out of the EU and closed its borders, and after all the student riots and destruction of the 2020s, the Lorders dealt harshly with rioters, gangs, and terrorists the same way, no matter their age: imprisonment or death. But as things settled down, they were forced to accept compromise with Freedom UK in the Central Coalition, and harsh penalties were banned for under-sixteens. Slating was brought in to give them a second chance, a new life. But Freedom UK became a puppet of the Lorders, who abused their power more and more. Free UK rose up in response, wanting to get rid of Lorder oppression by whatever means.

Whatever means.

The teeth *are* the terror. I shake my head, part of me rejecting what I know to be true. "I'm not a terrorist. Am I?"

He shakes his head. "None of us are. But you were with us in our fight for freedom, and you would be now, if Lorders hadn't snatched you and Slated you, stole your mind away. Or so they thought."

"Yet, here I am. And I know you. I remember some things. But I—"

"This is too much at once, isn't it? Listen to me, Rain: There is nothing you have to do if you don't want to. We're not like the Lorders. We don't *make* anybody do anything."

"Really?"

"Really. I'm just so happy you're all right. You're you, again." And he smiles, and I'm back in another hug.

More memory traces surface. Nico isn't known for his hugs or smiles. They are so rare, they're like a gift when you have shone enough in his eyes to get that much approval. We'd fight for his approval. We'd kill for it. All of us. We'd do anything to get half a smile.

"Listen. There is just one thing. I need to talk to you some more. I need to know how things have worked with you, so we know how we can help others survive Slating. You want that, don't you?"

"Of course."

"I've got something for you," he says, and reaches into a desk drawer. The back is false, and hidden behind it is a small metal device, thin and flexible. He shows me. "Look. It's a communicator: a com. See, you press this button here and wait for me to answer. Then we can speak. You can call if you need me."

Just as I'm wondering where I'm going to hide this highly illegal device, he shows me. It slips underneath my Levo and clasps to it. The thin controls are not visible; they are barely there by feel.

"It is undetectable here. Even if you go through a metal scan, they'll just see it as picking up your Levo."

I twist my Levo; I can't even tell it is there.

"Now, off you go. Have your lunch. We'll talk again when you are ready." He touches my face. "I'm just so happy you're with us," he says. His hand, warm on my cheek, sparks electricity through my body.

He unlocks the door. "Go," he says. And I walk as if in a daze into the hall. After a few steps, I look back; he smiles, then shuts the door. Gone.

The farther I am from Nico, the more the warmth and joy seep away, leaving cold and loneliness.

More bits and fragments are coming back. That training in my dream? *It was real.* Training with Nico, with Free UK. Hiding in the woods with others like me. Learning to fight. Weapons. Whatever we could do to strike at Lorders, we learned. For freedom! And every one of the girls was in love with Nico; all the boys wanted to be him.

All it took was minutes alone with him today for me to feel the same as I did back then. Seeing myself through Nico's eyes made me sure who I am; it made me become the Rain that he knew. Part of me wants Nico to take over, to tell me what to think, what to do. So I don't have to try to work anything out for myself.

The farther away I get from him, the more it terrifies me.

6

"KYLA? YOU HAVE A VISITOR," MUM CALLS UP THE STAIRS.

A visitor? I walk down, and there is Cam, a sheepish look on his face and a plate clutched in his hands. His sandy hair is almost neat, he wears a collared shirt, and there is a distinct air of aftershave about the place.

"Hi," he says.

"Ah, hi."

"I just wanted to apologize," he says, and holds out the plate. Chocolate cake? And I'm thinking *don't say anything* at him, really hard, but it doesn't work. "That detention you got was totally my fault."

"Detention?" Mum says.

I give Cam a glare.

"Oh, sorry! You didn't want her to know, did you."

Thanks for spelling out the obvious. I sigh.

"Kyla?" Mum says.

"Yes, I got a lunchtime detention today, and yes, it was Cam's fault. Happy?"

Mum laughs. "I can see you will have no secrets with Cam in the neighborhood."

"I'm really sorry," he says again, looking even more miserable.

"It's fine. Really. Thanks for the cake," I say, and take the plate, hoping he'll do the same with the hint, and leave.

"Come in," Mum says. "I think we need some tea with that."

No such luck.

The word *cake* tempts Amy away from the TV to join us. Luscious-looking dark chocolate cake, with buttercream icing.

"This is really good," I say, starting to thaw once I begin to tackle a piece. And it is: gooey with delicious bitter dark chocolate and just enough sweet to balance. "Did you make it?"

"Believe me, if I made it, you wouldn't want to eat it. My uncle did."

"Why have you come to stay with them? Will you be here for long?" Amy asks.

"Amy!" Mum says.

Cam laughs. Dimples appear when he smiles—one in each cheek. "It's fine. I'm not sure how long; my mum is off on a research platform in the North Sea. Depends how long it takes them to discover something important, I guess."

"What about your dad?" Amy asks.

"He split last year," Cam says, with no elaboration and a look on his face that suggests Amy has ventured into no-go territory. Mum quickly changes the subject, asking after his aunt and uncle.

Eventually they leave the kitchen when Cam asks me what we've done so far in biology. Like I've been paying attention. But I go get my notes.

"I'm sorry. I won't be much help." I give him my notebook and Cam flicks through, but soon realizes much of what is in it is nonsense. "I have trouble concentrating in that class," I admit.

"You were away with the fairies this morning," he says. "I just passed you a note to tear your eyes away from the Teacher God Who Walks Among Us."

"That's ridiculous," I say, nervous how much he noticed, how much anyone could.

"Oh, come on. You and every other girl were totally in awe of his swaggering magnificence; I notice these things. But Hatten is a mite creepy, if you ask me."

"How so?"

He pulls a piece of paper out of his pocket. Unfolds it to show a cartoon with the title *Survival of the Fittest.*

First a cute little bunny; then a fox chasing the bunny; then a lion chasing the fox. And chasing the lion, a dinosaur—T. rex? Who is finally chased by Nico. Dressed in skins like a caveman and clutching a club with a decidedly evil, manic look on his face.

I laugh. "Is that really how you see him?"

"Oh, yeah. He's all animal, that one. How'd he get a teaching license? I expect any minute he'll march us into a freezer and make us into sausages or something."

How *did* he get a teaching license? While he seems to know more about biology than I do, I'm sure he hasn't got one. Perhaps somewhere there was a real Mr. Hatten, biology teacher, who is no more. My smile falls away.

Absently I start sketching students in our Lord Williams's school uniform: maroon and black sausages, marching along.

"Wow. You can really draw."

"Thanks. Your stuff is good, too."

"Nah, I just do cartoons. Silly stuff."

"No, really; it's good. But I can see you need help in lessons."

"Oh?"

"For a start, this"—I tap on his cartoon—"isn't survival of the fittest. It's more the food chain."

"And?"

"Dinosaurs aren't in the food chain anymore."

He stays for an hour or so. He could talk for England: goes on about nothing, and everything. More cartoons of other teachers follow. I wonder how'd he draw Mrs. Ali?

"It's nice to see you smile, Kyla," Mum says as I go upstairs for the night.

And I think, wouldn't it be nice to stay this girl? Who has nothing more on her mind than school, making fun of teachers, and boys bearing cake. Cam is nice, funny; uncomplicated and silly. Nothing like Ben.

Ben. Stricken, I wonder what he would think of Cam. He might think Cam isn't just being friendly. And he might be right.

What was I thinking? All at once the evening fades away, the sense of another life that might be. Guilt and pain twist inside. I wasn't thinking of Ben at all. Mum said it was good to see me smile. But how can I smile, even at Cam, when Ben is . . . is . . . What is he?

The other night, Ben's mother wasn't smiling at anything. Mum couldn't help her, and she was in despair.

Maybe there is a way I can help. Give her something she *can* do: report Ben missing on MIA, with all the other missing children. Having something like that may give her hope, make her able to go on.

Maybe it will stop her from hating me if she learns the truth.

I run.

Sand slips under my feet. The salty tang from the sea rasps in my throat as I gasp for air. Run faster.

Through my fear I still hear gulls' cries, see stars glint on the water. The boat pulled on the beach ahead.

Faster!

So tired now, one foot not raised high enough catches in sand, and I sprawl. Fly through the air, land hard. Air is knocked out of lungs that already couldn't take in enough to keep running. Everything spins . . .

. . . and changes. The night is softer. More distant. I can't feel my frantic gusping for breath or my thumping heartbeats anymore, but the fear is closer, more complete.

"Never forget who you are!" a voice shouts, then cuts off. Disconnects.

Bricks rise all around, thunk-thud, thunk-thud. *Like a shovel dragging in sand.*

And all there is, is darkness.

Silence.

Thick, and absolute.

7

DARK JACKET, JEANS, WARM GLOVES. A DARK HAT, BOTH TO cover blond hair that might catch the moonlight, and to stay warm: It's cold tonight.

I slip like a shadow down the stairs, then carefully, quietly, open the side door and step out into the night. And I marvel at how I move, making no sound. Not such a mystery any longer, these hidden skills have an explanation: Learning them formed part of my Free UK training. They were tucked away inside and not recognized until needed. Who knows what else I can do?

A car goes past, and I melt into shadows. Where are they going at three in the morning?

I'm going to see Ben's mum.

Old walking maps found tucked on a bookshelf at home show the canals behind Ben's house link with the footpath above our village, just crossing a few country lanes on the way. No more than six miles. Maybe seven. A run should make it an hour, and I'm desperate to run. To shake off my dream. A dream that with some variation has haunted my sleep ever since I woke up in the hospital after I was Slated.

It is a slow start, hugging the shadows through the village in case any insomniacs pass a window. There is one tense moment as a sleepy dog gives a few halfhearted barks, but no doors open or voices follow, and it soon goes back to dreaming. Once I reach the footpath at the end of the village, I start to run: slower than expected, taking care not to trip on tree roots in the faint moonlight, then faster as eyes adjust.

This footpath, that Ben and I came up together.

This lookout spot, here, where he laughed at the mist-obstructed view, and was about to kiss me. Before Wayne interrupted.

Before Ben's levels crashed and he nearly blacked out; would have, if he hadn't taken a highly illegal Happy Pill. The pills that started all the trouble. And it was all because of Wayne: his attack, Ben's inability to help. Slateds can't use violence, even to defend. What would have happened if Amy and Jazz hadn't interrupted? Would my memories have come back then? I quail inside.

There is nothing to fear now.

No. Not since I started to remember all that Nico taught me. Just ask Wayne. My smile falters.

Before long the path branches. The left way I know; it goes back to the other end of our village. The right is new and leads to today's destination.

The run, the dark, the night: exhilarating! I've been locked up for too long. The cold air, the rhythm of feet and white breath, the here, the now, take over. Until all there is, is running.

But as I get closer, thoughts intrude. What will happen when I get there? What Ben's mum will make of me knocking on her back door at four in the morning is hard to predict. What should I say?

There is only one way to deal with it: I have to tell her the truth. I have to tell her what really happened.

She must know I love Ben. I'd never hurt him, not for anything.

But you did.

No! It wasn't like that. He was going to cut off his Levo, anyhow. I tried to stop him.

You should have tried harder.

There it is, face on: I should have tried harder. We were always told that any damage to your Levo would kill you, either from pain or seizures. And yes, he was so determined to try to be free of it that he wouldn't listen! But while the pain of Ben's absence is intense, the thought I should have been able to do something, anything, to stop him, is worse.

My reasons for helping him seemed right. With my help he was more likely to survive. Without it, he almost certainly would have failed.

He still failed, didn't he?

Did he? The Levo came off quick with my sure hands on the grinder, his wrist held still in a clamp. He still lived, then. But the *pain.* The slightest touch on a working Levo hurts like being hit in the head with a sledgehammer; the cut through must have been like an amputation without anesthetic.

I cannot banish what happened next, the last time I saw him. Ben's mother, home unexpectedly, found Ben writhing in pain, my arms around him, tears running down my face. His Levo off, body convulsing. No time for questions. She called the paramedics and told me to leave, to get out before they arrived. And I did it. I left, to save myself. Ben was lying there in agony. His body in spasms, his beautiful eyes clenched shut tight. At least he didn't see me walk away and leave him.

And then the Lorders came, and took him away.

I blink back tears as I run. Focus: on feet on path, on the night, on staying upright. Ben's mum deserves the truth.

My dark thoughts and the run have taken too much concentration. Their house is close now, but something isn't right. The air tastes wrong. A little at first, then more.

Smoke?

It gets stronger, and I slow to a jog, then a walk.

Very strong now: The air is thick and hazy, cutting the moonlight. My eyes are stinging, and it's only the will to stay silent that keeps me from coughing.

Caution. Go slow and silent.

Ben's road is visible now, dim houses beyond fences and hedges on one side of the canal path. Over one of them, smoke rises lazily, twists on the wind. It is an unreal silver and red, lit by moon above and red glow below. Though it is not a house any longer; now that I'm closer, I can see the absolute devastation. The remains of a house. A total ruin.

It isn't Ben's; it can't be. I scan those on either side from behind. None of them look like his, with the workshop on the side where his mum made her metal sculptures. It must be this one.

The wind shifts, and I pull my shirt over my face to breathe through, choking in the air, unable to hold back coughing any longer. There are no firefighters, nobody in sight. Whatever happened is mostly over; there is just a ruin, glowing ash. Smoke. How . . . ?

Stay back. Get back. There will be watchers.

Is it really Ben's house? Could it be? What has happened?

Leave. There is nothing to be done here.

Nothing to be done. Anyone who was in that house . . .

And I stare at the ruins. The houses around, untouched; this one, completely destroyed. No chance for anyone inside. None.

Were they in there? Ben's parents? Horror fills me. I never met his dad, but his mum was so full of life, of her art. Now so full of pain about Ben.

Not anymore.

Get out of here.

And the urgency and fear bite in. My feet start reversing, slow up the canal path, hugging the trees on the side of it. There will be wakeful eyes on this street tonight.

I pause. The path rises a little now; I can look back and see more.

Get out of sight!

If I can see down, eyes can see up. I slip into shadows of trees.

Every instinct is shouting *run, hide,* but I can't *not* look. I can't take my eyes off this smoking ruin. Were they in there? Burned to death? I shudder. I can't take this in, I can't . . .

Hands grab my shoulders from behind.

8

I SLAM MY LEFT ELBOW BACK INTO FLESH, WHICH GASPS AND sags into a tree. I spin around, kick with my right foot, right fist ready to crack skull against tree, and . . .

My hand drops.

A girl is bent double, gasping and clutching her stomach, long dark hair cascading down. Barely visible in this light, yet I know that hair. Don't I?

"Tori?"

She looks up. Familiar flawless features, beautiful eyes. Yet not the same. Hollow. Choked with tears.

"Tori?" I say again. She half nods and sags to the ground. "What are you doing here? How . . . ?"

She shakes her head, unable to talk, and I can't take this in. How is Tori here? How is she *anywhere*. She was returned to the Lorders. Tori was Ben's friend: Slated, like us. I barely knew her, but she was his girlfriend before I was, I'm sure of it. Though he said he never kissed her, I never totally believed him. How could he resist Tori? But she was taken by Lorders; nobody comes back from them.

"Bitch," she finally manages to cough out. "Why'd you do that?"

"I didn't know it was you," I whisper. "Keep your voice down. How did you . . ." I start to say, but my voice trails away. I don't know what question to ask first.

"I escaped, and I came to see Ben. But he . . ." Her voice breaks, and tears start down her cheeks.

Get away from here! It isn't safe.

"Tori, we've got to move. We can't stay here. We'll get caught."

"What does it matter now? Without Ben, I . . ." And she shakes her head. "They're all dead. They wouldn't save anyone. I saw it all!"

Get out of here!

But I have to know. "Tell me what happened."

"I got here hours ago; the house was alight, just, and I held back as fire trucks came rushing up, sirens on. But they didn't do anything."

"What?"

"Lorders were already here. They made them watch it burn. Just let them stop it from spreading to other houses. I could hear them screaming, Kyla. And I didn't do anything. I could hear them screaming inside the house. And one of the firefighters argued with the Lorders, and they shot him."

"They did *what*?"

"They just shot him." And she is sobbing harder. "Ben is dead, and I didn't do anything."

I know how that feels; the overwhelming guilt. She doesn't need it.

"Tori, he wasn't in the house. He wasn't there." Her shoulders are shaking; she is beyond hearing. "Listen to me: Ben wasn't in there. All right?"

Words are starting to get through. She looks up. "He wasn't? Then where is he?"

"I'll tell you everything. But first we need to get away from here."

"Where can I go? I can't go home; it's the first place they'll look. I have nowhere else."

"Come on."

I urge Tori to her feet. She is in bad shape. Wearing stupid light shoes, shivering in torn clothes, limping. Her bare arms shine white in the moonlight, a beacon to any eyes. I hold her hand to urge her along, then her arm—her skin is like ice. Then finally I link an arm around her waist to help her walk.

"What has happened to you?"

"I was all right until you karate-chopped me in the gut."

"Liar."

"I've walked a long way. I can't go much farther." Her voice is faint, and her body, light though it is, is becoming a dead weight on my shoulder.

"Stop. I need to rest," she says, and her words are slurred.

"We can't stop. Come on, Tori," I say, but then her body sags. I just manage to catch her, lower her to the ground.

God. What am I going to do? She escaped from Lorders; anyone caught helping her is in for it. Being anywhere near her is *danger.*

Leave her. Survival of the fittest!

No. I can't. I won't!

And I think of Cam's drawing, and Nico the caveman. There isn't really any other choice, is there? Even if she could walk that far, I can't take her home. I can't put that on Mum. Even if Mum would help, Amy could never keep a secret, and there'd be no way to hide it from her. And if Dad came home . . . I shudder. He was so suspicious of my involvement when Ben disappeared, he threatened to return me to the Lorders if I took even one step out of line. This would give him an excuse to get rid of me at last. Maybe Jazz and his cousin, Mac, would help. But there is no way to contact them or get her there. She could never walk that far. It has to be Nico.

He'll be furious.

Nico's fury isn't something to take lightly. But he said to call if I needed to. Why else give me means to contact him?

I fiddle under my Levo in the dark until I find the button on the com. Press it. *Be awake, Nico!*

Seconds later he answers, voice alert.

"This had better be good," he says.

9

"**Stupid move, Rain.**" **Nico hoists Tori into the back of** his car. "What am I supposed to do with her?"

I don't answer, shying away from thinking what he may come up with. I climb into the front seat next to Nico, exhausted from the effort of half dragging, half cajoling a semiconscious Tori up the footpath in the dark to this, the first lane crossing. The hastily arranged meeting point.

"Thank you, Nico," I say, and every bit of me means it. The relief when I saw his face was so strong, I'd wanted to throw myself in his arms. But he wasn't in a hugging mood.

His car purrs up the lane. It looks average, but the engine is something more. He keeps a careful eye when we get to a main road. What explanation could we have if spotted, an unconscious Tori in the back? We'd have to run for it.

"You reek of smoke."

"Do I? What time is it?"

"Nearly five."

"I've got to get home soon, or I'll get caught. Mum gets up early."

"Not smelling like that."

He drives fast. Tori whimpers, then is quiet again. We get to a dark house with a drive down the side to the back. On a hill, no neighbors nearby.

He carries her over his shoulder into the house. I follow. It is small, modern, neat. Not your usual Free UK hidey-hole.

"Your place?" I say, surprised.

He glares. "No time to take her anywhere else."

He puts Tori on the couch. Pulls heavy curtains across the windows before turning on a lamp.

That is when I really see the state of her. Thin colorful clothes in tatters, as if she'd set out to a party, not gone hiking in this cold. Covered in scratches, bruises. One ankle so swollen, it's a miracle she could walk at all.

She stirs, her eyes flutter part open, then all the way when they take in Nico. She sits up, panic on her face.

I grab her hand.

"Tori, it's okay. This is . . ." And I pause, not sure what name he wants to use. "My friend. He's going to look after you."

Nico comes over, smiles. "Hello. Tori, is it? I'm John Hatten. I need to ask you a few questions."

"Can't this wait?" I say, voice low.

"I'm afraid not. I'm sorry, Tori. But you can see what a risk I take for you. I need to know your story well enough to know what to do with you."

My blood runs cold. One wrong word and what he does with her could be permanent.

"Well, Tori?" he prompts, voice gentle.

She studies her hands, turning them side to side like they are unfamiliar, disconnected to her. "I killed him," she says in a low voice. "With a knife."

"Who?"

"A Lorder. I killed him, and I ran away." She closes her eyes.

"You're safe here. Rest, Tori," he says. Tori's head lolls to one side: out again.

Nico raises an eyebrow at me. She couldn't have found anything more *right* to say if I'd coached her. He probably wonders if I did.

"Go, take a fast shower. I'll look after her. But you owe me, Rain. Big-time. This is a huge risk, an unnecessary complication that could interfere with our plans. Now, go."

I run for the shower, grab the towel and nondescript dark T-shirt and bicycle shorts he chucks at me. *Our* plans? Does he mean Free UK plans, ones that somehow involve me? I wash and dry my hair as fast as possible, part of me noting things about Nico. I've never been in his personal space before. He likes nice shower gel, soap; it smells like him, and I can't stop myself from breathing it in deep. He has a hair dryer? His hair always looks good, but still. I stifle a smile, suddenly terrified that while I've been admiring his designer bathroom, Nico's version of looking after Tori might mean ending her life painlessly instead of otherwise.

But when I emerge, he's wrapped her in a blanket. It rises and falls slightly with her breath. She is in a deep sleep.

"Come on," he says. "I'll run you back."

"What if she wakes while we're gone?"

"She won't."

We are on our way up the road before I dare ask. "How do you know she won't wake up?"

"I gave her a shot. She won't."

"A shot?"

"Don't look so alarmed. It was just sedative and painkiller, both of which will help her." He curses under his breath. "If this goes horribly wrong, it is on your neck, Rain."

"I'm sorry," I say. My breath catches, both distressed to be the cause of Nico's unhappiness and scared of it, all at once.

"By the way, I thought you said she was Slated."

"She is."

"Well, she hasn't got a Levo."

I gasp with shock and think back. I held her hand, helped her walk. I didn't even notice. I had other things to worry about. And I've gotten so used to being able to ignore my own levels, I didn't think about hers. But with what she has been through tonight—and before tonight by the sounds of things—it would have been enough to make her black out for sure if she still had one.

"What happened to it?" I say.

"Just one of many questions she will have to answer soon. And I have some things to discuss with you. But first, tell me about the fire," he says.

I blink at the sudden tears. "Ben's house, his parents' house. It burned down. Tori watched. She said they were inside, screaming, but Lorders stopped anyone from helping."

He shakes his head. "Think, Rain; what is the date?"

"November fifth."

"The fifth of November. Guy Fawkes," he says bitterly. "This was not the only burning tonight. Reports were coming in when you called. Lorders have taken this day that used to belong to us. Remember, Rain. Mark this day."

I gasp as a series of images flood my mind. Fireworks. Raids. Bonfires! Guy Fawkes: Over four hundred years ago, there had been a plot to blow up Parliament. We had used the day to remind the Lorders that their power was not absolute. To remind the people they had a voice.

Now the Lorders used it to remind us he was hanged for his trouble.

"To think they dare act so openly against the people they should serve! Things are getting worse, Rain. The Lorder grip is tightening. Soon none will dare stand with us against them. The time of reckoning is nearly at hand." He stops at the bottom of our road. "You need to keep your eye on the bigger picture, Rain. We'll talk about this some more after school tomorrow. Now go."

I get out of the car and slip into the shadows, along the houses, taking care. It is still dark, but close enough to six now that people may be awake. Eyebrows would definitely go up if anyone spots me creeping about dressed like this. But I see no one. When I reach our place, something catches my eye: a movement across the street? I hug the side of the house and look back, but can see nothing. Yet I was sure something moved.

I slip into the side door, then go quiet and careful up the stairs to my room: safe, at last.

For now.

Sebastian is curled up on my bed, eyes open wide. I change out of Nico's things quickly and into my pajamas, then stuff his clothes into my school bag to get rid of later.

There is just enough time for about an hour of sleep, sleep which I desperately need, but there is no chance. Not with fires raging in my mind.

The night is full of questions. How did Tori get away from the Lorders? She'd been returned to them; Ben got that out of her mum.

Why, we didn't really know—she was there one day, then gone. One of the missing. What happened to her Levo?

What happened to Ben's parents I don't need to phrase as a question: I know the answer. They asked too many annoying questions of their own. The Lorders happened to them, that's what. And this, the night after Ben's mum came here to ask for help. My blood turns to ice when I remember what Mum said to her: "You shouldn't have come here." Did Mum turn her in to the Lorders? Mum's dad was the Lorder prime minister who started it all.

I can't get the sight of their destroyed house out of my mind. Their home became their tomb. Will they get the bodies out? They've already been cremated.

According to Nico, a picture that has repeated itself in other places this night. Other victims.

I want to cry for them, but I can't. All I feel inside is cold, blind rage at what has been done. It pushes all the hurt aside.

It wants out.

10

"Kyla, wait!" I pause at the library door, turn. Cam rushes up.

"Have lunch with me?" He looks both ways and drops his voice. "I've got cake."

"Hmmm, I dunno. Is it chocolate?"

He peeks in his bag. "Today it is Victoria sponge. My uncle is a frustrated chef; he loves to bake."

"Well, all right," I say. Sugar and distraction might help get me through the rest of this long day. All I can think of are Ben's parents, what Lorders did to them and others like them. And meeting with Nico at the end of the day; we have to *do something*.

Crossing the grounds, we spot an empty bench in a group of two. When boys sitting on the other one see us heading over, they quickly split up and spread their stuff over both of them.

"Nice," Cam says.

"I'm used to it. Are you sure you want to risk being seen with me?"

"Are you kidding? You're a babe."

I laugh. "A Slated babe, don't forget."

"Was that their problem?" He looks back. "Want me to go rough them up for you?" And he drops into a boxing stance, fists up.

"All three of them? What would you do if I said yes?"

He looks both ways. "Hide. But I have my ways of getting back at people, y'know. When they least expect it." And he laughs in a *mwa-ha-ha-ha* villain sort of way.

"Sure you do."

"Doesn't what they did bother you?"

"It used to. But . . ." And I stop.

"But what?"

"People around me have a way of disappearing. That might be their reason, and, if so, I can't really argue."

"Disappearing?" His face forms into a serious expression. So he does have one. "That happens everywhere," he says, with such bitterness that I wonder what lies behind it.

"Look, there's one." I point at an empty bench on its own, behind the admin building. "If you dare."

"Well, let me think. Have you got a portable Bermuda triangle that follows you about?"

I look side to side. "I must have left it at home today."

"Are you going to put invisibility potion in my sandwich when I'm not looking?"

"No!"

"Then I'll risk it."

And I don't tell him the other reason why it doesn't bother me so much anymore. The list of things bothering me has been well and truly taken over; high school boys being stupid seems low priority.

We munch our sandwiches in silence, and he pulls out the cake.

"There are two pieces here," I say. "Were you planning this?"

"Who, me? No. I'm a growing boy. I always take two pieces of cake. But I don't mind sharing." He hands one across, and I take a big bite.

Light, sweet. Yummy! "I wish my mum liked to bake."

"How long have you lived there?"

I look at him sideways. "Not long. Almost two months."

"Do you ever wonder about your other parents?"

"My other parents?" I stall, though I know what he means. This conversation is venturing into no-go territory, the sort of stuff I'm not supposed to think about, let alone talk about. Slateds have no past; they start over. Looking back is not allowed.

"You know. Before you were Slated."

"Sometimes," I admit.

"Would you track them down if you could?"

Uncomfortable with where this is going, I busy my mouth with eating cake. Tracking down my past life would be well and truly illegal. Just being overheard having this conversation could be dangerous for us, and who knows who listens, or how? I wouldn't put it past the Lorders to bug every bench in the school—they and their spies like Mrs. Ali are everywhere.

"What about you?" I ask when all that is left of the cake is crumbs.

"What?"

"You said your dad took off. Do you still see him?"

The serious look is back, and the pause is long.

"Kyla, listen." His voice drops a notch lower. "You know what I said before, about people disappearing everywhere?"

I nod.

"My dad didn't split. Lorders took him. They broke into our house in the middle of the night and hauled him away. Haven't seen or heard from him since."

"Oh, Cam." I stare at him, shocked. He seems so carefree, so uncomplicated. Yet he knows what it's like to have someone he cares for go missing. Like Ben.

"Yeah. He was involved in some things they didn't like. Something to do with finding missing people. Illegal websites and stuff."

MIA?

I look nervously side to side. No one I can see is close enough to hear, yet some part of me doesn't trust this conversation. But I can't stop myself. "And your mum?" I ask.

"I think she'd be gone and so would I if it weren't for her research. Don't know much about it, but they want her to continue. They shuffled me off to keep her under their thumb."

"How horrible. I'm sorry; I shouldn't have asked."

"It's not your fault. You weren't close enough to use your secret disappearing skills! Unless your powers extend up a few hundred miles north of here?"

And Cam is back to kidding around. But he's not fooling me any longer. There is more going on inside him than I ever imagined.

"Listen," he says. "Do you want to go for a drive later? I really need to talk. More than we can here."

Curiosity wars with caution. Yet no need to decide, not yet. "I can't today. I'm going to be here late."

"Why's that?"

"Things to do."

"What?"

"Stuff."

"What sort of stuff?"

"Look, Mr. Curious, I'm just busy; that's all."

He pauses. "I'll hang. Give you a lift home?"

"I don't know how long I'm going to be."

"Doesn't matter. I've got nothing else to do."

I try to talk him out of it. Last thing I want is for my disappearing powers to manifest if any trouble I land in spreads his way. His mother has had enough of that already. But he insists he'll wait by his car until I show, so unless I want him to still be there the next morning, I best turn up.

The hall is empty. I knock once; Nico's door opens. I go in and he locks it.

"How is Tori?" I ask.

"She scrubs up pretty good," he says. "A few hot meals and staying off her sprained ankle is all she needs. Physically."

"She's not been any trouble?"

"No. Not yet. If she is, you'll hear about it. I've got somewhere I can move her soon; just sorting details. Though she says she can cook. Maybe I'll keep her."

She scrubs up pretty good; she can cook. A flash of the green-eyed monster inside sees them sitting down over a cozy dinner tonight. Using the candles I'd spotted on his table and finishing the open bottle of wine on his counter.

Nico smiles as if he can see exactly what I'm thinking, a smile that says, *If you don't like it, it is your own fault.*

I flush, and when he points at the chair next to his desk, I sit down.

"I realized something last night," he says, sitting on the other chair and pulling it close in front of mine so we are facing each other. My eyes are locked on his. The long lashes that seem too dark for pale blue irises. The lock of hair falling across his forehead that I have to suppress the urge to brush back.

I swallow. "What is that?"

He leans in close. "Rain is back," he whispers in my ear, and his words, his breath, are shock on my skin.

He smiles and sits back in his chair, a small school chair that looks ridiculous under him. "She really is back. I wasn't sure how much of her was in you. But what you did last night was her, wasn't it? Sneaking out in the night. Kyla wouldn't have done it."

"No. She wouldn't have," I say, and realize he's right. I've changed, so much. I'm still changing. My head is spinning. The room is a kaleidoscope, everything shifting, moving inside. I blink, and the world, Nico at its center, snaps into sharp focus.

"Yet something isn't quite right."

"What's wrong?" I say. "I'll fix it."

"Will you?" He smiles. "That whole thing with Tori. Now, the Rain I knew wouldn't have risked any exposure to Free UK for the sake of one girl. She'd have dealt with it, and there'd be no Tori, and no problem."

The safety of the group is paramount; any risk of drawing Lorder attention must be dealt with by any means necessary. But could she—I—really have just twisted Tori's neck? Or smashed her skull. A vision of Tori, head bashed against a tree, floats into view, and I flinch. No. I could never have done that. Could I? But I almost did; I just stopped when I recognized her. With wondering, memories stream in my mind—guns, screaming, blood. They say, *Yes, Rain could have done* anything. And I never really even liked Tori; why help her?

"Tell me what you're thinking," Nico says, in a voice that doesn't allow evasion.

I try. "My thoughts argue with each other. Like there are two voices inside my head, and they see things differently."

He nods, his eyes thoughtful.

"Please explain what has happened to me," I plead. "I don't understand."

He hesitates. Smiles. "I have some things to ask *you* still. But I will explain a little. Sometimes you are more Kyla, and sometimes more Rain. That makes sense. Things are reordering. In time, Rain will take over; she is stronger."

A vision rises unbidden in my mind: Lucy, with bloody fingers. And Nico . . . holding a brick.

I gasp, hold out my left hand wonderingly. Turn it side to side. "Did you do that? To make me right-handed?"

"Do what?"

"Hurt my fingers." I hesitate. "Lucy's fingers."

His eyes withdraw, look away. There is a pause: one beat, two. He looks back. "Do you remember being Lucy?"

"No. Not really, just a few bits of dreams that don't make sense. Please, Nico, everything is such a confused mess inside. What happened to Lucy?" What happened to ten-year-old *me*.

He hesitates, considering, then nods. "All right. You were special to me, Rain. But being on the side of freedom, there was always the risk of getting caught. I knew I had to find a way to protect you if the Lorders got their hands on you."

"How?"

"By separating you into two parts inside, so one could survive if you were Slated. Rain was stronger than Lucy; she survived."

As he says the words, I know them. I have always known them. I was one who became two: Lucy, with her childhood memories, and Rain, whose life was with Nico and Free UK. The pieces of the puzzle slot in together. Lucy was made to be right-handed; she wouldn't cooperate, so Nico forced her to be. Rain was left-handed. And how Slating is done depends on handedness: Memory access is hemisphere dominant and linked to handedness. But who was I when I was Slated?

"I still don't understand. If Rain was stronger and in control, why didn't the Lorders Slate me as her, as if I was left-handed?"

"That's the beauty of this. Rain hid inside when you were captured; you were trained to do this. So the part of you that was Lucy was dominant."

"So as far as the Lorders knew when they Slated me last year, I was right-handed. And they didn't know about Rain. When they took my memories, they only took part of them."

"Exactly. Lucy is gone; she was weak. But you, special Rain, survived Slating, hidden inside. Waiting for the right moment to fight your way out."

"And this," I say, spinning my Levo, "doesn't work anymore now because I'm Rain again, left-handed. It's linked to the wrong side of my brain."

"Just so." He catches my left hand in his. Gently kisses my fingertips. "I'm sorry I hurt you all those years ago. But I did it because it was the only way to protect you."

Lucy: gone forever. That is why I can't remember her life. The ache of loss fills me, spreads into the emptiness inside. So much of my life destroyed, forgotten. But part of me is still here: Nico saved me. If it weren't for him, I'd be gone completely. I wouldn't even know what I missed.

"Thank you," I whisper. And I wonder: Does Rain being stronger mean Kyla is disappearing, too? All that she hoped and cared about? Like Ben. Tears prick at my eyes, and I blink furiously. *Don't cry. Not in front of Nico. Don't!* And then fear wars with pain: Nico doesn't like weakness.

But instead of anger, he takes my hand. "What is it?" he says, voice gentle.

I cling to his hand. It is much bigger, stronger. He could crush mine in an instant.

"Ben," I whisper.

"Tell me. I know a little, but you tell me. What really happened to him?" He stresses *really,* as if he knows there is more than the official story.

"It was all my fault. I did it." I say out loud, at last, what has been haunting, festering, inside.

"What did you do? Tell me."

"I cut his Levo off. With a grinder."

And as I tell him the facts, the events, Nico shifts his chair around next to mine, slips a warm arm over my shoulders. And the images fill my mind: Ben's agony. Me running away, leaving him to his fate. And what was that, exactly?

"What happened to him?" I ask, my eyes pleading for a chance, a hope.

"You know the ultimate answer to that question," Nico says. "You know what the Lorders will have done to him if there was any life left."

I nod through the tears.

"And you know what they did to his parents."

"Yes."

"Do you feel it, Rain? Inside: the anger."

And it springs to life, a fire, as if Nico had tossed a match of his own. The bonfire burns in my mind, hotter and angrier than the blaze that consumed their house. Than all the fires Lorders set that night combined.

"Now, listen to me, Rain. This doesn't mean you have to forget about Ben, or what he meant to you, or what the Lorders did to his parents. Any of it. Just use it; use it the right way."

Use the rage.

And it rolls through me, like a wave—a searing heat that ripples through every muscle, every bone. Every drop of blood that burns in my veins.

I grip the arms of the chair. "We must make the Lorders pay for what they've done. They must be stopped!"

Nico cups his hands around my face, tilts it up. His eyes study mine, searching, assessing. At last, he nods. His eyes are warm. A flush on my skin tingles, travels up my body.

"Yes, Rain." He smiles, leans down. His lips lightly brush my forehead. "But there is one question you still haven't answered. When did you get your memories back?"

The attack in the woods. Wayne. The words are working their way up my throat to tell him what happened, but I stop. He'll deal with Wayne if he knows. But why am I protecting Wayne? Isn't that what he deserves?

"It really should have been when you left Ben and the Lorders took him. That should have done it; it is exactly the right sort of trauma to break through. So why didn't it happen then?" Nico says the words almost like he is talking to himself, as if he has forgotten I am there.

I squirm, uncomfortable with his analysis, his sifting through my "trauma" to evaluate its effects. But if my memories didn't return that day, why didn't I black out and die? I look at my useless Levo.

Then I remember. "I know," I say. "It was the pills."

"What pills?"

"Happy Pills. Ben got them from someplace," I say. Holding back just where he got them, and unsure why. They came from Aiden, who is in MIA; they run the Missing in Action website I saw at Jazz's cousin's place.

Nico nods. "That makes sense. They'd block the full experience. Then, when they wore off, Rain made an appearance."

He grins widely. Laughs. "Rain!" He hugs me. "You were always my favorite, you know."

My heart sings. Nico never had relationships with girls in training camps—not that I saw. His power was absolute, but we all wanted him.

He pulls back. "Now, listen. There is something you can do for me. You're still going to hospital appointments in London, aren't you?"

I nod. "Every Saturday." New London Hospital is a symbol of Lorder control, and a frequent Free UK target; it is where they took me, and countless others like me, and deliberately erased our memories.

"I want plans. As accurate as possible, of every bit of the hospital you know. Inside and out. Can you do that for me?"

"Of course," I say, eager to help strike against the Lorders, even in such a small way. I can see the layout in my mind without trying, my memory and map ability so ingrained inside that . . .

And a memory comes back. Long and tedious training. "You taught me that," I say slowly. "How to memorize positions and places, how to draw maps." Consequences were dire if we made a mistake: I remember, and quail inside. But I don't make mistakes anymore.

He smiles. "Yes. That was part of your training. You will do it."

"Yes. I will."

"Now get going."

I stand, and he unlocks the door, looks both ways. "All clear. Go."

• • •

I run around the school track, not trusting myself to meet Cam for the drive home until I calm down. All the moments with Nico I hold to myself, inside.

I was his favorite!

He hugged me. My forehead still tingles where his lips touched.

He saved me.

So many reasons he could have been angry, but he wasn't!

But most of all: *I know who I am.* I know where I come from, and where I belong. What I must do. The Lorders failed. *I remember.*

Joy threatens composure, and I pound harder and harder around the track, until a wolf whistle pierces my reverie. I spin around.

Cam.

He claps, and I slow my pace, do another lap to cool down, then walk over to him.

"Geez, you can run. Is this what you so desperately needed to do after school?"

I'm breathing hard. Shrug. "Sometimes, I really need to run," I say, not answering the question directly. And it is true enough. It used to be that I'd run to keep my levels up. Curious, I look at my Levo. Still hovering around 6; running used to put it up into the 8s, but it really is useless now.

"Time to head home?"

I nod. "Sorry I'm all sweaty," I say, and grin, then try to remember to tone it down. At least I have running as an excuse for being giddy.

11

"ARE YOU READY TO GO?" MUM ASKS.

I look up from the homework I am pretending to do at the kitchen table.

"Where?" I say, my mind a blank.

She laughs. "What day is it?"

And all I can think of is Guy Fawkes. Hard to believe this is still the same day that started before the sun came up with a burning house, and Tori.

"It's Thursday," she says.

"Thursday?" I stare at her blankly.

"Group, right?"

"Oh. Sorry." I dash to brush my hair, grab shoes. How could I forget? Too many other things floating through my mind. Group is every Thursday night. All the Slateds from the surrounding area get together with Nurse Penny to support our transition from hospital to society. Huh. More like to spy on us and watch for any deviation that needs to be dealt with. Then I squirm at my thoughts. That may be true in some ways, but Penny is all right.

This is still a test.

Yes. I must be like the rest of them. Penny or any other hidden listening ears mustn't notice anything different or wrong. I cast my mind back. Last Thursday, I was so upset about Ben, I could barely stay level enough to remain conscious. She'll expect the same.

I focus on that day, being that person, pushing Rain and her memories aside.

Kyla, you're on.

Penny's cardigan is bright lemon yellow with purple trim, her face just as sunny. She is talking to a woman and girl, neither of whom I recognize. The girl is fourteen or so, and grinning like a lunatic: a new Slated. They are all like that to begin with. Full of joy that the Lorders have stolen their memories, their past; that no matter what crimes they have committed, here is their second chance and a new life. I was like that, too, though less than most. Was it Rain's memories hiding inside that always made me different?

The other nine are as always. No Tori anymore; no Ben. And I don't have to remind myself to be just Kyla, to act and look as she would. Here, in this place, I *am* her. Rain doesn't belong.

We gather our chairs into a circle, and it begins.

Penny stands at the front. "Good evening, everyone!"

Everyone looks at one another, hesitates. "Good evening," a few voices say back, and then the rest chime in.

"Tonight I want you to welcome Angela. She is joining our group. And what do you do now?"

She looks around and I groan internally, remembering my first day here. It was Tori who rolled her eyes and told everyone to introduce themselves, all sarcastic. Then Ben came late.

The memory catches inside. Jumps like a stone skipping on water. I can see him, dashing through the door. Shorts and a long T-shirt, clinging to him from running. Always running. I sigh.

"Kyla?"

Penny walks over, concern in her eyes. "Are you all right, dear?" she says.

"Sorry, just faded out a moment." She checks my levels, raises an eyebrow when she sees they are fine at 5.8. She goes back to the front.

I give myself a shake inside. Neither smile too wide nor sink into misery. Stay *level* is what I am really saying. What all Slateds must do, though it isn't the same for me anymore.

Penny is smiling at the new girl, whose grin is even wider. She looks so happy, she is in no danger of ever blacking out from low levels like I used to sometimes. The rest of them, too; they all look *too* happy. Happy the Lorders caught them, stopped them doing or saying whatever it was that wasn't liked. I glance across the open, blissful faces. Were any of them *real* criminals like they were supposed to be? Murderers, or terrorists. Like me. They're so happy—do they even care what they once were? If my Slating had worked like it was supposed to, I'd be smiling along with the rest of them.

I'd be happy, too.

I jump as a warm hand squeezes my shoulder. Penny. "Can you answer my question?" she chides.

"Ah . . ."

"Why are we here?"

"It's our second chance?"

"Exactly, Kyla."

I do have a second chance—but not the one she means. She doesn't know I've come back, that the Lorders failed. My Slating failed. I hold the knowledge tight, a small knot of satisfaction deep in my gut.

Back to addressing the group, Penny tells us that today, we're going to play some games. She opens a trunk, takes out cards, checkers, and other board games. There is an odd number of us, and she decides she and I will make a pair. Keeping an eye on me still?

"Have you played any of these before?" she asks, and I look in the trunk to see what else is there.

"Most of them. I like chess. I used to play it late at night at the hospital; a Watcher taught me."

She takes the chess box out, hands it to me to set up while she checks on everyone else. The box is inlaid wood; it opens and the pieces are nested inside, one set in light wood, one in dark. I take them out, then line them up on the board. Rooks in corners, then knights, bishops, king, and queen. The long row of pawns in front, lined up and expendable. Though with the right strategy, the right game, a pawn can make the difference.

Penny returns and pulls a chair across so we can play.

My hand is drawn to one of my rooks: I pick it up. *A castle,* something says inside. *You used to call it a castle.*

No. I frown. The Watcher—bored, stuck babysitting me late at night when I was having nightmares—taught me to play. Taught me the correct names for each piece, their moves, and was surprised how quick I learned. By the time I left the hospital, I even won sometimes.

"Kyla?" Penny looks at me curiously.

I give myself an internal shake, put the chess piece back into its square. We begin.

"Good night?" Mum asks.

"All right." She looks at me still, wanting more. "We played chess, Penny and I."

"Who won?"

"She did."

I didn't play at my best. I kept having this weird feeling as I touched the pieces. Something *right* in the way they felt in my hands. I kept wanting to pick them up, run my fingers over corners and rounded edges, to pick out the shapes of each by touch alone.

I fake a yawn. "I'm tired. I'm going to turn in."

But up in my room, my brain is jumping.

My second chance, but not as the Lorders mean. My second chance with Free UK. To strike at the Lorders.

Yet . . . what have I done before with Free UK? Whenever I *try* to remember that life with Nico, it is shy and hides away. Things seem to come when I don't hunt and search. I try to relax, to let my mind drift. The training camp I can see—yes. But not much else. Did I go out on attacks? The Lorders caught me somehow, so I must have. But of that I remember nothing.

Nico's face floats into view and won't go away. With him this afternoon, it was hard to think, to know what to say or do. I just was what he wanted.

I shake my head, confused. No. That isn't right. It is what *I* want, too.

Though tonight, playing chess, I felt more like *me,* whoever that is. In my own skin. Like holding a rook in my hand somehow made things start to settle down inside, start working themselves out.

I concentrate on the board, the carved pieces standing on their own squares. I chew my lip. Every move I can see will end in one of mine captured. I haven't many left. I reach my hand out, then pull it back again.

"I don't know what to do," I admit, finally.

"Want a hint?"

I touch my fingers to one piece, then another. Watching his eyes.

He winks when I touch the castle on the king's side. But there is no-where useful it can go; there are just a few open spaces between it and the king. The king is in an unguarded position, and will soon be under threat. Unless . . .

"What's that special thing the castle can do?" I ask.

"It's called a rook, Lucy."

"It looks like a castle!"

"It does, doesn't it?" He smiles. "It can slide up to the king. And then they swap places."

"I remember!" I do as he said, they swap places, and my king is safe.

The game continues: I finally win.

I know he let me. I hold the castle in my small hand, take it to my room when I go to sleep. It stands on my bedside table when Daddy kisses me good night.

I wake slowly; warm, happy, safe. Open my eyes. The rook is gone. I sit up in shock, the room folding and contracting, changing, to become Kyla's once again. Not Lucy's.

How do I still have this memory? It should have been Slated away with the rest of her, like Nico said. Confusion twists and pulls inside. I've had dreams of Lucy before, but never anything this real.

Never anything of her at home, safe and happy.

I grasp at the dream, but already it is becoming unreal, slipping away. I stumble across the room, switch on the lights. Find my sketch pad and pencils, and try, again and again, to draw his face. To hold on to him.

But he is gone. I can't. All that is left is vague and unsure, a sense of size and proportion. No details, no features anyone could recognize as individual.

I give up on the hopeless task of drawing Lucy's father. My father. And I start on Ben instead. Now that Ben's parents are gone, there is no one else left to remember him. I'll look at his drawing every day. That way I can never forget him; I will always be reminded when I see his face.

And there is something else I can do. Lucy reminded me.

There is one last chance.

One final way I can try to find out what really happened to Ben: MIA.

12

"**Don't you want to go with Cameron?**" **Amy smiles**—more of a smirk, really. "He's quite cute, don't you think?"

"No! I mean, no, I don't want to go with Cameron."

"So you agree he is cute, then."

I roll my eyes and get into Jazz's backseat.

I'd told them yesterday not to wait, to go and I'd come home with Cam. Mum didn't know and probably wouldn't approve. Not necessarily of him, but of Amy and Jazz being alone: I'm their chaperone. I'd already explained this to Cam so he won't think he is on regular chauffeur duty. Especially today, when I've got plans I don't want him in on.

We pull onto the road before I ask. "Jazz, do you think we could visit Mac after school today?"

"Sure," he says, and that is that. Mac is Jazz's cousin; the illegal computer in his back room is where I first found Lucy on MIA. Can they find Ben?

Amy starts babbling about all the gossip from the doctor's office yesterday. I tune out, but then something grabs my attention.

"Amy, what was that?" I ask, not sure I heard right; not sure I want to.

"You know that man I told you about, the one they found beaten up who was in a coma? He woke up in the hospital."

My heart skips a beat, an actual fluttering feeling deep in my chest.

Try to sound casual.

"Has he said anything? About what happened to him?"

"He was pretty out of it, according to the nurse whose friend works at the hospital. Might have amnesia from his head injuries. Lorders came to talk to him, but gave up because he made no sense."

Tell Nico!

But then what will happen? After he has finished being completely furious it is the first he has heard of it. After he gets over me not telling him about Wayne's attack when he asked what triggered the return of my memories. Wayne is a risk: If he talks about what I did, Lorders will come for me. Nico will have him dealt with, one way or another. *Dealt with* means *dead.* And then he'll deal with me.

I'm not doing it.

My instincts protest against taking such a risk. But wait and see: Maybe Wayne won't remember anything.

Maybe, he will.

That afternoon we file into the hall for year eleven assembly. Everyone takes their seats without fuss, and it is pin-drop quiet. Up front stands the reason: Lorders.

A cold shock of recognition travels down my spine when I glance their way.

Don't stare.

I fight to pull my eyes away. These Lorders I know: Agent Coulson and his underling. Coulson's cold eyes sweep the room and I struggle to avert mine, but they are locked. What is he doing here?

Coulson is not run-of-the-mill Lorder; he is something more. It was obvious when they came to question me after Ben disappeared. For a start, they'd be careful who they sent when Mum was involved.

They'd want to be sure how they dealt with the daughter of the Lorder hero, Wam the Man, prime minister before Free UK blew up him and his wife. Mum might not be involved in politics now or exploit her connections in any way I've seen, but they couldn't do or say anything that couldn't be explained if it needed to be. She'd been the only reason, I'm sure, that I hadn't been hauled off for a less gentle inquisition.

But more than that: Coulson exudes careful power. He isn't just a nasty bully, though I'm sure he would be if an occasion called for it. Everything about him is cold calculation.

His eyes rest on mine. Pinpricks of sweat break out on my forehead.

Look away!

I break the gaze, lower my eyes. Resist the impulse to check, to see if he still stares.

He's just a man. A nasty one.

He would bleed red just like anybody else. He should!

Assembly begins. The head drones on about student accomplishment, then sprinkles his usual warnings. His injunction to live up to your potential . . . or else.

But I am somewhere else.

In my mind, it is Coulson who drags Ben's pain-racked body away from his mother.

It is Coulson who holds a lit match. Tosses it to Ben's house.

Coulson who plucks Lucy from her family.

Rage fills me: roiling, hot rage. Outside, my face is calm, attentive; inside is something else.

If I had a gun in my hand right now, I could raise it. Shoot him. He deserves it. They all do.

The hard seat under me, the drone of the head's voice, and the hall full of listening students all fade away. My hands grip cold metal, my eyes take sight, careful aim. Index finger pulls the trigger. A blast of noise, a recoil as the gun slams back in my hands. The bullet flies across the room too fast for normal eyes to follow, but mine watch its progress to target.

It strikes his chest. His heart explodes: A red wave ripples out in all directions like a stone dropped in still water. He falls.

I smile, then realize assembly is over; everyone is filing out of the room. I'd stood and followed along without realizing. Cam has dropped back slightly from his tutor group and walks beside me. He must think I'm totally mad to smile here, now.

I am.

The spell, if there was one, is gone. We approach the doors of the hall. The other Lorder stands there, watching students leave, one by one. Coulson stays at the front, door duty beneath him. I'm relieved. And then lunch twists in my stomach as images of Coulson's bloody body replay in my mind.

"Are you all right?" Cam whispers as we step out of the hall. "You've gone all pale."

I just shake my head, run to the toilet in the next building, and throw up, again and again. When I'm finally sure there is nothing left to come up, I splash water on my face and stare in the mirror.

What the hell happened in there?

My hands are shaking. I'm not that person, I couldn't do that. Could I? I wouldn't cry if he died, but not by my hands.

But then what was all that training for?

And visions flow through my mind like a movie on fast-forward. Shooting practice. Targets. Knives and their uses. Faster it spins. I was a good shot, the best of my cell. A cell that was, itself, the best.

No!

Yes. What is being a terrorist about? Political discussions over cups of tea? The Lorders are evil. He deserves to die. They all do.

I look at my hands. I can feel the cold weight of a gun in them. I know what to do with one. He deserves to die. Why not?

13

"I'LL LET YOU IN ON A SECRET." JAZZ IS SMILING, SO I'M guessing this isn't bad news.

"What?"

"Before you asked this morning, I was planning on us going to Mac's today, anyhow. He's got a surprise for you."

My stomach jumps. Jazz is still smiling—he must know what it is, and it must be good.

"It's not Ben, is it?" I whisper quietly. Knowing it won't be, it can't be, but unable to stop myself from asking the question.

Jazz's smile falls away. "I'm sorry, Kyla. If I find out anything about him, you'll be the first to know."

I lean back against his car, unable to stop the wave of disappointment, however unreasonable. Aiden promised he'd send news through Mac if he found out anything about Ben, so my brain instantly flipped to that. *Wrong.*

Amy appears across the parking lot. She walks to us and slips her arms around Jazz. He turns and kisses her, and I try not to watch.

"Are you all right?" she asks me.

"Fine."

"A friend of mine saw you running to the bathroom, looking sick."

"Oh. I just had an upset tummy, no big deal. I'm fine now."

"Sure you don't want to go straight home?"

"I'm sure!"

"Don't look so fierce! We're going already."

"In you get, ladies," Jazz says, holding the car door open.

We drive down back country lanes, through stubbled fields. Past farms and woodland, to Mac's place. It is down a narrow lane, isolated. His huge backyard is full of bits of cars that he scavenges and salvages for parts to build into new cars. Like the one he made for Jazz. But he isn't just a mechanic.

What could the surprise be?

It knocks me over when we go through Mac's front door.

Skye! Ben's dog, a gorgeous golden retriever, jumps up and covers my face excitedly with great sloppy dog kisses. I drop to my knees and wrap my arms around her, sink my face into her fur. Fur that smells smoky.

Jazz takes Amy for a walk to get her alone as usual. Mac watches me and Skye, her tail thumping on the ground, sprawled half on my lap. Something is hiding behind the careful look on his face.

"How?" I ask him. A one-word question that covers so much. How did she survive? How is Ben's dog at Mac's?

Mac sits next to us on the floor. He rubs her ears, and she flops down between us, her head on my knee. "That's the happiest I've seen this dog look since she got here last night."

"Do you know what happened?"

"Some. The rest I can fill in. What I can't figure out is how come you don't look surprised to see her here, and why you are the one asking me if I know what happened."

"I heard something," I say guardedly.

Mac puts up one hand. "You don't have to tell me how you know about Ben's parents. You do know, don't you?"

I nod, slump into Skye once again.

"Skye here is a lucky dog."

"Yeah. First the boy she loves, then the rest of her family are gone: very lucky."

"She's a survivor. Not sure if she was out, or got out, or what. But Jazz's mate found her the next day. Jazz brought her here. None of the neighbors wanted to be seen to keep her in case anyone official got offended she escaped." The way he says the words, I can tell he thinks about as much of that as I do.

"Stay there," he says, gets up, goes into the kitchen. Comes back a moment later with a bowl in his hand. "See if you can get her to eat."

And so I sit on the floor with Skye, feeding her bits of meat. She eats some, then closes her eyes and goes to sleep.

Her solid warmth and doggy smell, even with smoky undertones, feel good, real, and I don't want to move. But I have other business with Mac. I ease her off my legs, and find him in the kitchen.

My breath catches when I see the owl on top of a cabinet: the metal sculpture Ben's mum made from a drawing I did once, then gave to me. So beautiful—and deadly. So much talent she had, and this is all that is left of it now. I run fingertips across its feathers; inside, pain is welling up, wanting out.

I fight to contain it, hold it inside. I'm here for a reason.

"Can I look at MIA?" I ask.

Mac stares levelly back at me, then nods. I follow him to the back room, and he uncovers his highly illegal, not government issue computer. It doesn't block websites that the Lorders don't want to be seen, like legal computers do. Soon the MIA website fills the screen: Missing in Action. Full of missing children.

It was me asking Mac about Robert that made him show me this computer the first time. Mum's son, Robert, is on the memorial at school as being killed on a bus with thirty other students when they got in the way of an AGT attack. But Mac was there, too. He knew Robert didn't die on the bus, and thought he was probably Slated. It was when he was showing me on MIA how many children go missing in this country without explanation that we first stumbled on Lucy. Me.

Somehow I have to do it, to check again. I enter into the search box: *girl, blond, green eyes, 17.* Hit the search button.

Pages of hits come up, but it isn't long before I spot her and click on her image to enlarge the listing.

Her face—my face—fills the screen. Lucy Connor, ten years old, missing from school in Keswick. Seven years ago now, but you can still tell it is me. She looks absurdly happy, smiling at the camera holding a gray kitten.

A birthday present.

I gasp as the knowledge hits me. The kitten was her—my—tenth birthday present.

"Are you all right, Kyla?" Mac asks.

Tears are smarting my eyes. I've never had a memory like that, of Lucy's life, just appear in my mind before. Ever. Only snippets in dreams. Mostly nightmares of horrible things, until the chess-playing dream the other night. But dreams access the unconscious. This time, I was awake. She should be gone, completely gone; Nico said so. What can it mean?

Mac puts a hand over mine. "What is it?"

"It's just that for a second there, I thought I could remember something. That kitten." I sigh. "I must be going mental."

"Have you changed your mind about MIA?" he asks. He looks at the screen, and I follow his eyes. There is a button, marked *Found*. One click of the mouse and I could find out. Who reported Lucy missing? Maybe my dad. Maybe we could play chess again.

I shake my head. No. My life is enough of a mess, and apart from a few fragments of dreams, I don't even know my real family. Anyhow, I can't risk Free UK or Lorders following me to them: They are better off missing me.

Time to get to my reason for being here. "Are you involved with MIA?"

"I'm more of a . . . relay than anything else. Why?"

"I was wondering something. Can you get Ben put on MIA?"

Mac stares back. He knows Ben's story, more or less. Even if he doesn't know my role in it. That Ben was taken by Lorders. He must think it will be a waste of time, that there is nothing left of Ben to be found. He's probably right.

But he nods. "Of course. Have you got a photo?"

I shake my head. "No. But I've got this," I say, and pull my drawing of Ben out of my pocket. I'd spent hours on it, making it as lifelike as possible. "Is it good enough?"

He whistles. "It is more than good; it's him. It's perfect. But it'll have to be scanned, and I haven't got one here. I'll get Aiden to do it. All right?"

I force reaction from my face, hide dismay. "Thanks," is all I say. Mac's friend Aiden was the one whose stories of Slateds cutting off their Levos gave Ben the idea to try it in the first place. It was Aiden's Happy Pills that made the attempt possible. Aiden was also the one who wanted me to report myself found on MIA, such a breach of the rules Slateds must live by that it would be a certain death sentence if

Lorders found out. He wasn't a terrorist, he said, but an activist—trying to change things in other ways.

A no-hoper.

Maybe. But at least he doesn't kill people. Thinking of Robert earlier reminded me of all those students who died. Killed by stray AGT bombs meant for Lorders. I'd had nightmares of that bus attack when I first learned of it, but I couldn't have been there! I was only ten years old when it happened.

But Nico could have been.

No. Nico would never do that, not a busload of innocent schoolkids. He wouldn't. His fight is against the Lorders. *My fight.*

I convince Mac that I'm all right, to leave me alone to compose myself, and stay looking at Lucy on the screen. What happened to her? I can't work it out. One minute she is a happy kid with a kitten, a dad who lets her win at chess. The next? I shake my head. She disappears at age ten, then somehow there is a huge jump, a gap in time. Rain's memories don't begin until about age fourteen, training with Nico and other teenagers, off in some boot camp in the woods. Learning how to shoot guns and blow things up.

What happened to her the four years between to take her to that place?

Amy and Jazz get back from their walk. As we leave, I touch the owl Ben's mother made for me. It holds a secret. A note from Ben, still hidden. Knowing where to look, I can see the tiny white speck, the corner of paper that if pulled reveals itself as his last words to me. But I can't bear to look at it, not today.

Mac holds Skye when she tries to follow us. I twist to look back at her. Her mournful eyes follow us until she is gone from sight.

• • •

Green trees blue sky white clouds, green trees blue sky white clouds . . .

But different.

Fields of long grass. Daisies. Alive with detail, movement, and sound, like never before. Trees, but not from underneath: top branches rush past as I dive. There is a rustle that says mouse, but when I get there, it is gone.

No matter.

I beat my wings and climb up again, the sun warm on my feathers. I should hide, wait for dark and better hunting.

But I want to fly to the sun. Leave this earth behind. How high can I go? I face the open sky, glide on a warm updraft, then beat my wings to reach the next one. Almost effortless, higher and higher. I can fly forever.

Trees are merging into field, a uniform green far below, when it happens. First a gradual sense of stiffness, making my wings have to work harder to beat at all. Then, a trap. As if my flesh is inside an owl-shaped box that gradually compresses and grows smaller, tighter, and heavier, no matter how I struggle. Until it isn't flesh and feathers inside a trap, but sinew and blood and muscle all thickening, slowing, stiffening. Becoming metal. The trap isn't around me. It is me.

The sky is not my friend anymore. Air whistles past, and trees rush closer. Plummeting down, down, down . . .

14

THE NEXT MORNING, MUM IS DRIVING US THROUGH LONDON streets that I now see with different eyes.

I see the menace. This close to the hospital, there are Lorders in black operations gear at every corner. They stand in twos and threes, more of them than the last time we came this way. With machine guns. I see the signs of conflict: boarded windows, damaged and abandoned buildings spaced between ones full of life. And most of all I see the real damage, the eyes of a beaten people. In the way they hold themselves, where they look, where they don't. It is much worse in London than in the country.

"All right?" Mum asks, and I nod. "Your dad will be home when we get back; he called earlier." She says the words casually, almost too casual to be anything but contrived.

"Is something wrong?" I ask, the words out before I can censor.

"Why do you ask?"

"You seem funny when you mention him, that's all." And I remember how she changed the subject the last time his name came up.

She doesn't answer, eyes straight ahead on traffic, until I think she isn't going to.

She sighs. "Grown-up stuff. It's complicated, Kyla," is all she says.

We continue in silence until the hospital rears up, a great ugly sore on the landscape among old buildings and twisty streets: a modern monstrosity. This hospital is a Lorder symbol of power; it is an obvious target, where Slating takes place.

I study the number and positions of towers on the perimeter. I promised Nico accurate maps, outside and in. I am going to deliver. Anyone could note this, and I'm sure they already have. The inside arrangements, likewise. Someone in the multitude of medical and other staff could be bought. Nico must want confirmation from eyes he has trained, eyes he trusts. Mine.

We continue to the main entrance and wait in the line. Lorders at the gates are searching cars. Visitors must get out and go through a metal detector on foot, before getting back in their cars and driving below to park.

Unease twists my stomach. What if Nico is wrong and the com on the underside of my Levo isn't undetectable? Maybe I should have taken it off before I came. Can I even get it off? I haven't tried.

We inch forward. Finally, it is our turn; the Lorder on this side of the gate puts up his hand to stop us. He makes a deferential gesture to Mum, as daughter of the Lorder hero: hand touching heart, then held out. An apology on his face that this time we must comply like everyone else.

We get out of the car, and my feet are like lead as I walk to the metal detector. An alarm goes off as I step through, and I almost panic, until I realize it is my Levo. A Lorder with a handheld scanner gets me to hold out my arms and runs it across my body. It beeps again at my Levo, and he nods for me to go through.

That was it? Inside, I snort. How obvious is it that the one place to hide metal on a Slated is on or in their Levo? What if it were an explosive?

Though the com is well disguised. If I didn't know it was there, I couldn't even find it by touch. And I suppose it wouldn't be possible to have something like this on most Slateds. If their Levos were working properly, putting it on would cause pain and levels to fall.

We get back in the car and spiral underneath the hospital to park. Nerves are twisting in my stomach: Can I pass muster in Dr. Lysander's eyes? Every Saturday I see her; she digs and pokes around in my mind. Checks up on me, looks for cracks. Places where I am different from other Slateds.

I am *so* different now. How will I get through this?

She is smart, the brainiest person I've ever known. She sees what you try to hide.

Easy. Don't hide anything. Tell her about your inner terrorist.

Yeah, right.

I must be Kyla, the girl she knows, and only her. Nobody else. I focus, concentrate, think of Kyla.

"Kyla?" Dr. Lysander stands at the door to her office. "Come in."

I sit on the chair opposite her desk, glad of the door closed behind me: There is a Lorder guard in the waiting area once again. They must be on alert for another attack.

When the last one happened—several weeks ago today—Dr. Lysander was whisked away at the first sign of trouble. She vanished before the terrorists came on their killing spree. One pointed a gun at me before his mate told him not to waste a bullet on a Slated. Where did they take her to get her hidden away so fast?

She taps at her screen a moment. Looks up. "You look very thoughtful. Perhaps we could begin today by you telling me what you are worrying about."

The truth, but not too much of it; lie to Dr. Lysander at your peril.

"I was thinking about all the security we came through to get in today."

"Ah, I see. Does it worry you?"

It certainly did today. "Yes."

"Why is that, do you think?"

"It makes me feel like they are going to haul me away and lock me up."

"Guilty conscience?" Then she laughs; she thinks she is telling a joke. Slateds never do anything wrong. Almost never, that is; what about Ben? Anyhow, if being Slated means you can't be a danger to self or others, then why are we all watched and monitored so carefully?

And I am different. More so now, but I always have been. Is this why she is my doctor? Dr. Lysander is famous, the one who invented Slating in the first place. In all the times I've seen her, there has never been another patient in her waiting room. And without being able to define how I am different, she somehow knows something is wrong, and tries to find out how, and why. Yet even she has no grasp of the degree of difference, the implications. The ticking time bomb I was, and am.

A terrorist bomb, like the one that hit Robert's bus.

My stomach twists.

"What is it, Kyla? Tell me what is upsetting you," she says.

"The terrorist attack here," I answer.

She tilts her head to one side, considering my words. "Still thinking of that day, are you? Don't be frightened. You are quite safe here now, I promise you. Security has gone to new measures." The way she says it: She thinks they're going too far, being too careful. She's wrong.

Find out.

"Do you mean the new security gates we had to walk through to get in?"

She nods. "That, and some other things. Technological things. The whole hospital is protected."

How?

But I can't ask. Excessive curiosity is not a Slated trait.

Then, I see. Her telephone and intercom on the desk have changed; they are not cordless anymore, but hardwired. Her computer, too: A snake of wires reach out from it and run along the room to the corner and out through the wall. But isn't that old technology?

She taps at her screen. Looks up.

"I've got conflicting reports from your school."

"Oh?"

"Apparently you've been both distant and miserable, and a happy bundle of energy, sometimes all on the same day." She half smiles. "Care to explain that?"

"I'm not always the same person." The truest thing I've said so far today.

"Being a teenager can be hard work sometimes. Still, I'd like to schedule some scans, see how things are. Perhaps next time."

They might see the memory pathways have changed. Scans must be avoided!

But how?

Dr. Lysander closes her computer, folds her hands and faces me. "Now, Kyla. Have you thought any more of what we were speaking about the last few visits?"

"What do you mean?" I ask, stalling.

An eyebrow goes up. "We were talking about difference. Deviation.

What is happening with you inside that is outside of the usual. You said you would think about it, and speak to me."

Give her something.

I swallow. "Sometimes . . . I think I remember things. That I shouldn't."

She considers. "That is not unusual with Slateds. It is human to abhor the void, the absence of accessible memory. To make things up to fill it. Yet . . ." She pauses, thinking. "Tell me what you remember."

Without meaning to, without thinking or choosing something either real or made up, I go straight for the one I want to hug to myself and not share. Dr. Lysander has that effect.

"Playing chess with my dad. My real dad. It was long ago, my hands were small. I was much younger."

"Tell me about it," she says, and I do. Everything. The feel of the rook in my hand. The sense of warmth and security when I woke.

"Just a dream, most likely," she says.

"Maybe. But it was so detailed. It felt real."

"Dreams can be like that sometimes. Anyhow, I'm glad you've left nightmares behind." She smiles, looks at the clock. "Nearly time," she says. "Is there anything else you would like to talk about?"

Keep her curious.

I hesitate. Then shake my head.

"There is something; tell me."

"It's just that before I had the dream, I was playing chess. And I kept picking the rook up in my hand, feeling it."

She sits forward. "You felt drawn to touch and hold it?" I nod. "That is interesting. Perhaps a physical memory lingers? Triggering the dream, which may be a subconscious fabrication, but still; very interesting."

"I don't understand. If a memory is gone, it's gone. Isn't it?" And I know I should leave this alone, shouldn't make her focus more closely on it, but can't help myself. I want to know.

"That is the popular understanding of what happens with Slating. It isn't quite accurate." She sits back. "It is more like this, Kyla: Your conscious *access* is what is destroyed. The memories are still there, you just can't find them."

They are still there? Trapped like Rain was, behind a wall. Does that mean Lucy is somewhere inside me still, screaming to get out? I shudder. "Is that why things come out in dreams? My conscious mind can't get at them, but when I'm asleep . . ." I stop, not liking where this is going, not liking what she will think of it. Slateds don't have memories, awake or asleep. Do they?

"Rarely, this can happen. It is far more likely that your dreams are made up in that overactive imagination of yours." She taps her fingers on the desk a moment. "We'll leave doing scans. For now. Away you go."

It isn't until I'm back in the car with Mum, driving away from the hospital, that I trust myself to think. What happened? One minute Dr. Lysander wants scans, then she doesn't.

If I'm accessing old memories, and the pathways show up on scans, she'd have no choice but to tell the board. I'd be terminated.

But if Dr. Lysander realizes something has gone wrong with my Slating, surely that is what she is supposed to do? I think about our conversation, what was said and not said, her facial expressions. All I can come up with is that she is curious.

She can't study me if I am dead. She wants to know what makes me tick.

Tick like a bomb.

15

DAD'S CAR IS OUT FRONT WHEN WE GET HOME. HE AND AMY are arm in arm on the sofa with cups of tea when we walk in.

"There's my other two girls!" he says, smiles, and holds out a hand. I walk across. "Give your dad a kiss on the cheek," he says, and with no obvious escape, I do.

He's in a good mood today.

"Sit down, Kyla. I'll make us some drinks," Mum says, and disappears into the kitchen. No kiss on the cheek from her.

Third degree follows.

"So, how is school?"

"Fine."

"Who is this new boy I've been hearing about?" he says, and winks.

I glance at Amy. *Thanks a lot,* I say with my eyes. But she just smiles, oblivious to the look I give her.

Amy doesn't seem to get that some things should be said, others not. It used to be when I first got here that I was the one with that problem, when it came to her and Jazz, before they were officially allowed to see each other. But the more I understand, the less I realize Amy does.

"What new boy?" I say.

Amy smirks. "Cameron, of course."

"He's just a friend, no big deal. His uncle makes fantastic cakes."

"How about you bake us a cake now and then?" Dad says, calling out to the kitchen. Mum doesn't answer, but teacups clatter loud on the counter.

"Where've you been?" I ask, before he has a chance to ask me anything else.

"Oh, here and there. Work, you know." He smiles again, and I can see he is very pleased. Anything that has him that pleased makes me nervous.

As Mum brings in our tea there is a knock at the door. She turns to answer it, but Dad jumps up. "I'll go," he says.

She plonks down in an armchair, hands clenched on her cup. She is *so* not happy.

Sebastian is asleep on the back of the sofa. I pick him up and put him on her lap. He protests sleepily, then flops down, and her eyes meet mine. A half smile. Cat therapy.

"Well, look who's here." Dad comes back in, and following him is Cam. I groan internally. He is a master of brilliant timing.

He has a bicycle helmet dangling from his hand. "It's a gorgeous day; come for a bike ride? You can use my aunt's if you haven't got one."

An escape?

Best to look neutral.

"Perhaps I should stay. Dad just got back."

"No, no; you go on," Dad says. "Have fun." He smiles, and everything about him is friendly, open, caring. Is this the same dad who threatened to return me to the Lorders when Ben disappeared?

"You can use my bike, out in the shed," Mum says. "Don't forget to wear a helmet."

Dad follows us to the door. "Can you get Kyla's bike out?" he says to Cam, and points out the shed at the side of the house. "She'll just be a moment."

Cam heads out the door, and Dad and I are alone in the hall. Now comes the warning?

He smiles. "Kyla, I think we've gotten off on the wrong foot. If I've seemed harsh before, it was just because I was worried about you getting into trouble. You know I'm here for you, to help you if you ever need it. Don't you?"

"Sure," I say, surprised. This is more Dad like he was at the beginning, when I first got here. Maybe he regrets overreacting?

"Go on. Have a good afternoon," he says, and holds the door open.

"I'm not sure I know how to ride a bicycle," I say to Cam, but as I grip the handlebars and push it to the road, I feel that I do.

Cam pushes his bike down on the grass and holds mine upright. He has me get on and pedal slow on the pavement while he runs alongside, one hand on the handlebars. I laugh and pedal harder until he falls behind. I drop off the curb and onto the road.

Faster!

But I hold the speed in check until he catches up on his bike.

"You learn in a hurry!"

I laugh. "Let's see how fast we can go." And take off.

The day is crisp, clear. A cold rush of November air hits my face and body, but I'm pedaling hard enough to be warm. Freedom!

I hold back, just a little, so Cam can keep up. Eventually as we crest a hill he yells out to take a break. I coast to a footpath on the side of the road and stop.

He's breathing hard when he catches up. "Not only are you fit, Kyla. You are also *fit*!" he gasps out.

I laugh. We lay our bikes down on the grass and sit on a crumbling stone wall. From this high point we can see the Chiltern countryside folding out in all directions: an area of outstanding natural beauty, or so they say.

Lucy went missing from the Lake District; there would have been mountains where she lived, not just hills. Once, not paying much attention to what I was doing, I drew a picture of her with mountains behind. But if I try to think of them deliberately, there is nothing. Is this another memory trapped inside me?

"Everything all right?" Cam asks, looking at me curiously, and I wonder how long I've been staring off into space.

"Sorry. Yes, I'm fine."

I look back at him and realize a few things. He is staring into my eyes; he is sitting very close. And I like it. And then, all at once, I don't.

I shift, move away a little. Look back over the hills.

"Listen, Kyla. I think we need to have a talk."

"What about?"

"About Ben."

His name tears a hole inside. "What do you know?"

"That he disappeared. And I heard a few rumors, that you were involved somehow. What happened? You can tell me. No one can hear us here."

I close my eyes tight. There is a part of me that longs to talk about it, tell him everything. He'll understand. His dad got taken by Lorders, didn't he?

There is another part—Rain—that says *no*. Don't trust. Never trust.

I shake my head and look back at Cam. His eyes are disappointed. "Well, if you ever want to talk, I'm here. And I understand something else."

"What's that?"

"We're friends, that's all. Don't worry on that score. It's obvious you are still hurting over this other guy. I'm not trying anything. All right?"

I look at him again, and all I see is friendly concern.

Yeah, right.

But I'll take him at face value. For now. "Friends, then?" I say, smile, and hold out my hand.

Late that night, the house is quiet. Dad is gone. He stayed for dinner, then after Amy and I went up for the night, he and Mum argued in the kitchen. Voices kept down but you couldn't mistake the tone. After that the phone rang, and he left.

The compulsion to draw is on me: The hospital, the towers, the new security at the gates, all begin to take shape on paper. I wonder about the hardwired computers and phones. Mum said her cell phone wouldn't work there today, and when I asked she said it usually does.

My Levo has its own secrets: Would my com have worked there if I tried? I spin it around and feel nothing. Dead as it has been since my memories came back.

Some of my memories, that is. Though I remembered the birthday kitten. I couldn't if Lucy were truly gone like Nico said, could I? I stare at my left hand, move the fingers, the ones that were broken like I was inside. A hand is one thing; what would have been enough to split a person in two? I flinch at a vision of a brick and hold my fingers tight together.

Maybe if I hadn't seen Lucy on MIA, her memories would have stayed hidden. Nico must know more, but something inside says *don't ask.* He was a bit weird when I asked him about Lucy—some mix of surprise that I knew who she was, and something else.

He said he did it all to protect me, because I was special; he was harsh to be kind. But why am I special? Why did he track me down in this new life? I can't imagine anything I could do for Free UK that would be worth that effort. It must be something else. I have to know.

I hesitate. Why not? I slip out of bed and close my bedroom door. Hit the button under my Levo. Seconds pass.

There is a tiny click. "Yes?" he answers.

A thrill rushes through me with his voice as he tells me where to meet him tomorrow. I'm excited to see him, ridiculously so. He isn't angry with me about dumping Tori on him anymore, I can tell. He sounds happy, chilled, and I'm so relieved. Then I hear Tori's laughter in the background.

16

"**Sure you don't mind?**" **Mum hesitates at the door,** umbrella in hand. It's pouring.

"I'm sure. Go."

Mum is off to Aunt Stacey's for a long Sunday lunch, collected by another friend, wine in hand. She won't be back anytime soon. And Amy is off with Jazz's family for the day. An empty house, and no need to sneak out.

I consider calling Nico and getting him to pick me up closer, then dismiss it. It is just a little rain, and he is unlikely to be sympathetic.

I'm upstairs looking for a raincoat when there is a knock at the front door.

Standing out of sight at the side of the window, I peek down. I can just work out that it's Cam under that umbrella.

He might be hard to get rid of, and the house is dark and quiet. Let him think I'm not here. I wait silently; eventually he gives up and goes back across the road.

I fold up the drawings I made last night for Nico, plans of the hospital. Wrap them in plastic and tuck them in an inner pocket.

After chewing on a pen a moment, I leave a short note: *Went for a walk.* Just in case Mum or Amy get home early, so they don't panic or create a fuss.

I realize I'd best go out the back way in case Cam is watching and demands to know why I didn't answer the door. The back way is not appealing in this weather. I sigh. Outside I march across our long, muddy backyard in the deluge, then push through the scraggy hedge and fight my way through brambles to get to a path that will take me around to the bottom of our road.

"You're soaked," Nico says, and makes me wait to get out of the rain while he pulls a towel from the back and puts it over the passenger seat.

We drive on, quiet except for low music on the car stereo. Classical. Not what I would have thought Nico would like, but then what do I know about him, really, as a person?

"Is everything all right, Rain?" he says.

I nod. "Yes. Just exhausted; it's been a hard few weeks."

He laughs. "You're getting soft. What you need is a good endurance course in the woods for a few days."

"All right; I will if you will."

He shakes his head. "If only we could. Those were the good days, weren't they, Rain? With the Owls."

My eyes open wide. *The Owls.* That is what we were called, the code name for our cell. Is that why I was so fascinated by owls? To draw them, follow them, no matter where they led? Images fly through my mind.

The Owls were the best!

There were seven of us. Well, eight, but one died early on in an accident with explosives, and I shy away from thinking of her. Three girls and four boys. I was the youngest, not quite fourteen when I joined, the oldest fifteen. We were so tight: best friends, fiercest competitors. We lost our old identities and picked new names from the woods when we joined; mine was Rain. A face floats in front of my eyes, then vanishes. Who was he? The best part of things, until . . . until . . . something went wrong. Then he was the worst. What happened? The memories vanish.

"What happened to everyone?"

He glances sideways. "Some were captured, like you, and presumed Slated. Others died on missions. Do you want to know who—"

And I interrupt him. "No. Don't tell me." I don't want to know who died, to remember their names only to know they are gone.

"They fought for what they believed in," he says. "It is a good death."

Easy to say when you are alive.

We dash into Nico's house in the rain. I start to walk in from the door, but Nico pulls me back. "Don't drip everywhere," he says. And I shuck off jacket and boots, still half-soaked and shivering.

Tori is curled up on the sofa, reading, warm and dry. Her scratches and bruises are less apparent, and her dark hair shines.

"Hello," she says, then turns back to her book.

I don't know what to expect from Tori, exactly. We were never close. She didn't particularly like me before, and that probably had something to do with Ben. Yet I did risk my neck to save hers, so somehow expected more than this.

"I've got some calls to make. Why don't you two get reacquainted for a moment," Nico says, and disappears down the hall.

I perch on the edge of the sofa.

"So. How're things?"

She shrugs.

I try a few other conversations, getting nowhere. Somehow I want to crack into wherever she's hiding inside. I want to know how she got rid of her Levo. After what happened when I cut off Ben's . . . I shudder. Maybe she knows how to survive it. Maybe she knows if there is any chance he did.

Ben: That's the way to reach her.

"Skye is alive."

Her eyes widen. "Ben's dog? Where is she?"

"She is . . ." I start to say, then hesitate, not sure if I should use Mac's name. "She's with a friend."

"Ben loved that dog," she says, eyes dropping. Looks up again. "Ben loved me," she says, a challenge in her voice.

There is nothing to be gained by arguing, by saying, *He loved me really, not you,* is there? She is in pain. Let her keep her memories as she likes.

"Do you know what happened to Ben?" I ask.

Her head lowers. She nods. "Nico told me he cut off his Levo and the Lorders took him. But I don't understand. Why would he do it? He was never the sort to question things, to do anything to get in trouble. Why? If only I'd been there. I could have stopped him."

And I don't say anything, uncomfortable with it but afraid of her reaction if I tell her I was there. She's not asking about it, so Nico must not have told her that part of the story. She doesn't know how close Ben and I were.

"What did Ben say when I disappeared?" she says.

And I remember it didn't really register with him at first that she was gone. Until I asked him where she was, and then he tried to find out. But she doesn't need to know that.

"He went to see your mum."

"He did? Did he tell you what happened?"

I hesitate.

"Tell me if you know anything. Please. I need to know." And she is gripping my hand. Mine are cold, and she pulls her blanket around both of us.

"All right," I say, and slump back. I know the agony of wanting to know things you have no way of knowing. "Ben said he asked her where you were, and she said you didn't live there anymore. I think he thought she meant you'd gone to live with your dad in London."

She snorted. "As if. She wouldn't have let me near him. Then what?"

"She said you'd been returned."

"Returned? That's a funny word for it." She lowers her head.

"What happened, Tori?"

"Well. They didn't stick a 'return to sender' on my forehead and dump me in a mailbox. One night, Mum was out, and they came and took me. I was at home, asleep. Suddenly there were these two Lorders in my bedroom, and they hauled me away."

I reach a hand to her shoulder, but she shrugs me off.

"She said that? I was returned?" Her eyes fill with tears.

"I'm sorry, I shouldn't have said anything. I'm sorry."

Tori hunches forward, head on knees. "We used to be so close, Mum and me. When I first came to live with her, she used to dress me up in outfits like hers. Take me to all her parties with her friends. Then, the last year, it all stopped. It was like I took too much attention away from her, so she didn't want me around."

Like a doll she didn't want to play with anymore.

Tori shakes her head side to side. Sobs creep into her voice. "And I liked being the center of attention; I played up to her friends. It's my fault—I shouldn't have done it! But still. Some part of me . . . really hoped . . . I mean, I never thought she would do that. I wondered if she didn't know what happened to me, you know? That she has been crying over me being missing, and . . ." She throws her book across the room. "That bitch," she says.

She pulls the blanket off and limps into the kitchen.

"Tea?" she asks.

"Uh, yeah."

She slams the cups about. Nico appears out of a door down the hall, a mild look on his face. Curiosity. "Everything all right?"

But he isn't saying it to me. He goes up to Tori, puts a hand on her back. And it is there, in her eyes: She adores him already.

She nods. "Fine. Thanks, Nico. Do you want some tea?"

"Later."

He turns to me. "After you have that, come and talk to me in my office." He disappears back down the hall.

She called him Nico. He must have told her John Hatten isn't his real name. How did she do that? Nico doesn't trust people, he doesn't. It was months in the woods of torture and training before he even *began* to trust me. And somehow, he has told her his real name.

I shake my head.

"Sugar?" she asks.

"Look, I'm not really thirsty."

"Suit yourself." She dumps my cup out in the sink. Goes and picks her book up off the floor and starts reading it again, tea in one hand.

There were so many other questions I wanted to ask her. How did she get away from the Lorders? What happened to her Levo?

But her shutters are back up. Time for talking is over.

I knock on Nico's door.

"Come in."

I open the door. There is a sofa, a desk with a computer folded out of it. I'm guessing it disappears back inside it in a clever fashion as if it didn't exist at all. Bookshelves, apparently full of biology books? Maintaining the teacher cover.

And there is Nico. He smiles. "Show me what you've got."

I pull the hospital drawings out of my inner pocket. He unfolds them on a low table in front of the sofa, gestures for me to sit there next to him. Grills me on the positions and defenses drawn, the security on the way in.

"You must know these things already."

"Mostly. Though the entrance security has been increased. Anything else?"

"I think there is something new. Someone said there are technological defenses."

"Any details?"

"No. But the phones and computers have changed. They have cables and wires running from them into the walls. And Mum's phone wouldn't work there. She said it usually does."

"Interesting. A signal block installed, over the whole hospital, perhaps? Makes coms useless."

"And remotes?"

He looks at me.

"Like remotely detonated explosives."

He half smiles. "Clever Rain. True enough. Though nothing we can't get around one way or another, I'm sure."

"There's something else."

"Yes?"

"There must be a hidden way. At the last attack, some Lorders got doctors out of the way, fast. Too fast. Like they were hidden in plain sight."

"Interesting. You must watch, observe. Find out what you can."

"Yes."

"Perhaps we can plan a dummy attack—a threat—one time when you are there, and you can see what you see."

The last hospital attack comes back to me. My head feels fuzzy, and I shake it. Bombs. Bullets. Death. Slipping on blood sticky and cooling on the floor. My stomach twists, and I have to fight to breathe, to calm down, to avoid being sick.

"Rain!" he says, and grips my shoulders. "Stay with me."

With the firm pressure of his hands, heat seeping through damp clothes to skin, the blur around the edges vanishes. All is stark and clear. "Yes. I'll do what you want, anything you want. I promise."

"Good. My special Rain!" He hugs me, and I'm filled with warmth. The questions I wanted to ask him fade away.

He lets go. "Now, about Tori."

"Yes?"

"She may be useful to us. We'll see. She has a lot of rage; I don't know if she can learn to control it, channel it. But remember this: She is still a risk, and you brought her. Anything goes wrong and it is on your pretty head." He kisses my forehead. "It must be time to take you home by now."

That night, I replay it all, everything said and done. And it's all still confusing.

Why am I special to Nico and his plans? Why didn't I ask Nico the questions I wanted to ask? It is like when I'm with him, my will is gone.

And when I thought of the hospital attack I witnessed, I almost lost it. Even now I can't think of it without nausea, panic rising up again. *Blood.* With Nico's touch—calling my name, *Rain*—it was gone. Calm control returned.

I know the hospital is an evil place. What they do, stealing minds and memories, is evil. Lorders are evil. They must be stopped.

They will be stopped.

But what have I done before, with Nico? And the Owls. The memory of blood on the floor at the hospital attack last month is stark, clear. The horror that rises from it. Yet of anything before . . . nothing beyond a glimpse.

Nico's path is the right one. My path. True, he can be cruel. He doesn't value life. Not just Lorders' lives, or innocent bystanders, but even those of his followers. What was it he said earlier? That those who died had a good death.

What about Ben: Did he die a good death, trying to break away from a life dictated for him by Lorders? I flinch, part of me still rejecting the possibility, while more is racked with pain.

On my bedside table stands a rook. The house was still empty when I got home this afternoon. Restless, I'd prowled around downstairs and found a dusty chess set on a bookshelf. Not as nice as Penny's set; the pieces are plastic, not wood. But I took one of the rooks and held it in my hand. Somehow, it was soothing. I kept it in my pocket after Mum and Amy got home, during dinner, patting it now and then to make sure it was still there.

Now I take it from the bedside table and grasp it in my hand.

I run. With each step, sand slips away under my feet, but I fly as fast as I can. Terror gives me strength I don't normally have. I run, but there are limits. Strength ends.

"Faster!"

I trip and go sprawling, gasping for oxygen. Collapsed in a heap.

He tries to drag me to my feet.

I shake my head. "I can't. Go. Save yourself," I gasp.

"No. I'll never leave you." He wraps arms around me. Arms that make me feel warm and safe for the first time in so long. But only for seconds.

Terror approaches.

He is ripped away. Where there was warmth, there is only cold.

I scream.

I open my eyes wide and wider. It is dark, quiet. No sound except the frantic beating of my heart. There are no movements or footsteps that say I screamed out loud in my sleep like I sometimes do. No one is coming to comfort me.

There is pain in my left hand. My fingers are clasped tight in a knot and I can't unclench them. As my heart rate slows, I pry my fingers open, one by one.

On my palm is the rook. I'd clenched it so hard, the battlement spikes that top the castle have cut my hand. There is a perfect ring of six indentations in the skin, filling with pinpricks of blood.

I've had this nightmare many times before. But this time, it changed.

At the beginning when I run, terrified, the details are always as clear as the sharp edges of crystal: I can feel the sand slipping away under my feet. Each ragged breath I take as I run. The fear that makes me go on, beyond endurance. But after I fall, it *changes*.

In the past, it has always gone misty, vague. I am still terrified, but the details become remote and unreal. Blurry around the edges. And someone is yelling to never forget and to put up a wall: the wall of bricks. A concrete representation of what hid Rain inside me. Was this when I was taken by Lorders and Slated? What else could be so frightening?

But tonight, it changed. The clarity stayed through to the end. The man with me was also different. He wasn't yelling, he was holding me, and I was clinging to him until he was torn away. My eyes were clenched shut, but I could feel the grit of the sand, the cold salty breeze off the sea. Hear the pounding of my heart and the crash of the waves. It felt *real*.

Who was the man who ran with me, who said he will never leave? Never became seconds; he was torn away almost as he said it. And what happened to him, to me? What came next?

The fear that lingers from the dream turns to frustration, then anger. I slam a fist into the mattress. Why can't I remember what *really* happened, now that I have these other memories back? Why?

So much is still missing. Inside, I feel empty, hollow. Suddenly limp, I sag back in bed, tears trickling down my face that I don't even bother to wipe away.

17

Bzzzz!

A muffled vibration at my wrist pulls me out of sleep, confused. My Levo . . . ? But it doesn't work anymore. I squint at the numbers in the dark: 5.6. Even if it did work, my levels aren't low enough to make it vibrate.

Bzzzz!

The com underneath; it must be. A call from Nico? My stomach swirls with nervous butterflies.

I fiddle under my Levo to press the hidden button. "Hello?" I whisper.

"Took you long enough." Nico's voice radiates tension.

"Sorry. I didn't realize it was you." And how clever to make calling sound like my Levo vibrating. No one would blink unless they saw the numbers weren't low.

"Can you talk?"

"Yes." The house is quiet, dark. Everyone asleep but me and Sebastian. He stalks across the bed and stares at my wrist, keeping a safe distance as if some danger lurks there.

"We've got trouble."

"What is it?"

"Tori is missing."

"What?"

"I had a meeting. And when I came back just now, she was gone.

She seemed pretty settled until you were here yesterday. What did you talk about? Where do you think she's gone?"

Nico is keeping control now, but there is a definite edge to his voice. Whatever she does is my fault. Whatever she might say if forced or otherwise about where she has been, or who with. My fault she was there at all.

"I don't know. We talked about Ben and his dog. That's about it."

He curses. "If you think of anything, call me." There is an abrupt *click,* then silence.

I lie back and stare at the ceiling. Where could she be? I review yesterday, the little we said. Tori was held in tight most of the time, contained. The only time cracks really showed was when she spoke about Lorders taking her from home, and her mother.

I sit bolt upright. I told her that Ben had been to see her mother, that her mother said she had been returned. Tori was furious with her. That's it, isn't it?

She's gone to confront her mother. Call Nico!

I should call him. But I'm already up, pulling clothes out of drawers, getting dressed in the dark.

This is my mess to fix, and I'll not do it his way.

Careful and silent, I creep down the stairs, out of the house. No time for anything else, I ease Mum's bicycle out of the shed. The door clunks when I shut it, and my heart jumps in fright, a flutter inside. But no lights go on, no curtains move.

There is no time for discretion. On the bike I head down the road as fast as I can go, hoping no one watches.

Ben had pointed out Tori's street once when we ran, on the other side from here of the hall where we have Group. I don't know which house, but I remember Ben saying it was the big one at the end. Hopefully that will be enough to work it out.

If Nico has her address, it is one of the first places he will go.

And if he doesn't already know it, he will soon. I pedal harder.

The night blurs past. If she is there, I can understand why. She'd hoped her mother was missing her, didn't know what happened to her, and I crushed that hope. Stupid! She'd wanted to know Ben's reaction to her being taken. That was the evidence, but why didn't I just say he went on about her, and not tell her he went to see her mother? He did talk about her often enough. Enough that it made me jealous. Is that why I didn't tell her?

I reach her street and slow down, trying to control my breathing after such a mad dash. It's after midnight, yet the big house at the end is lit up. There are cars parked everywhere, and an unseen piano tinkles in the background. Some guests have spilled out onto the lawn, and there are voices, laughter. I tuck my bicycle in some bushes and slip closer, through the shadows. There are too many eyes about, but at least this should have stopped Tori. She couldn't be crazy enough to go in with all these people. Could she?

After the big house, the road ends; there is a footpath sign, woods. That is where she'd hide.

On the opposite side of the street I slip behind front garden hedges, hoping the neighbors sleep despite the party noises and are not looking out their windows.

Tori is easy to find in the dark trees that overlook her old house, in a pale blue hoodie that almost glows in the dark. I creep up next to her and touch her arm. She jumps, turns, and sees it's me. Turns back to watching the house. "You have to learn to dress for these sorts of things," I say.

She doesn't answer, eyes fixed. I follow them: There is a group of a half dozen, talking, laughing. One woman, the rest are men in tuxes. She must be freezing in that slinky black dress, arms bare. Laughing at something one of the others said, her head thrown back.

"Is that her?" I whisper.

Tori nods.

She is beautiful, like Tori. Both have long dark hair. Had she asked for a Slated with similar features? I've heard rumors some do that, request a designer son or daughter. Perhaps when Tori got older she took too many eyes away from her mother; a younger, more beautiful version of herself.

"Why are you here, Tori?"

She doesn't answer. I take her hand, ice cold, in mine.

"Come on. Come with me," I say. "There is nothing for you here."

No reaction. Her eyes are fixed and staring, straight ahead. Then a tear glistens and runs down her cheek.

"Tori?"

"I just had to see her. I wanted her to tell me why I was returned, to hear her say the words. See what justification she has."

"Busy place tonight."

"Yes. Maybe that would be even better. In front of all her friends. Imagine the embarrassment!"

"The Lorders would take you again."

She flinches. "It might be worth it."

I tug her hand. "Come on. Before we're spotted."

She tears her eyes away from the woman who had been her mother.

"What did I do wrong?" she says, and another tear spills out, chases the other down her cheek.

I shake my head. "Nothing. Nothing at all."

She lets me lead her away, listens when I tell her to bend down and slip along the hedges, out of sight.

We get to where I stashed the bicycle. "Come on, I'll double you," I say, and she gets on the seat behind me and I cycle, standing up, down the road. Legs protesting after the dash earlier.

"Where is there to go?" she says in my ear.

"Nico. Where else?"

"He's going to be really pissed."

"Yes. He is."

Nico isn't home when we get there. The house is locked, but Tori knows the door combination, and soon we are inside.

She is shaking. I find his whisky, pour her a glass. After a moment have a sip of it myself.

Then I call Nico and tell him where we are.

Tori is sound asleep on the sofa.

"What did you give her?"

"Sedative. Knock her out for a day or so while I work out next steps," he says, his voice cold. "That was too close to disaster. You should have told me where she was."

"I didn't know; I guessed."

"Your guesses are good, Rain. You should have told me." He walks closer; much taller, he looks down, and I fight the urge to back away.

I stand my ground. "She was my responsibility. It was up to me to deal with it. What are you going to do with her?"

He stares back a few heartbeats, then nods, as if to himself. "I still think there may be a use for her. In the meantime, I need to put her someplace more secure." He sighs. "What am I to do with you?" His lips curve up in some semblance of a smile, but the ice is still there behind it.

"I'm sorry, Nico. I just wanted to fix it; it was my fault."

He stares at me, for one beat, two. His eyes soften. He puts a hand on each shoulder, pulls me close, and I nestle in against him. Afraid to move, afraid to breathe, to do anything to spoil this.

"Your heart beats so fast," he says at last. Pushes me away, looks into my eyes. "I'm not angry with you, Rain. At least not the way you think I am."

Relief swells through me. "You're not?"

"No. I was scared."

"You? *Scared?*" Even saying the words sounds wrong. Nico isn't afraid of anything.

He half smiles. "Yes. Even I have fears. I was scared of something happening to you. What if you'd gotten caught? You should have told me where she was so I could deal with it. You need to stay safe, Rain. *I* need you to stay safe."

I stare up at him in wonder. "I'm sorry."

"Don't be sorry. It was brave of you. But promise me something: Don't rush off to rescue anyone again without checking with me first. Deal?"

"Deal."

"One more thing before you go. Those plans you did of the hospital are wonderful, but I want the people, too. Faces. I know you can draw them. All the faces from the hospital. Nurses, doctors, security. Everyone you come in contact with now or have in the past."

"What will you do with them?"

He doesn't answer, and all I can think of is that nurse who died the last time Free UK attacked the hospital. Her blood pooling on the floor. My stomach twists, and I fight to keep it down. If they can identify them outside the hospital, they are easier targets.

"You know, Rain. But don't waste your sympathy on Lorders' servants. Remember whose side you are on. Think about it. If you're not with us, then you are with the Lorders and everything they stand for. You might as well have handed Tori over to the Lorders yourself. Snatched Ben and ended his life. Tossed the match that burned his parents alive. Think about it, Rain. Now, go."

I head for the door, the long bike ride home. Anxious to escape into the night. But force myself to look back. Tori's chest rises and falls; her face peaceful in sleep, a marked contrast from the pain it held earlier.

"She'll be all right?" I can't stop myself from asking.

"For now."

Back home, I feel my feet are fighting for purchase, slipping down a long and sandy slope. Nico wants faces. But giving them to him would be like handing out death sentences for nurses and doctors.

They're not innocent!

No. They Slated me, and countless others like me. What happened to Ben lies square on their shoulders.

They do what they are told. And I know that isn't good enough! But some of them are nice, more than nice. But what else can I do? Nico is right. They're all part of it.

I can't sleep. I spread sketch paper around me. Every time my pencil touches the paper, a real face soon stares back. Like the messy gray hair of Nurse Sally from the tenth floor. My floor, and she was one of the ones who looked after me at the beginning. She was always laughing, told me about her new grandson when he was born. Showed me his photo.

One day, he may not be safe. Her grandson—was it Brian, Ryan, something like that?—might say something the authorities don't like, and then go missing, and be Slated himself. Then be returned or terminated if anything goes wrong. Like Tori, whose life—no kidding myself about Nico's slight reassurances—now hangs in the balance.

Would Sally sacrifice herself for her grandson? Can I make that decision for her? For her grandson and all the other children and grandchildren whose lives are limited, controlled and threatened by Lorders.

I keep drawing, compelled. I can't stop.

18

"KYLA? SO, WHAT DO YOU THINK? KYLA? KYLA . . ."

"Sorry, what was that?" I turn to Cam, realizing I've heard an echo of my name for a while. Lost in my thoughts while I ate my sandwich, his voice a comforting sound but the meaning not registering.

Cam mock glares. "A simple yes or no is all."

"Hmmm, let's see: You might be offering me cake, and then I should say yes. On the other hand, you might have suggested *anything*."

"Take a guess."

"Uh . . . yes!"

"Okay, I'll come get you at about ten."

"For what?"

"Going for a walk tomorrow."

"What about school?"

He waves a hand in front of my eyes. "There is something seriously wrong with your memory." Then his face falls as he realizes what he said. "I'm sorry. I didn't mean that the way it sounded."

"Don't worry. There *is* something seriously wrong with my memory. Slating kind of does that." Not to mention all the rest of it.

"But that's only for stuff before then, right?"

"Right." Though not so much in my case. "Besides, if I actually listen, my short-term memory is okay."

"What is it like?"

"What?"

He hesitates. "Sorry. Forget it."

"There you go again!"

"Oh, sorry, I . . ." He looks stricken, so I let him off.

"I'm kidding. Go ahead and ask whatever it is. I don't mind."

"What is it like, not having any memories?"

"Well, to start with, it's fine. Because you don't know any different. And everyone in the hospital is the same as you."

"And then?"

I frown. "For me, things got worse when I got out. I wanted to know things I couldn't know. And then it's like you fill stuff in because too much is blank. And then you can't tell what is real, and what isn't."

"Most Slateds look pretty happy about it."

I laugh. "True enough. They monkey with our happy settings, didn't you know? Plus you learn to stay happy so your Levo isn't buzzing and blacking you out all the time."

"Being happy and forgetting things sounds good," he says quietly. Thinking about his dad? I lean back, considering. I'd be happier if I didn't remember anything from before. If I didn't obsess about Lucy and her broken fingers; if Rain's memories never appeared. But then the Lorders would have won.

"The thing is, if you're making yourself pretend happy to stay level, you don't know what you feel anymore. Nothing feels real. There may be some things it would be good to forget. Yet it is frustrating missing pieces of myself I want to remember!"

For someone who talks so much, Cam has a good listener's face. There is something about him that makes me want to tell him everything.

"It's nice to have a day off school in honor of your affliction, though," he says.

"What are you talking about?"

"Are you pulling my leg, or do you really not remember?"

I aim a punch at his shoulder, but he jumps away.

"Tell me already!"

"There's no school tomorrow. It's Remembrance Day."

There is a special afternoon class all about it.

We scan in, take our seats.

Our teacher glances across our faces. "Can anyone tell us why there is no school tomorrow?"

"Remembrance Day," several voices call out.

"But what are we remembering? Anyone?"

He spends minutes on the original meaning: remembering those who fought and died for this country in wars, so long ago almost none living can remember. The numbers are dizzying. The population of the UK is less now than then, but still.

"And what else are we remembering?" he asks. But this time he doesn't wait for an answer. He turns the lights down and a film begins. Horrifying images fill the screen. Angry mobs, out of control, destroying everything in their path. The student riots of the twenties.

Windows are broken, shops emptied, fires burn. A girl younger than me is dragged off screaming by a gang of hooded youths, and though you don't see anything else, you get the idea. An old man is pushed and trampled. A child knocked from a mother's arms.

I close my eyes to shut it out. A flash of memory: Nico. He showed us this same film! I remember. Then he showed another one.

Whoever is in charge changes history to suit themselves.

That is what he said. The Lorders took every bit of evidence they had of out of control riots and destruction, pieced them together, and made it mandatory viewing for the population. They didn't show Nico's version. Lorders—police, they were called then—beating students. Causing many of the injuries and deaths shown, then deleting their involvement so it looks like the rioters were responsible for it all.

Yet the students weren't blameless. They caused damage and injury. Many deserved to be punished for their part. And criminals and gangs joined in, took part in thieving and murder.

But it wasn't one-sided. And I wonder: If Free UK are successful, and the Lorders beaten down, how will history be rewritten? For a start, they wouldn't be generally called AGT anymore; they'd be Free UK to everyone. A more palatable name, dropping the *terrorist* right out of it.

I feel the lights come back on through my eyelids, and open my eyes. Everyone in the room is quiet, sobered by the violence even though they must be shown this every year.

Just a few weeks from now, the twenty-sixth of November is Armstrong Memorial Day. This year will be twenty-five years since the deaths of the first Lorder PM and his wife. Mum's parents. They were killed on the way to their country house at Chequers to celebrate five years in power; so thirty years, now, of Lorder control. Our teacher tells us about the celebrations planned.

Celebrations of a Lorder government that twists and destroys minds.

As I leave to meet Jazz and Amy to go home, the irony isn't lost on me. The Lorders are saying remember those who died defending the country from itself almost thirty years ago.

Yet now they make people go missing, make sure they are

forgotten, that no one asks any embarrassing questions. They steal memories, like mine.

Lest we forget.

"You're quiet today," Jazz says, watching me in the mirror as we pull into our village.

"I'm all right."

Jazz and Amy kiss good-bye, and I slip in the house.

Amy dashes in for a quick change of clothes while I make her cup of tea. I hold it out when she gets downstairs.

"Thanks, Kyla. Are you sure everything is all right?"

"Yes. Fine; go on." And she dashes out and up the road to work.

But the house is so quiet; there is too much darkness in my mind to be alone. I wander room to room, then finally settle down with my sketch pad. No one will be home for almost two hours. I want to draw, yet I don't. I extract my hidden drawings from the other night: Nurse Sally and friends. I sigh.

What does this say about me, about where I stand? Am I so weak that I can't do what I see is right, just because it is hard? And I owe everything to Nico. After all he did to save me, protect me, I can't let him down.

But if I give him these drawings, what about all of them?

I won't draw faces this afternoon. The hospital—that's it. I have already given Nico plans, but something is still niggling away inside. Dr. Lysander vanished from danger so quickly during that attack. There must be a secret way out, but where? I start to draw the hall outside her office.

I'm concentrating so hard, I almost don't hear the knock downstairs.

I put down my pencil, pull the curtains, and look down. A delivery person? With a huge bunch of flowers. Perhaps Dad is trying to get back on Mum's good side.

I run down the stairs, open the door.

"Delivery for O'Reilly?" he says.

"You must be in the wrong place. There isn't anyone here by that name."

He pulls out some paperwork, studies it. "Janet O'Reilly?"

"No. Sorry."

He rolls his eyes. "Sorry to bother you. Do you know what time it is?"

I look at my watch, and he peers close to see it. Slips a small square of paper in my hand. Winks, and is gone.

Back inside, door shut, I unfold the paper. *Meet me at the footpath lookout over your village as soon as possible. Very important. Destroy this note. A.*

A . . . Aiden? My feet are frozen to the floor. I read the note again, barely able to breathe. Mac was going to get Aiden to scan my drawing of Ben to put it on MIA. Now Aiden wants to see me.

Ben! They must have news of Ben.

I swallow, hard. News can be good, or bad. Bad is more likely. But Aiden could have sent a message through Mac if it was bad news. Couldn't he? But he is *here*.

I fly up the stairs, chucking school uniform for jeans and boots and rushing out the door. Daring to *hope*.

I force myself to walk at a normal pace through the village, to look as if I'm just out for a stroll. Fighting the urge to run.

No one is in sight at the start of the footpath. I hesitate, all of Mum's warnings to avoid these places on my own echoing in my ears.

But I'm not afraid anymore, not since my memories came back. I'm good at self-defense.

I run up the footpath, past the fields and hedges, through trees as it rises. The air is frosty and clear, afternoon sun low in the sky. As I get closer to the lookout, I slow down to a walk. Afraid, now, to hear what Aiden has to say. Until I hear it, it can be what I want to hear. Once I see him and he says the words, it's over. I go slower and slower, stop and make myself breathe in and out to calm the rapid thudding of my heart that has nothing to do with the run.

I walk slow and silent under shadow of trees as I round the final bend of the path. His head is turned the other way, but the fire of his red hair glints in the setting sun. Aiden. I step forward, and he turns. Smiles.

He's smiling.

"How are you, Kyla?"

I search his eyes for the answer I'm looking for. Blue eyes, but nothing like Nico's pale color; Aiden's are an intense, deep-water blue. Reassuring eyes. Not bad news?

Legs unable to hold me up anymore, I almost collapse next to him on the log where he sits. "Tell me, please. What have you heard?"

"There's been a possible sighting of Ben."

"A sighting?" I whisper, not daring to think he means what I think he might.

"Yes. It's true, Kyla. I can't believe it, I really can't. I thought it worse than a long shot to even bother. But I put that drawing you did of Ben on MIA, and someone who looks like him has been spotted a few times. I can't say for sure that it will be Ben. But the person making the report is very reliable."

"Really?"

He nods. "Really. This isn't how MIA generally operates, by the way. Normally we only tell that someone is found if they agree to it first. But as I sort of feel I had a hand in things with you and Ben, I've made an exception."

And I can't move or speak, or even take it in. Could it be true?

"Say something," he says.

I shake my head. "I just . . . really?" And I grin.

He smiles back, and without thought I launch myself at him. His arms curl around me in a hug. And all at once it is too much, way too much. Emotion works its way up from inside, and I'm shaking, then I'm crying. "It can't be him. I can't believe it. What if it is a mistake?"

"You're not good with good news, are you? Are your levels okay?"

"Yeah, fine. I ran here so my levels are up," I say, and embarrassed now, move back. I tuck my hand in my pocket so he can't see my Levo.

"But you're right to be careful. As I said, it could be mistaken identity."

"What happens next?"

"We'll try to get a photo of him to show you. Then get you to see him if it still looks like it's Ben. All right?"

"Where is he? Where did they see him? When can I—"

"Slow down a little. I'll tell you what I can. He was seen not far from here, twenty miles or so. If it is him—it was at a distance, at a running track. So—"

"That's Ben! He loves to run. It must be him. When can I see him?"

"We need to do some planning. Sit tight. Not a word to anyone. Right?" I nod. "We'll be in touch."

"Another flower delivery?"

He laughs. "This time I was in the area, and a friend of mine owed me a favor. But best not to use that trick more than once. Mac will know if anything is up, all right? I'll be at his place Friday night; I can pass any news on then." Aiden gets up. "I've got to go. It really is good to see you, Kyla." His smile is warm; he touches my hand. "Take care."

He starts to walk away. I haven't seen him since the day I all but accused him of taking Ben away. But it wasn't fair. He didn't make Ben do anything he didn't want to do, and now he's trying to help.

"Aiden, wait." He pauses, turns back. "Look. I'm sorry about what I said the last time."

"It's all right. I understand how upset you were. It's natural to lash out." He stares levelly back, calm and steady.

And he disappears down the footpath, the other way. I walk back the way I came, head spinning. Could it be true? Could it really be Ben? Only twenty miles away; so close. If it is him, what does it mean?

The Lorders wouldn't just let him go. There must be a catch.

19

WHEN I GET HOME, SOMETHING ISN'T RIGHT.

The front door isn't locked for a start. Dad's car isn't out front; Mum and Amy are both at work. Could I really have left without locking up? I think back, and I'm not sure. When I left to meet Aiden, I was in a hurry of panic in case he was gone by the time I got there. Yet I would have done it automatically, without thinking. Wouldn't I?

My instincts are screaming *danger.*

I open the door and push it forward without stepping in. The hall is empty, and I listen, not moving, not breathing.

There! Footsteps, upstairs. My throat constricts: my drawings! I didn't hide them away before I went out, did I? Stupid.

Careful, quiet, slow: up the stairs. My door is open: I scan the room. Drawings still all over the bed, the one I started of the hospital faceup. Not quite the way I left them, I'm sure. My stomach sinks.

Footsteps, behind me! I spring around, ready for, well, anything.

Amy jumps about a foot in the air. "Oh my God, Kyla! You scared me. Why don't you yell hello or something when you come in?"

I shake my head. "I scared you? You scared me! You're not supposed to be home yet."

"You were so out of it this afternoon, I asked to come home early to spend some time with you, you nitwit. But when I got here, no sign. Where've you been?"

"I . . . I'm sorry. I went for a walk to clear my head."

Her face softens. "Are you all right? Really? You've been so odd this week. And ever since Ben . . ." And she looks away, doesn't finish the sentence.

"Let's go downstairs and have some tea," I suggest.

"Not so fast." And she walks past me to my room, pushes open the door I'd left ajar. Goes straight for my bed and the hospital drawing I'd left. "Tell me about this first," she says.

I shrug, stomach in knots. "Just the usual. You know me: I draw everything. And what were you doing snooping around in my room, anyway?"

"You didn't answer the door; I thought you might be upset, or that your levels had dropped and you couldn't." She sighs and sits on the bed. "I'm worried about you." She holds out her hand and I take it, sit next to her.

She is dangerous.

No. This is Amy, not the enemy.

She picks up my drawing of Dr. Lysander's floor of the hospital. "Explain this to me," she says, and there is no way around it, really, so I do. About the attack, and how doctors disappeared and I wondered where. I was curious, it was a puzzle, and I was drawing it.

She shakes her head. "Kyla, you are *so* stupid. Think of the trouble this could land you in if the wrong person saw it! Why waste time drawing boring stuff like this, anyway, when you're so good at people and faces?" And she turns over Nurse Sally. "This is gorgeous. She's so warm and alive. Who is it?"

"Nobody. Just a made-up face."

"Really? Funny, she looks familiar. Can't place her, though."

Was Sally at the hospital when Amy was Slated? When was that: five years ago. She could have been.

"But this," she says, and picks up the hospital one again, "has to go. And don't do anything like it again. Promise?"

I do, and together we tear it in half and in half again and again, until all that are left are tiny squares. She flushes it. "That is the end of that," she says. "Time for that cup of tea?"

Downstairs in the kitchen I put the kettle on.

"Where'd you walk?" Amy asks.

"Oh, you know. Just around the village," I lie, the footpath being off-limits solo.

"Mum would have a fit if she knew you went walking alone. Ever since that Wayne Best was found."

"Have you heard anything else about him?"

"Oh, didn't I say? He is talking and remembering things now."

I turn to get the cups out of the cupboard, not trusting myself to keep a neutral face. He is remembering? Oh, God. The room seems to darken and spin in my eyes, as if it's turning into a black pit that will suck me in. I shake my head and my vision clears.

Tell Nico.

My stomach squirms. Nico will be furious it is the first he's heard about it. I can't tell him now. It's too late.

"But he's got, like, traumatic amnesia," Amy says.

"What's that?"

"He can remember everything, except why he was in the woods that day and what happened to him there."

"Oh?"

"He might remember eventually, the doc said. I heard Lorders were annoyed with him for not answering." She shuddered. "That'd be enough to get your memory back quick, I should think."

The phone rings as I'm pouring the tea, and Amy runs to answer. I

130

dash upstairs and carefully gather the rest of my drawings and hide them in a folder with others.

Amy almost recognized Nurse Sally. I shouldn't have lied about who she was; what if she remembers that she works at the hospital, and puts it together?

Did Amy actually say she wouldn't tell anyone about the drawings?

I think hard. Not in so many words, but she got me to destroy the one of the hospital. What would be the point if it wasn't then secret?

I shrug, uneasy, but the moment to make her promise not to tell has passed. If I bring it up again, she'll wonder why. Silence is best.

Late that night I creep out of my room to the dark study downstairs. Shut the door and turn on the desk lamp.

Mum is a bit of a local history buff. The shelves in here are stuffed with books on local villages and towns, current and historical, and maps: both usual road ones, and detailed ordinance survey maps that show every footpath and canal.

I can't wait for Aiden's careful investigations. Is it really Ben? *It has to be.* I cannot accept any other alternative. My thoughts twist around one another over and over, jumping between bubbles of joy and anticipation, and fear that it will all be a lie. That any hope will lead to disappointment.

A running track, twenty miles from here. I visualize a circle and carefully go over each village and town that fits the distance. The footpaths and lanes to reach them from here.

I'll find you, Ben.

20

THE NEXT DAY IS CRISP AND COLD, WITH A FEW CLOUDS light and high enough they shouldn't cause trouble.

I strap on my bike helmet. "Are you sure you don't mind switching to a bike ride today?"

"Your wish is my command," Cam says, bowing down. "Where do you want to go?"

"Follow me!"

We head out. The roads are quiet today with the holiday, if Remembrance Day can be thought of that way. I'd memorized the map grid. We should be able to check at least three possible locations of Ben's running track today. I shrug off the doubting voice that says even if I find the right village and the right track, I won't know it unless he happens to be running at the exact same time. At least I'm *doing* something.

Amy had been *so* pleased to hear Cam and I were going cycling. Mum, off with Aunt Stacey for the day, thinks we are chaperoning each other, and I wonder what Amy and Jazz will get up to. Amy had smirked at Cam and I when we left. She assumes things about us that aren't true.

But I'm dancing inside because Ben has been spotted; there is no other reason. This is just going for a bike ride. Cam said he understands about Ben. We're just *friends*.

At a small bridge I duck off the road to a canal path. I glance back to make sure Cam follows. Something is coming up fast behind him on the narrow country lane. The sun in my eyes makes it difficult to see, and I squint. A black van?

We disappear down the canal path, and I shake off unease. If that even was Lorders, they are all over the place. It's just coincidence.

A few miles later we are back on a country road, cycling side by side, close to the first village to check. There is a rumble, a car coming behind, and Cam slips in front. There isn't much room for passing cars and we both move as far to the left as possible. It is getting closer, and Cam glances back. His eyes widen.

I turn just in time to see a blur of motion. A black sliding door opens, an arm swings out and connects with my shoulder. And I'm flying through the air in a slow-motion tumble, then landing, hard, half on the side of the road and half in a hedge. Tangled in my bicycle.

I look up. My vision is swimming, but I can't mistake what gets out of the van and stands over me. Big as a mountain and dressed in black: a Lorder.

"Get up," he says.

I try to push myself up with my arms, but struggle to move with my legs under the bicycle. He kicks me in the side.

I groan.

Another blur of motion and Cam is there, grabbing the Lorder by the arm. "Leave her alone! You're making a big mistake," Cam says.

No, Cam, no. Terror finds strength and I push the bike away, pull myself to my feet.

Something you don't see every day: a smiling Lorder. "I think you'll find, boy, that you are making the mistake. This has nothing to do with you." He turns and shoves Cam, easily landing him on the ground.

"You, get in." He points at me. I don't move and he bends over, grabs and twists my arm, pushing me to the van.

Cam struggles to his feet. "Leave her!" he shouts.

The Lorder sighs as if an annoying fly is buzzing around his face, lets go of my arm, and swings at Cam. His fist connects with the side of Cam's face and makes a sickening sound. Cam crumples to the ground, slow. Something inside says *run while the Lorder is distracted, do it now,* but I can't leave Cam, and I'm filling with rage, hands clenching into fists.

He is too big. Wait.

And the moment for running is past. Now it's not just me shoved into the van, but Cam, too.

Two Lorders. The mountain is in the back with us, while the other, a more normal-sized woman, is driving.

We drive up bumpy roads. Cam is groaning on the floor, eyes closed. I hold his head in my lap. His cheek is bleeding. He coughs, tries to say something.

"Silence!" the mountain says.

Where are we going? Why?

I always wondered what really happens to people snatched by Lorders. Looks like we're going to find out.

I count the time. We've gone perhaps two miles on bumpy lanes, then eight or ten on fast smooth roads, when the van pulls off again to a lane. No windows in the back; we could be anywhere in that radius.

Cam's eyes are open now, looking at Mr. Mountain, judging. Back to me. I'd expect him to be blank with terror, but his eyes are calm. Pain twists inside: Cam stood up to this wall of muscle for me, and look what it got him.

"Sir?" I say, and Mountain turns, surprise registering on his thick face.

"What?"

"Please. Can't you let him go?" I say.

"How sweet. Shut up."

"But—"

And a hand swings out, checks itself to stop at the last second before hitting my face, just as I feel Cam tensing to jump. *No, Cam! Don't be such an idiot.*

"Silence!"

We come to a stop. The door is opened from the outside, where there are more Lorders in black ops gear. Mountain gets out and has a few words with them, then disappears through a door. One reaches for me and another for Cam, pulling us out of the van. The rage is there, so much inside me. Mountain is gone and these look more my size.

I spin around and jump kick one of them in the head. He crumples to the ground. Cam struggles with the one holding him, and I swing around and chop his captor in the back of the head, but then there are footsteps, too many, running into the room. Arms holding me. I struggle, but then something jabs in my arm. Everything starts going black. I fight to keep my eyes open. Cam is being dragged across the floor, not moving. There are four—no, more Lorders. Their faces blur in and out until each one looks like a whole group of identical expressionless faces. I slip to the ground.

I wake slowly, but I don't want to. As I do, I start to remember. I was in a car, feeling it bump along the road the only clue because I could see nothing, couldn't move. Head still so thick. It was that drink they gave me, wasn't it?

I frown to myself. Before that, how did I get in that car?

Memory trickles in, and I panic. I was supposed to meet Daddy, but it wasn't him. Somebody else that I didn't know said they were taking me to him, that it was part of a game.

Daddy is a secret agent. He is going to free the world, he said so. And not to tell Mum, like when I was drawing those signs for him. She got mad.

My head thuds; everything feels disconnected. Mouth dry, and I try to swallow.

"She's coming around." A man's voice. Who?

I open my eyes.

"There you are, Lucy. Welcome to your new home."

I sit up in a rush and everything spins.

"Where's Daddy? Who are you?"

"I'm your doctor. Doctor Craig."

"I'm not sick!"

"No. But you will be." He smiles, but it isn't a nice smile.

I start screaming, and a woman comes in, a nurse. She fusses, says I'll be all right, to go back to sleep.

Soon after the door clicks shut. A key scrapes in the lock and turns. Footsteps thud down the hall.

21

"WAKE UP!" A VOICE YELLS, AND A COLD SHOCK FOLLOWS. Wet. Bucket of water?

I crawl back from black through gray, slowly feeling my body and wishing I didn't. Everything hurts. My hands are behind my back; I pull, nothing. Tied together. My head is flopped forward. I'm sitting—on a chair? A hand yanks my head upright by the hair.

Play dead?

What is the point in dragging things out? I open my eyes.

"Ah, there you are. Kyla, is it? Answer!"

"No," I say, voice feeling thick and wrong. Mouth dry. Who is Kyla? I frown, concentrating. Lucy, the child: That was a dream, from before. But now I am Rain. Aren't I?

"It is definitely her," a second, quieter voice says. "But she shouldn't be able to lie with that in her system."

"Who are you?" the first voice yells.

Ah. Truth drugs can be overcome if you believe what you say. I am Rain. But I am also Kyla.

"Kyla," I say. "Yes. I am Kyla."

"Good girl."

The yelling voice moves behind me, out of sight, and the quieter voice comes around. Pulls a chair in front of me. "Now, Kyla, I'm just going to ask you a few questions, all right?"

"Sure," I say. "Knock yourself out."

"I hear you like to draw things."

I stare back at him.

"Well?"

I form my face confused. "Is that a question?"

"Oh, sorry; you are quite right. Do you like to draw?"

"Yes."

"Now, I've heard you like drawing pictures of the New London Hospital. Where you were Slated. Is that true?"

And I frown, concentrating. I don't like drawing the hospital; I felt I had to. Ah. "No," I say.

He looks at someone out of sight behind me. "Be more specific," a third voice says.

"Did you draw the hospital yesterday?"

And I can't see a way out of answering. Think.

It wasn't a drawing of the hospital I did yesterday. Just a hall inside of the hospital. My face clears.

"No," I say.

"Give her more?"

"Any more and it will knock her out."

"Let's try something more . . . painful." Another voice.

A face appears in front of mine. One eye is closed, swollen. He touches my eyebrow. "I'd like to do what you did to me. How'd a Slated learn to kick like that is what I'd like to know." He traces around my eye with one finger as if setting the place for a kick, and I feel sick inside.

There is a door opening somewhere behind me, a movement of air.

The one next to me jumps straight to attention.

"Sir!" he says.

There are more voices, but my head is too fuzzy to pick them; it can't concentrate, it wants sleep. One new voice is cold. There is something about it; I know who it is, yet I don't. It is telling them to leave me, to go along, to talk. Footsteps retreat. It is silent. My eyes close.

When I wake again, I am lying down. My head feels like a football in the middle of a game.

Don't move; listen.

But there is nothing to hear. A ticking clock, that is all. I open my eyes cautiously.

An office. A desk. I'm on a sofa along a wall opposite the desk. There is a Lorder in a gray suit using a netbook. He looks up, sees my eyes are open.

"Awake, I see."

His face I cannot forget. Thin lips, almost as if his skin has just been slashed by a knife to make a mouth. It is Coulson.

So it was his voice I'd recognized earlier.

I struggle to sit, to face him. Pain everywhere, but things seem to be working. No lasting damage. I touch my face, around my eye: still whole.

"This has been most regrettable today." He shakes his head. "Not the way things should have gone." He sighs. "Don't worry, there will be an investigation. Punishments where necessary."

"I don't understand."

"Well, I am going to explain things to you, Kyla. It's like this. I've been keeping my eye on you for a while. Something isn't right about you. You've been up to things you shouldn't. For a Slated, it is very worrying, indeed." He sighs again. "We so want all of you to succeed, you know. Your second chance. Of course, my interest in you started with the Ben Nix situation. The Happy Pills he had. Obviously you have been taking them as well, or you wouldn't have been able to withstand what has happened today. You'd have blacked out long ago."

I say nothing, blanching at Ben's name.

"Poor Kyla. I know you are a pawn. Being used by the AGT to draw the hospital that keeps all the dedicated medical staff and patients safe. But we wanted to follow you, you see. To the AGT and their plans. So I was very angry when I learned you'd been picked up today. It wasn't time, and now, things have changed."

He pauses, sips a cup of tea, and I stare back at him, mind numb. *He knows about the drawing.* Amy is the only one who saw it . . . No. She wouldn't. Would she?

His thin lips curve in what might be taken for a smile, but it's all wrong. "But let's make the best of things, shall we? This is what I think we should do. We'll let you go. You continue along with the AGT. Find out their plans, and tell us about them. What do you think?"

"I don't know what you're talking about. I don't have anything to do with terrorists."

He shakes his head sadly. "We know, Kyla. There is no point in lying. And what has this boy Cameron to do with things? What should we do with him, then?"

I panic inside. "Nothing! This has nothing to do with him. We were just cycling."

"Your desire to protect a friend does you credit, Kyla. Yet why should I believe you?"

"Because it's true."

"What about Ben?"

"What about him?"

"Wouldn't you like to know where he is?"

So it is true: He is alive! Part of me sings inside; part is gripped by fear. If Coulson knows where he is, that can't be good.

"Where is he?"

He shakes his head. "I don't give things away; they must be earned. Yet if you lie about some things, how am I to know when you speak the truth, and when, lies? Now tell me again about the terrorists."

Lying is useless when he knows, isn't it?

"I don't know their plans. I don't! I'm just drawing things. That is all."

He nods his head. "I am inclined to believe they would not trust you with any serious information, yet I am also aware what a resourceful girl you are, Kyla. You will be able to find out more if you try. And despite all your wrongs, I'm inclined to be lenient. This isn't an easy task we are setting you.

"This is what I propose: We'll let you and Cameron go home today. He will remain safe, for now. Just as your old friend Ben will remain safe. For now. You will find out what the AGT are planning and who is involved, and you will tell me. If you succeed, if you prove your loyalty to us, we'll take you to Ben. You can start over. Tell you what: We'll even remove your Levo, as Ben has done."

He stares back, waiting, calm. The clock ticks, counting seconds down, and I'm frozen. Numb.

"What do you say? Will you do this?"

There is only one answer, and the smug look behind his eyes says he knows it. Only one way to save Ben. Only one way to save Cam. And myself.

"Yes."

. . .

Not much later, Cam and I are dumped by the side of the road next to our bicycles.

"Your poor face," I say. Touch a hand to his cheek, cut and swollen.

"It'll heal." His eyes hold mine. Cam, who leaped to my defense when it was obvious he could only fail. Hurt and under threat because of me.

"I'm so sorry," I start to say, but the words catch in my throat. Now that it is over and the Lorders gone, the horror, the fear wash over me. I start to shake.

He catches my hand, holds it and pulls me close. We just stand there by the side of the road, not moving, not speaking. And I try to breathe slow, to get myself under control, to not cry. But having him there, his arms warm about me, just makes it harder. I pull away.

"Now," he says. "Are you going to tell me what is going on with you and the Lorders?"

Cam has earned the truth. He has, but I can't tell it. It would just put him in more danger if he knew about Coulson's deal. About me and Free UK.

I shake my head. "There's not much to tell. The Lorders thought I was in some trouble. But then they worked out they made a mistake, so they let us go."

"Do you expect me to believe that? Don't lie to me," he says, his eyes full of hurt.

And I wince inside. But I'm not saying anything, not when knowledge is so dangerous. The less he knows, the better for him.

"If there was anything I could tell you, I would. I'm sorry."

He gets up, checks that my bicycle survived its collision with the hedge, but doesn't look me in the eye. I so long to tell him everything, just to take away that withdrawn look. To have someone know what I know. Hold me and make things feel better, even if just for a moment.

That won't make anything better. Don't trust him.

This is crazy! He's just been hauled off along with me; his only crime was standing up to that Lorder who knocked me off my bike. Hasn't he proved he can be trusted?

No. Until you work out who has betrayed you, trust no one.

That is what occupies my mind the long ride home. The sun is getting low in the sky—late afternoon. Well after we should have been home.

Who told the Lorders about my drawing of the hospital?

Amy is the one who saw it. But she wouldn't. Never! Anyhow, it doesn't make sense. If she was going to report me to the Lorders, why get me to destroy it, or even admit she saw it in the first place?

Yet . . . what if she told someone about it without meaning to get me in trouble, and they told somebody else?

That is possible. But it was just yesterday she saw it. With no school today, the only people she has seen since then are Mum and Jazz.

It must be one of them.

No! I can't believe it. But who else could it be?

And I have no answer to that. Whether unwittingly or deliberately, either Amy, Jazz, or Mum must have turned me in to the Lorders.

There are so few people in this world that I trust and care for, and one has betrayed me. I don't know which one, and I can't believe any of them would do it. Especially Mum.

The mum you've had for less than two months.

Yeah.

The one whose parents were killed by terrorists; her son, too, as far as she knows. You don't think she'd turn you in if she thought you were one of them?

I squirm inside. Maybe, but . . . No. I can't believe it.

But something else sings inside: Ben is alive! He really is. Not just Aiden's sighting confirms it now; Coulson said so, as well.

He could be lying, but why would he bother? His threats against me and Cam were enough. And Coulson doesn't know that even if I don't manage to track Ben down by myself, I can find out where he is from Aiden. All I have to do is find Ben and warn him about Coulson's threats. Maybe we can disappear someplace together, someplace the Lorders won't find us.

Like the moon?

I push the doubting voice away, ignore it. Hug this little hope inside and hold it tight.

Without it, I have nothing.

When we get to our street, Cam gets off his bike in front of his house. Says nothing, starts pushing it up his drive.

"Wait," I say. He stops, turns. "What are you going to say happened?"

"I fell off my bike. You?"

"I won't say anything."

He turns away.

Tears are pricking in my eyes. He is my only friend here now, apart from Amy, Mum, and Jazz. And at least one of them is not really my friend.

"Cam, I'm sorry," I call softly.

He turns again. Nods. "I know," he says. And goes inside.

I breathe in and out to steady myself, then push the bike into our shed. Unlock the front door.

"Hello?" I call out. But there is no answer. The house is quiet.

I run for the shower. At least I will look normal by the time anyone gets home; I'll see who looks surprised to see me here.

I watch them all carefully at dinner. Jazz is here yet again, so all the suspects are in attendance. But everyone is as they always are. Either someone is a good actor, or I've got it wrong. But what else could be the answer? It must be one of them.

22

Next morning is misery and gray drizzle. Not helped by how I ache, everywhere, from head to toe. Getting thrown around and drugged by Lorders takes a lot out of you. Not to mention fighting. Part of me grins inside at the thought of the swollen face of that Lorder I kicked; part of me winces.

I wilt over the breakfast table, stirring cereal this way and that, and not eating much of it.

"What's with you this morning?" Mum says.

"Too many late night sighs over Cameron, maybe?" Amy says, and smirks.

I scowl. "You've got it wrong; we're friends." At least, we were. I sigh. Wonder if he is even talking to me?

"See?" Amy laughs. And Mum smiles as if she agrees with her conclusions. How could they think that, so soon after Ben disappeared? Butterflies flutter inside with his name. *Ben, will I see you soon?*

And what does it matter what they think. Better that than they know what really troubles my sleep. Of course, one or both of them do, if they called the Lorders.

Yet watching, listening to them again this morning, I find it impossible to believe they could have had anything to do with what happened yesterday.

And what about Nico? If I tell him about Coulson, he'll know what to do. But what will he make of me leaving that drawing where it

146

could be found in the first place? Coulson said he was watching me already. Perhaps my slipup tipped us off, put us in a stronger position: Now, at least, I *know* I'm being watched. But somehow I doubt Nico will see it that way.

Nico goes past in the hall when I am changing classes that morning. He tilts his head slightly, then walks on toward his office. He wants me to follow.

Does he somehow know what happened yesterday already? Indecision and fear hold me still.

Better to know.

I check no one is watching and knock once on his office door. It opens and he pulls me inside, shuts it again.

"Rain! How are you?" He is grinning.

"Uh, fine."

"I've got a surprise for you. Don't look so alarmed! You'll like it," he says, and there is nothing in his eyes to alarm me, yet I am.

"What is it?"

He shakes his head. "Not so fast. First we're going on a road trip at lunch today."

"Where to?"

"Wait and see, impatient Rain. Wait and see." And he tells me where to walk out of the grounds at lunch, where he'll pick me up.

"What about my afternoon classes?"

"Give me your ID at lunch and I'll take care of it. No one will notice."

When the lunch bell rings, I head through the side gate and rush down the road. As I hurry along I wonder *why* I'm even going. If he knows, this is dangerous. If he doesn't, I should tell him. Either way I'm in deep trouble. Yet somehow, even as I'm wondering if I should turn around, my feet take me to our meeting point. Somehow I can't *not* do what he says.

When I reach the bend he described, I barely have time to take a breath when his car appears and stops. The passenger door opens. I get in.

Soon we're off the main road, twisting down single lane tracks, overgrown and unfamiliar. Nico remains silent. My stomach twists inside. Maybe this is all just about getting me out somewhere quiet, alone, to deal with.

"We're nearly there," he says, but all I can see are trees and more trees. The track narrows until the car barely fits, and he stops. Nothing in sight. He points out an almost invisible path hidden in the undergrowth. "You'll find answers to why I brought you here about a ten-minute walk that way. I'll come later."

He reaches for my school ID where it hangs around my neck and pulls it over my head; his warm fingers brush my face. "Go on. Take care," he says.

After I get out he starts reversing back down the lane, and the farther away he gets, the more I can breathe.

I walk under the trees, along the faint path. Careful, quiet, slow; not sure what lies in wait. Having to concentrate to not lose the way.

With Nico long ago we did all sorts of deep woods training, like how to move through undergrowth and make no noise. How to mark or follow a path no one else will see. Here, there are only faint bends in plants to mark the way, at irregularly spaced intervals. Once I lose track and have to go back.

Out of practice.

Yes. And I wonder if I'm walking into one of Nico's traps. *Take care,* he said; what did he mean? He used to test us, introduce unexpected dangers. Maybe he is checking to see if I'm still up for it?

As I get close to ten minutes' walk, I double off the path and back, in loops. Creeping and checking as I go forward.

It is on one such diversion that I see a small clearing. To one side under overhanging trees, a green tarp and loose branches cover something bulky. And to the other side, someone is waiting, sitting on a stump, watching the path where I should have emerged. He glances down at a watch. Wondering where I am?

I blink, and again. My eyes feel wrong. Like I'm wide-eyed awake and in deep sleep at the same time; standing here, and lost in a dream—or a nightmare. Goose bumps creep up my arms and spine. The back of this head is familiar, so familiar. His dark hair is long now; his shoulders are broader. My heart is beating fast. Wondering is it really him, and who is he, all at the same time. I step forward, hesitant, not looking where I place my feet. A twig snaps.

He whips around at the sound. Eyes widen, and he stares for one beat, two. Emotion crosses his face, too fast to identify; he shakes himself. "Well, I don't flipping believe it. Rain?" A scowl covers his face, one I'd nearly forgotten, but now it is stark in my memories. The jagged knife scar down the right cheek has faded little since I last saw it, and prompts memory to whisper the name he chose for himself.

"Hello, Katran."

"I never thought I'd see *you* again." His jaw is clenched; a little muscle twitches up the side of his face.

"That makes two of us. Nico didn't tell me you'd be here."

"Same. He just told me to meet someone. What rock did he find you under? I thought you were Slated."

I hold up my wrist, pull the sleeve back. Levo in place.

"Shouldn't you be blacking out at the mere sight of my handsome face?" He smiles.

"I hate to disappoint you, but you're not *that* frightening. Besides, this thing doesn't work." I spin it on my wrist.

"Aren't you the special one."

I glare. Echoes of past taunts burn in my ears. *Rain is too special to come with us; Rain is too special for this; Rain is too special to do that.* It's coming back: Nico stopped me from going with my cell a lot of the time. Until—I frown. The memory is gone.

"Come on. Best get going."

"To where?"

He doesn't answer, pulls the tarp up. Underneath are trail bikes. "Remember how?" he says, challenge in his voice.

"Try to keep up," I say, and take off ahead of him up the path. It is rough and bouncy; not great with yesterday's bruises, but I don't care. It is like flying! Faster than Katran—this is all that matters.

Before long I get to a fork in the path and I wait to see the way. He takes off past me to the left, then soon slows, crosses a rocky creek. We get off and push the bikes through dense trees. And there is a house. It looks like a ruin from the outside, and would from the air: ugly, crumbling concrete, decades old. Pre-riot it looks but not by much. There is a track road to one side of it.

"A safe house?" I ask. Free UK have them all over the country, in unexpected places. To hide both people and weapons.

He nods.

"Why am I here?"

"Nico knows," he says, his words an old expression, familiar yet forgotten until he said them. "But he told me to leave you alone for a while with our latest recruit."

"Who?"

He rolls his eyes. "Princess Pea."

We hide the bikes under trees. "Watch it; there's a trip wire all around," Katran says, pointing out the almost invisible wire set to warn the house if any uninvited guests come by.

We step over it and to the front of the house. And there, lounging on a deck chair in the late autumn sunshine, is Tori.

Tori, a recruit? I can feel my mouth hanging open and shut it. When Nico said he had somewhere to stash her, I never thought he meant *this*. That she was to be one of us.

Katran takes off, muttering something about finding his group. Leaving us alone. From his backward glance and Tori's icy look, I get the feeling they don't get along.

"So. How're things?" I ask, finally breaking the silence.

"All right." She stares back, eyes unreadable, long enough for it to be uncomfortable. She finally stands and picks up a box of throwing knives. "Come on," she says. "There're some targets. I hear you're good at this."

We walk around the back of the house; a tree behind has faintly marked rings. I draw a knife out of the box, the weight and feel in my hand so sure, so familiar. It prompts a memory of winning a throwing competition, beating Katran. I smile. "Knives are my specialty," I say.

"I always knew there was more to you than met the eye, Kyla. But I don't understand who you are."

"Neither do I!" I laugh. "But I'm not Kyla, not here. I'm Rain. Who are you?"

She rolls her eyes. "They said pick a name from something around, but I wasn't quick enough, and that jerk started calling me Princess Pea." She scowls. "It seems to have stuck."

We flick knives at the targets.

"Are things all right here?" I ask Tori. Watching her carefully with one eye while pretending to concentrate on the target.

"Yes. It's great!" She grimaces. "Apart from the name."

"Princess I get. But why Pea?"

"I complained about things when I got here a few days ago," she admits, sheepish look on her face. "Katran said I was like a princess whining about a pea under her mattress."

"But it's all right now?"

She smiles. "Out here, middle of nothing and nowhere, you can do and say what you like. Scream if you want! No one cares, no Lorders." She hefts a knife in her hand. "I can look at that target, and whoever I like is there. Mum." She throws the knife. *Thud*: perfect shot. "Or a Lorder." She throws another, but it's off center. She clucks, annoyed.

We walk to the tree, pull the knives out, and walk back again. "Try standing farther away this time," I suggest, and we move back. "Any particular Lorder? Planning revenge?"

"Too late for that; he's already dead." She throws a knife, but distracted, it wobbles, misses the target. She curses. Tries again and hits dead center.

"You never told me what happened."

We go back to the tree, pull our knives out. Instead of walking back she sits down, leans against the tree, and closes her eyes.

I follow. She is silent.

"Tori?"

"You're not supposed to use that name here. I'm not her anymore. Too many bad things happened to her. I'm leaving them behind."

She leans forward, pulls out a blade of grass and tears it into little pieces. "You know the start. I was taken. In the night, from my sleep. Hauled off by Lorders. They wouldn't say why." She sighs. "I was taken to a place with other Slateds. There were half a dozen of us. So scared. Never heard so many Levos buzzing at once. One of the Lorders read out something about how we had violated our contracts, but they wouldn't let us say anything. And then . . ." She stops, her face twisting.

"Don't tell me if you don't want to."

"They were killed," she whispers.

"What?"

"Terminated. By injection. And dumped in a hole in the ground. Of course by the time one was dead, most of the others blacked out, so they didn't know what happened to them."

You guess these things, what happens to people who disappear. But to hear someone who knows, who saw it happen? I feel sick.

"But what about you?"

"I was last. I didn't black out. After, I wished I had." She gives a thin smile. "I was given an injection. I struggled and kicked, but they still got it in. But it wasn't what the others got. It was Happy Juice."

"What? I don't understand."

"I didn't, either. Then one of the Lorders snuck me out in his car."

Rescued, by a Lorder? Unbelievable. But when she said it, her eyes narrowed.

"Why?"

"At first, I thought he had a conscience. Wanted to save me, though why me and not any of the others I couldn't understand. He hid me in his house and had a doctor come and take off my Levo. That was so amazing! And he gave me stuff. Clothes, nice things. Treated me like a daughter." Her face turns away. "But it was all a lie. He was a total sicko. The things he did. Just little things at first, then worse and worse. I won't tell you what—I can't."

Oh, Tori. Her face, even filled with hate as it is now, is flawless. The same beauty that may be why her mother returned her has hurt her in ways she can't say, that I can't bear to even think about. I hold out my hand, and she grips it. Holds on tight.

"And then, one day, I took my chance. I stopped fighting. Pretended to go along with him, with the things he wanted me to do. Then, when he was . . . distracted, I killed him."

She lets go of my hand and picks up one of the knives, runs her finger lightly across the blade. "It wasn't as sharp as this. A dinner knife. Messy, and slow. He suffered, and I was glad."

She looks up again. "Then I ran away. Didn't think I'd get far, didn't care. Was going to kill myself so they couldn't do it to me when they caught up. To take that away from them, you know? But then realized I wanted to see Ben before I died." Her eyes fill with tears.

My insides clench. If she knows of my involvement in Ben's disappearance, the knife won't stay in her hand.

She grips the handle so tight, her knuckles turn white. "I didn't want to talk about this. Do you know why I've told you?"

My mouth is dry, my body prepared to react, to defend myself if necessary. "Why?"

"Nico asked me to."

I relax, just a little. Is this the real reason why he brought me here? Why would he do that?

"I had to tell him," she says. "He insisted he had to know what happened to let me stay. He got more out of me than I thought I'd ever say out loud."

"He's got a way of doing that," I say.

She nods, a half smile on her lips as she thinks of Nico and his ways. Jealousy twists inside.

Then her smile falls away. "And in return, he told me that Ben cut off his Levo, and that Lorders took him. I was too late. He's probably in a hole in the ground someplace like those other Slateds."

Her head drops to her knees, her arms wrapped around them tight. Her body shakes with sobs, and I slip an arm across her shoulders. I should tell her Ben has been spotted. But I don't. Is it because it isn't definite, it might not be him? To protect Aiden? Or some darker reason. I'm not sure.

She lifts her head, wipes her face on her sleeve. Looks up and smiles.

"But now I'm in Free UK, and I'm going to kill more Lorders. And that is why I like it here." She jumps to her feet. "Come on. I need to practice."

And practice she does. She has a good eye, and it is seeing Lorder blood.

23

Tori holds the pistol in both hands. Takes careful aim, and pulls the trigger.

The bottle explodes as her arms jerk back with the recoil.

She raises a fist in triumph. "At last!" She is a wild shot, not a natural like with knives, and this session has been long, frustrating, and occasionally dangerous. We're both laughing when we turn and realize Nico is there, watching.

"Bravo!" he says, and Tori flushes with pleasure. And I wonder in annoyance if he saw any of the previous dozen shots that missed?

Nico tosses my school ID at me; I catch it.

"Did everything go all right with this?" I ask, and slip it back around my neck.

"Of course. You were in every class as required, or so the school computer will insist if anyone questions. Come," he says, pointing at me, and walks into the house.

I follow. Through the door are rough sleeping quarters, bedrolls on the floor. Crates, boxes. Weapons? No running water by the looks of things. Tori wouldn't like that; no wonder Katran started calling her Princess. But after what happened to her, being here must be paradise.

"Sit," Nico says, points at a box and sits on the one next to it. "We need to talk. Did Tori tell you her story?"

"Yes."

"But do you understand why I asked her to tell it to you? Rain, you know how we must work in a group: total honesty. I had Tori tell you her sad tale; you needed to know. To know her strengths and weaknesses, her motivation. To work with her."

He is putting Tori and me in the same category, the same level. As if we are on the same team. He barely knows her! And I'm hurt inside and can't work out if that is the reason, or if it's something else. It isn't total honesty. If Tori knew my story—everything that happened with Ben—she'd never accept me. I sigh.

"Poor Rain. You know I'm on your side, don't you?"

He takes my hand, holds it, and I grip on tight, overwhelmed by feeling isolated, alone. Mum and Amy can't be trusted, Cam isn't speaking to me—or, if he is, must be avoided for his own good. Earlier I'd felt Tori and I had the beginnings of a fragile friendship, but it will go in an instant if she learns the truth about Ben.

There is only Nico. I look up and meet his eyes. They hold mine, steady. They are always the same. *Total honesty:* I have to tell him everything.

"Now," he says. "How are your drawings coming along?"

"I've got some; I could have brought them today if I knew I'd be here. I'm at the hospital on Saturday. I need to check some details, and do more. They must be accurate."

"Indeed. But soon, Rain. Soon."

I take a deep breath. "I need to talk to you about something else. I—"

"Wait." There are footsteps, a murmur of voices outside. "Go out and meet your new friends first."

When I walk out of the house, Katran is back, and with him an exhausted crew of nine. Newish recruits by the looks of them, all about fourteen or fifteen years old. Some are half-known faces from school, and I may be surprised to see them, but they are even more surprised to see me. Eyes focus on my wrist: my Levo.

When Nico walks out behind me, all whispers cease. They stand up straighter.

Nico glances at Katran. "Report."

He shakes his head. "Useless bunch, this new lot of fodder. They were goofing off when I got back from my *diversion*." He glares at me.

The fear around me is tangible, a slimy, choking thing you can almost reach out and touch. We all started that way, in terror of Nico. Bit by bit as we achieved and he approved, it changed: The fear remained, but the rest of it followed. We started to understand everything he did, he did for us. To make us stronger. To keep us safe.

But Nico just raises an eyebrow. "It's your group, Katran. What do you think you should do about it?"

Katran smiles. "Night training again tonight." He raises a hand to tell them to go, and a few start making hesitant steps away.

"Wait," Nico says. "There is one more problem."

They all stop, still, eyes back on Nico.

"We've had a serious breach of security. One of you has slipped away, told some tales about us. Who is it?" His voice is ice, and though I know it isn't me, that it is one of this group, their fear is so contagious it has me in hold with them. Dread pools inside at what will happen next.

He glances at the white faces, one by one, and holds their eyes. I spot the guilty one before he gets to her: a dark-haired girl, in year ten at school I think. She shakes and can't meet his gaze.

Nico sighs. Gestures at Katran, who grabs her, pulls her forward from the others. Holds her in front of Nico.

"Holly, aren't you?" Nico says. He reaches a hand forward; she flinches, but he just lightly touches her cheek. He smiles. "Tell us what you've done," he says, his voice gentle.

She looks up, desperate hope in her eyes. She doesn't know him as well as I do; angry would be safer. "I'm sorry, Nico. I had to see him, to say good-bye."

"Who? A boyfriend?" Nico glances at Katran, who rolls his eyes.

"No. My brother."

"Holly. I seem to remember you telling me with great passion how you hated the Lorders, that you'd do anything to overthrow them. That we were your new family."

"You are! This is all I want to do, to be. You have to believe me. I'll do anything."

"Anything?" He nods to himself. "We shall see. But you've put us at risk."

"He won't tell anybody!"

"Then how do I know about it?" His words sink in. Her face, if it could get any paler, does. "We don't make the rules lightly, Holly. Holding on to past ties twists loyalties. They make you vulnerable, and weak."

Nico looks over their heads. Waves a hand. The group parts down the middle without discussion; from the woods come two men, and between them, a boy. Thirteen at most, an arm held by each. Struggling.

Nico scans the faces. "Everyone, meet Holly's brother." He turns back to Holly. "Now, here is my dilemma. You tell me things, you make promises, then you break the rules." Nico smiles. "Yet you say you will do *anything* for our cause."

He nods at Katran, who lets her go. She is trembling.

"You have created a security risk. You must eliminate it."

Nico reaches under his jacket. Takes out a gun. Checks it. Hands it to Holly.

No. She won't. He won't make her. No!

Her brother realizes before she does. He stops struggling. Stares at her with huge brown eyes, at his big sister who holds a gun in her hands. Looking at it like she can't work out how it got there.

Nico puts a hand on her shoulder, pulls her hair behind one ear, and speaks softly. "Know that you did this to him, whether you pull the trigger or somebody else does. You did it. Finish what you started," he says.

The gun shakes wildly in her hands, and I fight for control, to not throw myself at her and take it from her. To then get held myself between those two men like that boy is now.

She finally looks up. At Nico, into his eyes. He nods.

Her face is blank. She holds the gun in both hands, tries to steady it.

"Bang!" Katran yells. Everyone flinches, then he laughs, takes the gun from her hands. Opens it and shows everyone: not loaded.

Holly collapses on the ground. Nico kneels down next to her. "I'd never make you kill your brother, silly girl. I care for all of you far too much. But you had to be taught this lesson. You all did." He stands and looks at each of the group in the eye, one after another.

He nods at the men, who release Holly's brother. He's smiling now, runs to his sister, and they cling to each other. "I'm sorry," he says. "I had to play along to be able to come. So I could join Free UK, too."

Nico reaches out a hand, pulls Holly to her feet. I'm shaking with relief. Of course I should have known better, should have had faith in Nico. I believed the whole thing. I shouldn't have fallen for it, not like all these new recruits. Katran was either in on it the whole time or worked it out. I should have, too.

Holly clings to Nico's hand, her eyes full of gratitude. "Thank you, Nico, thank you so much. You won't be sorry for giving me another chance."

"I won't be." He says the words with calm assurance, and Holly may not realize the thin ice she is on, but I do. No one crosses Nico and gets away with it. My stomach sinks. What she did, telling her brother, is nowhere near as bad as what I did. If Nico finds out my carelessness led to Lorders picking me up . . . well. That gun would have bullets in it.

I can't tell him.

But what about Ben?

Nico faces the group. "While you're all here, I have some special news. A great honor for you all. Thanks to some information from Princess, here"—a grin twists at the corner of his mouth as he says the name, and he gestures at Tori—"we've managed to pin down the location of a Lorder RTC. A Recall and Termination Center, where they take and murder so-called contract breakers. You'll attack in a few days."

The center where Tori was taken? Where Slateds were killed, and dumped in the ground. My fists clench, full of pain at what was done to them there. Was nearly done to Tori, before a fate that may have been worse stepped in and claimed her.

Everyone smiles nervously, then cheers. Their first? Are they ready? I look at Katran, who quirks an eyebrow. He's not sure, either.

But I'm ready. Maybe I can escape the mess with Coulson by leaving it behind.

"Nico, can I—"

"Wait." He puts a hand on my shoulder. "Come along inside, special one. Time for us to finish our talk."

I follow him back in the house, feeling eyes on my back. *Special,* and labeled as such in front of them all. Katran's taunt rings in my ears: *too special to come along.* We'll see about that.

"Now. What did you want to talk to me about?"

"Let me help. I want to stay here, be part of things."

Nico smiles. "I'm so pleased to hear you say what I already know, Rain." He leans forward and kisses my forehead. "But you can't stay here."

"But—"

He raises a hand. "Not yet. You can't stay here *yet.* There are things you can do for us if you stay in your other life a bit longer. Big plans are coming, Rain. Soon I will tell you. For now, just know this: The Lorders and their ways are in jeopardy. There will be concerted attacks on many fronts. And you will play a vital role. You must stay safe."

"Please let me go on the RTC attack. Please! I'll do anything." I hear the echo of Holly's words earlier, and inside, deep down, some part wonders: Would I really do *anything*? She almost did.

He stares back, considering. Drawing the moment out for so long that I almost jump into the silence with more pleas. Then he nods his head.

"I can go?"

"Yes, Rain. You can go," he says, smiling at me, and I bask in his approval. "Now, was there anything else?"

Ben. Help me find him; make him safe from Coulson. Take Coulson's hold on me away. But standing there under Nico's eyes, I can't do it. I can't tell him about Coulson. He'll be so furious. All I want is to be part of this cause. Our cause. For Nico to keep looking at me as he is now, with warm favor. I'll keep away from Coulson and tell him nothing. I'll work out what to do about Ben by myself.

"No, Nico. There is nothing else."

"Then come on, it's time for you to go."

Back outside, there is no sign of Tori or the others, but Katran waits by the door.

"Take her home," Nico says.

Katran nods, and I follow him to our trail bikes.

Without a word he takes off fast down the path, and I follow. We go the same way we came until the fork after the creek, then go the other way.

We continue on, and the path we are taking hooks up with a canal path, one not much used by the state of it. Twice we have to stop and lift our bikes over fallen trees.

After a fork it starts to widen and look familiar; the other way it links with the path by Ben's house, I'm sure of it. Or where his house used to be. Which means this way links with the footpath over our village.

Katran soon stops. "We've put a hide in here for a bike." We go off the path, push through trees and brambles. "You can leave yours here so you can get to us if you need to."

"Thanks."

"Nico told me to take care of it." He shoves my bike in, points out a box behind painted to look like leaves. "Usual stash of supplies. Water, food, fuel," he says, then pulls a tarp and branches back over the lot. "Never knew this was for you or I might have thought twice."

I scowl at the acid in his voice. "Just what is your problem with me?"

He gets back on his bike. "My problem? I haven't got a problem. You, on the other hand, are nothing but problems, *special girl*." With that, he starts his bike and disappears up the path.

Great. The one person from my past I can totally do without, and he is the one who is here.

The sun is getting low in the sky as I trudge home, hurrying now to avoid questions about where I've been if I'm too late. The last few miles disappear while I think.

I chickened out.

There it is, faced straight on: I was afraid to tell Nico the truth.

Look what happened to Holly. If that is what Nico does to one of his own whose only sin is telling her brother why she left, what will he make of me? I won't be special anymore if he finds out about Coulson. Especially when I didn't tell him about it at the first opportunity. I might not even be alive.

We are your family now. Nico would have no interest in helping me find Ben. To him, Ben would be another security risk: He makes me careless. *Past ties twist loyalties.*

I am twisted tight: between Nico, and Ben.

There is only one way to know what to do. I need to see Ben.

24

"YES, DEAR?"

Cam's aunt is older than I expect, gray hair swept up on top of her head. Anxious eyes peer through thin wire glasses.

I shift my feet on the front step. "Is Cam home?"

"Yes, I think so. Come in, dear."

I follow her into a chintzy entranceway that leads to their front room: the whole place is crammed with cottage kitsch; frills and china animals *everywhere.*

"Cameron? You have a guest," she calls.

He comes down the stairs and my breath catches at the sight of him. A day later and what the Lorder did to him looks worse, far worse: Half his face is bruised, purple, and swollen. He has the shiner from hell, and it's all my fault.

"Thanks," he says, and looks at his aunt; she seems a little flustered. Disappears into the kitchen and shuts the door.

"Er . . . nice place."

"Cut the crap. It sucks."

"Want to get out of it and go for a walk?"

"Sure." He smiles at me with the half of his face that can still smile. We head out, and I think we have more in common than I realized. The atmosphere in that house is weird. Watchful. He is stuck here with relatives he doesn't really know, in a strange place. Not that different from what happened to me a few months ago when I landed across the street. At least Mum has better taste in home furnishings.

But why did I go and knock on his door, today of all days? After the afternoon with Tori, then Katran and Nico, I just had a compulsion to do something *ordinary*: to see a friend. If he still wants to be my friend after what happened. Or maybe it's not wanting to be alone with my thoughts?

We're past the edge of the village before he starts.

"Didn't see you at school today."

"Sorry."

"Missed you at lunch, as well. Where were you?"

"Around."

"I waited outside your last class at the end of the afternoon. Never saw you."

"I think I liked it better when you were giving me the silent treatment," I say, then immediately wish I hadn't. His face looks hurt in more ways than one. "I'm sorry."

"Look. If you tell me what is going on, maybe I can help." We've reached the edge of the village now, and I turn to go back, but he pulls my hand toward the dark footpath along a field. "Come on," he says, and I'm uneasy. This path leads to the woods where Wayne was found, a place I never want to go again. But once we're out of sight of the road, he stops and leans against the fence.

"Kyla, listen. I understand that right now, you feel you can't tell me anything. And don't say there is nothing to tell. I won't believe you."

"All right."

"But if there is ever anything I can do to help, anything, just ask, and I'll do it."

I stare back at him. My throat feels thick, like I'm going to cry, and it's because he cares enough to offer help that could land him in any sort of trouble. He's not stupid enough to not know that, not after yesterday. But at the same time I wonder *why*. Why is he so willing to risk himself for somebody he barely knows? Is it just friendship, or something *else*. I reach out and lightly touch his bruised cheek. "Isn't that what got you this?"

"Well. If I'd had another second, I'd have bested that jerk. He was on the ropes, wasn't he?"

I smile. "Sure he was. Not a mark on him, but he was quaking."

"He won't dare bother us again," Cam says, and drops into a boxer's stance.

I laugh. "Yeah, I'm sure you're right. And thanks again, for sticking up for me. Even though it was completely mental."

"I'd do anything to get back at the Lorders," he says, face back to serious. His eyes turn inward, focus someplace else, some other time, and I don't think he is talking about yesterday. He shakes his head. "What about you?" He looks up; his eyes are here again, and hold mine.

I hesitate. "I have some things to work out. That is all I can say."

"Cryptic Kyla," he says. "Come on, we'll be late for our dinners."

He holds out a hand, and I take it, hold it a little too tight as we walk home. A lifeline to another life. One that is slipping away.

At Group that night, Penny continues with the games theme. She's found some more chess sets, evidently having decided that if one Slated can manage to play it, the rest of them can work it out, too.

She splits us into two groups, me with one and her with the other, and we go over the board setup, the pieces, and how they all move. We start some games, but it is all so distant, so unimportant, I can't concentrate. As if moving chess pieces around—one player's move, then the other's, in sequence—has anything to do with real life.

My mind wanders in circles and back again. Nico always seems to be at the center of things, directing and controlling the action. A chess master knows so many moves in advance, the other player's positions and goals can always be predicted. But even he doesn't know about me and Coulson.

Who will win? Is it just a game to them both?

That night I focus on Ben's face, try to hold it in my mind, but it is frustration. His features are slippery.

He is everything to me, yet he is just one. One victim out of many the Lorders destroy every day they stay in power. What is one when the fate of many hang in the balance? Nico said I am to play a vital role in Free UK plans. The thought fills me with both pride and nervous fear at what that role may be. If Nico is right—if the Lorders really are under threat—how can I put that in jeopardy, even to save Ben?

How can I not.

I despise my weakness, that everything is so mixed up inside. But there is always only one answer: I have to see Ben. I have to warn him about Coulson.

I'm running as fast as I can.

But it is never fast enough.

Sometimes I am still running when I wake, chased by nameless, unseen fears. Other times it is worse, and I've fallen, and he won't leave me.

Even when I'm in it, I know this is a dream now. It comes so often.

But knowing doesn't stop the terror.

I fall. And he won't leave. My eyes are clenched shut tight; I can't look, I can't see what happens next. I can't . . .

And I'm screaming, but a hand is tight around my mouth, stifling the sound. I struggle, but strong, warm arms hold me firm, rock me side to side. A voice murmurs soothing sounds in my hair: "Shhhhh, Rain. It's all right. I've got you."

I open my eyes, and as reason returns, he takes his hand off my mouth. Katran is here. It was just a dream.

"Same one again?" he asks.

I nod, shaking, still unable to speak, gripped by another fear. Of losing more bits of myself, wrapping them up and shunting them away.

My eyes snap open in the dark. The fear from the dream is quickly replaced by shock. My recurring dream, the one I'd always thought must be from when I was Slated? It can't be. Not if tonight's version holds any truth. If I had this nightmare when Katran was there, then I must have had the same recurring dream when I was still training with the Owls. *Before* the Lorders caught me. *Before* I was Slated.

But Katran comforting me, holding me: This *must* be made up by my unconscious mind. It couldn't have been that way. But even as I reject this caring Katran, one I don't know, and wonder if the rest of the dream must then be fiction, too, I know that it can't be. It felt more real, more true, than anything ever has before.

And there is something else, something hidden in that dream. It is so close I can almost reach out and brush it with my fingers, but still it dances away.

Even as my fists clench, even as I want to scream in frustration at these gaps in my memory, there is a cold nugget of truth inside.

I don't want to know.

25

"**Come.**"

Just one word in a low voice, that is all. The Lorder isn't one I recognize; he walks ahead and doesn't look back. He has no doubt that I will follow. I consider running for it, but what would be the point? I drop behind, just keeping him in sight through the crowd of students changing classes. Easy to do as they give him a wide berth: just follow the blank spot in a crowded hall.

He opens an office door in the admin building, goes inside and leaves it ajar. I look quickly in all directions; even though Nico should be in science block, you never know. But there is no sign of him or anyone else I recognize.

When I reach the door, it is unlike the others I pass on the way. There is no nameplate or number.

I knock once and go in.

The Lorder I'd followed stands at attention to one side of a desk. At the desk sits Coulson.

"Sit," he says. There is only one chair, on this side of the small desk facing him. Too close for comfort, but I sit. "Speak."

I swallow, throat suddenly dry. "Nice office," I say.

He says nothing, but the ice factor in the room increases by enough for me to know I'm in trouble. The silence is brittle.

The best guide to lying is to stick to the truth as much as possible. "There may be some plans, but I don't know when, or the details."

He inclines his head slightly, his face blank, as always. Considering.

"Not good enough," he says, finally. "What sort of plans?"

My brain isn't cooperating; it has gone cold with fear. What I should or shouldn't say is an unprepared mystery, and the more his eyes rest on me, the more my brain stops working. Until I find Ben, until I warn him to hide where Coulson can't find him, Coulson *must* think I'm sticking to our deal. He must. I have to tell him *something*.

"There may be concerted attacks planned. But that is all I know. I don't know where, or when." I say the words in a rush, then flinch inside. Nico is part of these plans. I can't say anything to lead them to him or the others.

He stares back. The clock on the wall behind me ticks loud, and seems too slow, like seconds are stretching beyond their usual limits. His eyes bore in, see the holes in what I say, the things I leave out.

"There have been rumors of this. A few . . . confessions, that suggest similar. What else?"

"That is all I know," I say, the words almost sticking in my throat.

The bell for next class rings, and I jump.

There is something in his eyes. He knows I'm holding back, that I haven't told him everything.

The blood drains from my face.

He smiles, but it doesn't make me feel better. "Go now. You can't be late for math."

I almost leap out of the chair and reach for the door. He even knows my next class?

"Oh, Kyla?"

I pause.

"Consider yourself lucky today. I am not a patient man. The next time we speak, I want more. I want the *whole* story.

"Go!" he barks, and I bolt out the door.

I dash down the hall, glad to be late, to have an excuse to run.

In the door of my math class I scan in, sit, get my notebook out. Pretend to listen to the teacher go on about statistics while my mind churns over probabilities of my own.

It has only been two days. Coulson is impatient already? Somehow he knows *something*. That I wasn't where I was supposed to be yesterday afternoon. How? He has been watching, or someone is spying on me.

We file in for assembly that afternoon as we do every Friday, but this one is different. Coulson is there again with the Lorders, and this time I know I'm not imagining things. His eyes really are resting on my head, marking me out. Like a neon sign stamped on my forehead: *See the Lorder Spy.* I feel like a butterfly pinned in place under a lens, a hot lamp burning my wings.

Can anyone else see how he watches? I glance about, then with a start spot Nico sitting with his tutor group, off to the left and several rows back. His eyes flit to mine and then away. Did Coulson see?

Dangerous games.

Face carefully blank, I focus on the head as he goes on about school inspections. Inside, all is turmoil: those two, together, breathing the same air in the same room. Perhaps I could point them out to each other and let them get on with it.

No. It isn't fair to put them together in my mind like that. Lorders are evil: Thinking about what happened to Tori in their hands turns my stomach. And to so many others, who go missing without explanation. Nico is right to want to put an end to them and their ways.

Yet what Nico is to me . . . *that* is complicated.

I should have told him. Right from the start, as soon as it happened, I should have told Nico about Coulson and his deal. Let Nico decide how to handle it, how to turn it back on them. The old Rain would have done so.

But I didn't. I couldn't risk Ben; or Cam either, for that matter. But that isn't the Free UK way. They will rescue their own if they can without undue risk. Otherwise, all are expendable; we know this. It's part of the deal. The safety of the group—the cause—is more important than any individual, in the group or outside of it.

I feel sick. It is too late to tell Nico about any of it; I'd be damned by the delay. He'd see I am divided. That I am weak.

No matter what I do, it is wrong.

26

JAZZ WINKS AND SLIPS AN ENVELOPE IN MY HAND WHEN WE get home after school. I race up to my room and shut the door. He made sure to do it when Amy wasn't looking. What could it be? My hands are shaking so hard it takes longer than it should to open, and I almost rip it.

Inside is a photograph. A runner: slightly out of focus, taken on a track from some distance. His hair, his build, the away look on his face as he runs.

It's Ben.

Flipped over, a few words are written faint in pencil: *Is it him?*

I open the envelope again—nothing else, no instructions, no explanations.

I bite my tongue, hard, to keep myself from a therapeutic scream. Not. Good. Enough. This can't wait.

The last time I saw him, Aiden said he'd be at Mac's on Friday: today. Maybe he's still there? If he isn't, maybe Mac knows where Ben is.

Minutes later, I'm cycling up the road.

I knock on Mac's front door. No one comes, yet I could have sworn I heard someone inside as I walked up to the house. I try it, but it's locked. I scramble over the high gate down the side of the house; a white telephone van is parked on the other side. Aiden's? Then Skye bounds over and almost knocks me off my feet to lick my face.

"Where is everyone?" I ask her. She wags her tail.

I bang on the back door. "It's Kyla. Let me in!" I yell. "I know you're in there."

There are footsteps inside, the turn of a lock. The door opens: Aiden.

I pull the photo of Ben out of my pocket and hold it up. "Where is he?"

"Come in." Aiden takes my hand, pulls me inside Mac's kitchen. "Sorry I didn't answer the door; didn't know it was you. Mac is out, and I shouldn't be here. Skye doesn't make much of a guard dog, does she?"

"No." She leans on my legs so hard, she almost knocks me over again, tail thumping madly.

"I was just about to make some tea." He gets an extra cup out, holds it up. I nod and he puts the kettle on, then turns and leans on the counter. "So. I'm guessing by your appearance that you think that photo is Ben."

"Yes. It's him."

"Careful, now. Are you sure? It isn't just that you hope it to be so, so you see it? Look again."

I take out the photograph. Study it, but it is him. Even in the way he holds himself as he runs.

"I'm sure," I say. "Where is he? When can I see him?"

"Not so fast. It may be . . . complicated."

"What do you mean?"

He hesitates. "He's going to a boarding school. The surrounding area is infested."

"Infested? By what?"

"Lorders."

"I don't understand. Why?"

"I don't know why. But there is a high presence of Lorders in the village where the school is located. We're looking into it."

"I need to see him."

"You need to wait."

"No. Tell me where he is."

"Kyla, until we work out what is going on there, it's far too risky. Have some patience."

I stare back at Aiden. He is being reasonable, and cautious, but he doesn't know the stakes.

"If you won't help me, I'll find him myself."

"Really?" He raises an eyebrow, skeptical.

"Yes. You said a running track, twenty miles away. I've done a search. There are exactly nine possibilities. I've already been to three of them." I'm exaggerating, but I would have been the day we went cycling if Lorders hadn't interrupted. But I can do it.

His eyes widen. "You've done *what*?"

"You heard me."

He shakes his head. "You're one crazy girl," he says, but there, in his eyes: grudging respect. Maybe he's impressed, even. And I start to believe I can convince him.

"I'll do it with or without you. So, are you going to help me, or what?"

He hesitates, thinking, and I manage to keep quiet and leave him to it. Staring steadily back at his blue eyes. Hoping and hoping, so hard. For all that I said, it is a bit needle-haystack, and he and I both know it. I could have missed a track on the maps; the track may be new and not even on a map. I could go to the right place and not know it if he isn't there. I could get caught trying.

"It would be better to wait," he says at last. "Until we have more information."

"But . . . ?"

"I'm as crazy as you are." He grins.

I launch myself at him for a hug. "Thanks, Aiden! When?"

"How about Sunday? It may be dangerous."

"I don't care."

"I do. You have to promise to do what I say on the day, Kyla, and mean it. Or it's off."

I stare back at him, hesitant to make a promise I may find hard to keep. Yet he is taking risks here, too. "I promise."

Aiden holds out the photo. "This was taken last Sunday, training at the village track. So we can hope he'll be there same time and place again. You can at least confirm if it is him. What do you think?"

"I'll do it," I say again. Aiden tells me where he'll pick me up, what time, and I note the details, but all the while I'm staring at Ben's photograph in my hands.

It *is* him. I don't know how or why he survived being hauled off by Lorders. But it really is my Ben.

27

THE NEXT MORNING I WAIT, NERVOUS, IN DR. LYSANDER'S
waiting room. There are so many things I have to try to hide from her
now. I try to remember what it feels like to just be Kyla, before the
memories, but it is slipping away. She mustn't notice how different I
am, how changed; if she orders scans, I'm in big trouble.

Once again there is a Lorder standing guard outside Dr. Lysander's
door. A nurse comes out of the office next to it, her face one I don't
recognize. I store her up, some part of my brain busy collecting people who work in the hospital to draw for Nico. That is when it hits me:
What about Lorder faces?

I force myself to study the guard. It is uncomfortable, trying to
overcome the automatic urge to look away, to avoid eye contact and
stay out of notice. Apart from Coulson, whose face is ingrained in my
memory, and those ones when Cam and I were taken in, I can't say I
know what many Lorders look like, exactly. Men and women, they all
dress the same: identical gray suits most of the time. Or in black operations gear like this one has on now while on guard duty, with a
black vest over top, a weapon at his hip. The vests are bulletproof,
Nico says. And the way they stand and carry themselves says, *Stay out
of our way.* Faces generally expressionless; hair either short or tied
back. Nothing to distinguish them as individuals. If you came by him
on his day off in blue jeans, would he look the same as everybody
else?

He is young, and I'm surprised. Why? I suppose the whole uniform and stance of authority makes me assume older. His face is blank, staring straight ahead, not noticing any lesser beings like myself around him. But he looks no older than Mac or Aiden, early twenties or so. Average height and build. Thin tapering fingers like a musician, not for holding guns. I shake myself internally: Stop being so fanciful. Hazel eyes, short light brown hair. Average features in an average face that would be hard to distinguish in a drawing, but I store it up so I can reproduce it later, and—

He rolls his eyes. Shifts and turns a little, face still blank.

I nearly fall off my chair.

Dr. Lysander appears in her door. "Kyla? You can come in now."

Saved. I scurry past him and through the door.

Dr. Lysander smiles; so she is in a good mood.

"Good morning, Kyla. What is on your mind today?"

"Are Lorders human?" I cringe after I say it. I was so busy studying her Lorder guard, I hadn't prepared what to say.

"What?" She laughs. "Oh, Kyla, I do enjoy our talks. Of course they are."

"Well, I know they're *human*. That isn't what I meant, exactly."

"Please explain."

"Are they ordinary: Do they have pets, hobbies. Do they play musical instruments or go to dinner parties. Or do they just march around scowling all the time?"

She half smiles. "I expect they have lives beyond those that we see. But now that you mention it, I've never had one over for dinner, unless you count the one guarding the door."

"You get guarded having dinner?"

"I get guarded most places these days. But this isn't about me."

"Well, I don't get guarded. I get ignored and scowled at." *Kidnapped, and offered impossible deals.* I stuff the thought down before it can show on my face, but she doesn't seem to notice, and turns to her screen. Taps at it a moment, then looks up.

Watching me very carefully. "Have you had any more memories? Or dreams you thought were real."

"I might have."

"Tell me."

It is impossible to lie to her, and even if I could, I shouldn't. She has to believe me or she might want to do scans. "I dreamed I was having a nightmare. And . . ." I hesitate.

"Yes, Kyla?"

"A boy was holding me when I woke up. But I didn't wake up. It was part of the dream." I can feel my cheeks burning.

"Oh, I see." Amused. "That sort of dream element is a pretty common fabrication at your age."

Even though it makes sense to leave it at that, I can feel myself bristling inside. It is a real memory. As much as I'd rather it weren't Katran, somehow, I know: It happened.

She looks at the screen again.

"Are things all right at home?"

"Yes."

"Really?" She turns, and I'm pinned under her eyes again.

She's heard something. There is a pang inside: Mum. Must be; she must be giving reports. It really *is* her. Dad hasn't been home, and who else could it be?

What can I tell her?

"Well . . ."

"Go on."

"I'm not sure, but I think Mum and Dad aren't getting along that well."

"I see. Are you troubled by this?"

"No. I don't mind him being away more."

She tilts her head. Thinking position. "It is a requirement of your contract that you have two parents to guide your transition to home and community."

My eyes open wide in alarm. "I do, just not as often!"

"Don't worry, Kyla. As long as things are stable at home for you and your sister, I feel there is no need to report that at this time." She glances at the clock. "Time is about gone. Is there anything else you wish to talk about?"

And her eyes are pinning into me again. There are so many things that want to spill out when she looks at me like that. I manage to shake my head no and get up. Head for the door.

"Oh, Kyla?" I turn. "We will talk about whatever is on your mind there next time," she says.

I scurry out, escape made good.

The Lorder is still at her door. Standing at attention and staring straight ahead. I can't help myself glancing back at him before leaving.

He winks.

I just about trip over my feet.

Well! I'm pretty sure winking at a Slated could get him into trouble.

"Your dad called last night," Mum says, one eye on the road home and one on me. London traffic this close to the hospital is, as usual, so slow it doesn't need much attention.

"Did he? How is he?"

"Fine. He asked about you, how things are."

"Really?" I say, surprised. "What did you say?" I ask, unable to stop myself.

"Just what you tell me: School is fine, Cam is just friends, nothing is wrong." She sighs. "I wish . . ."

"What?"

"I wish you wouldn't feed those lines to *me,* though. We used to talk, really talk, didn't we, Kyla? What is going on with you these days?"

I bite my cheek. *Focus.*

"Nothing, really." I smile, and I have gotten better at faking it, yet somehow, she doesn't seem convinced.

"If you need to, we can talk. Just between us, all right?"

"Of course," I say. "I know."

But what I don't know is who turned me in to the Lorders. And even if I could be sure it wasn't her, what should I start with? Perhaps that I'm in Free UK. The same organization that blew up her parents. Or that I'm not, really—I'm a Lorder spy, infiltrating Free UK. Either way, I don't think she'd be much impressed.

I watch her as she drives. Daughter of the first Lorder PM: Is she one of them, or isn't she? But apart from all of that, there is one thing that bugs me most of all.

"I don't understand you," I say, finally breaking the silence.

"What's that?"

"Why did you take in Amy and me? We might have done anything, you don't know. We might be terrorists, or murderers."

"You don't strike me as the bloodthirsty type."

Appearances can be deceiving.

"How can you know?"

"I can't. But I do know who you are now. You and Amy both."

I stare out the window. Does she know who I *really* am? Did she turn me in to the Lorders because she found out? "But what about your parents? And your son. They got blown up by AGT." I stumble over the words, nearly saying Free UK instead of AGT. *Take care.*

She says nothing, keeps driving. Traffic slows to a stop.

"Kyla, what do you know about Robert? My son."

I turn and look at her, startled to see her eyes welling up.

"His name is on the memorial at school. He got killed when their school bus got bombed." That is what I say, though Mac was there and had a different version of events.

She shakes her head. "No. I believed that for a long time, but it isn't true. I found out he survived the bombing, but I never saw him again. I think he was Slated, though I haven't been able to prove it. I've done everything I can to find him, but nothing."

I stare at her in shock. *She knows.*

There is the *toot-toot* of a horn behind us; traffic starting again. Mum continues up the road.

"That is why, Kyla. Do you see? It is because I hope that some-where out there, somebody looked after Robert. Somebody loved him. That is why I do that for Amy and you."

28

THE VAN DOOR SLIDES OPEN. "QUICKLY NOW," AIDEN SAYS, and I climb in. "Sorry, it isn't very comfortable back here." He shifts a toolbox across. "Have a seat?"

I perch on the edge of it. He knocks on the wall to the front compartment, and the van rattles off. It is chock-full of technical stuff, parts, tools. Things hanging from the ceiling, on shelves, and on the walls. There is barely enough room for the two of us among it all.

"Is all this the other half of your double life?" I ask. "Telephone repairman by day, superhero by night?"

Aiden laughs, an easy, natural sound, likes he laughs often. "Something like that," he says, and smiles. And I'm struck by the risk he is taking now, to find Ben. The same risk he takes all the time to find other missing people.

"Thanks for doing this," I say.

"Don't thank me yet. I've seen the photo and I'm still not convinced it is definitely Ben. But we'll check it out. I've arranged an emergency repair at a house opposite the training field."

"Really?"

"Well, it'll turn out to be a simple job, though it can last as long as we need it to. Won't take long to actually fix, since I know exactly what's wrong. Since I was there in the small hours indulging in a little superhero sabotage."

"Naughty!"

184

"Don't get your hopes up too much. There is always the chance he won't be there today, though he has been the last two Sundays."

"Ben would never miss training."

"If it really is him," he cautions again, eyes serious.

"Where are we headed?" I ask.

Aiden finds a map book on a shelf and shows me our destination: about twenty miles up country roads. I quickly commit the way to memory. The van hits a pothole and lurches to one side; my bottom smacks on the toolbox.

After what feels like forever but is actually thirty minutes or so, we switch to a smoother road and go faster. There is a window at the back, but with Aiden and so much stuff in the way, all I can catch are glimpses of trees, blue sky.

We slow down, take a few turns.

"Nearly there, I think," Aiden says, voice low. The van stops. Moments later there is a knock and the door pulls across. The driver nods, and I say hi. Aiden doesn't introduce us, and the driver turns away, moves so fast that I barely get a look at him.

"Come on," Aiden says. Shielded by the van, we go around the back of the house, and the driver stays behind, getting out equipment. He starts making a show of checking wires outside the house as we go to the back door. Aiden reaches under a potted plant and holds up a key.

"No one home?"

"Yeah. It belongs to friends of friends, but they've arranged to be out. She said if we go up the stairs to the front bedroom, that is the best place to see. That is where she took the photograph."

Upstairs, the bedroom window overlooks a green field, a track surrounding. At the far side is a large building: a sports hall? There is a group of a few dozen or so boys, a coach, some onlookers. The boys are standing around, doing stretches.

"Can't we go over there? Get closer to see?"

"Wait. They'll run around," he says. "Then you can get a closer look. For now, try these." He passes across binoculars, and I eagerly peer through, try to see faces, but they keep moving around and turning their heads, and—

There.

"I think I've got him. Far side of the group."

I pass the binoculars to Aiden. He looks, considering. "Could be," he says a moment later. He hands them back, and I look again: *Is it really you, Ben?*

After what seems like ages, they start running around the track. The closer they get, the more sure I am. It is his body and the way he runs as much as what I can see of his face: a loping, easy gait that quickly leaves the others behind.

"It's him!"

I stand, turn for the door. A wide smile stretching across my face. Just this glimpse from a distance and my heart is pounding, blood rushing *swoosh* through my veins. All I want to do is run to him, throw my arms around him, and—

"Wait." Aiden puts a hand on my arm.

"But I've got to see him."

"Not so fast. You were too busy looking at Ben to notice."

"Notice what?"

"A black van just pulled up. Focus back on the buildings on the other side of the track. What do you see?"

With a sinking feeling, I hold the binoculars up again and sweep back to the far side of the field. A few figures. Men. In black. Standing, watching the runners on the track on the return loop get closer to them. A cold shiver runs up my back, and I pull away from the window without thinking. They wouldn't be able to see us this far away, unless they have binoculars of their own. Which they very well might, if they have a reason to look. Anything suspicious, like, say, a telephone van. On a Sunday. My mouth goes dry.

"Why would Lorders be here?"

"I don't know. I'm sorry, but they're too close for you to get anywhere near Ben today. They're too close for us to even be here. I don't like this, not at all."

Cold dismay fills me. "But I can't leave without saying something to him, seeing if he's okay. I can't. I have to see him!" *I have to warn him about Coulson.* Sooner or later, when I don't serve up Nico and the Free UK plans to Coulson, he'll make good on his threats.

"I'm sorry. It's too dangerous. We're getting out of here, pronto."

Aiden times it so most of the runners are on their next lap on the other side of the field, between Lorder eyes and us. We slip out of the house and I get into the back of the van, fighting my instincts—which all say to run to the track. To see Ben. Fighting to keep my promise to Aiden.

I'm on my own in the back this time, Aiden in front with the driver, wanting to see with his own eyes what is going on.

I count the turns as we go around the field, realize we've had to drive right past the Lorders. My stomach feels nauseous and I crouch down, away from the back window. But nothing happens. We carry on.

Once I'm sure we've cleared the field, I push through a jungle of equipment and wires hanging from the van roof and peek out the back window. There is a collection of what looks like school buildings on the other side: the boarding school that Aiden said Ben is going to? And past it, a canal. We go over a bridge, and a trail hugs the banks as far as I can see.

Ben would run there. Early in the mornings. I know he would.

Disappointment is creeping up my body, making me shake. I collapse back down on the floor, pull my knees up. We were so close! Tears are threatening to come up, and I fight them, hard. But I give up a battle I can't win.

The van slows, comes to a stop.

Moments later Aiden pulls open the door. I wipe my face on my sleeve.

"I dropped my coworker off at that last junction. Pulled in here for a break, all right? Come out," he says, and holds out his hand. I take it, duck forward and out, legs stiff, and find the van is pulled into a passing place on a single-lane road, trees making a green tunnel overhead.

"Stretch our legs?" he says. We cross the road to a footpath and walk in silence a few minutes to a creek, then along it until it reaches a clearing. There is a rough bench on one side.

"Let's talk," he says, and sits on the bench. I join him. "So. That really was Ben? You're sure?"

"Yes."

"Hold on to that. There was every reason to think he . . ." And he hesitates.

"That he was dead."

"Yes. Yet there he is. We need to play a waiting game now, and see what else we can find out about Ben and this boarding school he is going to, what the story is. Work out a safe place for you to meet him. As soon as I know anything, I'll tell you. All right?"

"When will that be?"

"I don't know for sure; I'll do what I can. Tell you what: I'll be at Mac's again next Friday. Come up straight after school, and if there is any news, I'll tell you then."

"I have to see him, speak to him. I have to," I say, and I can hear my voice is desperate and pleading, but can't stop it. I'm past just needing to warn Ben; seeing him today made every bit of me scream to be close to him. My hand grips tight to Aiden's arm.

He unhooks my fingers, holds my hand between his.

"I know," he says, voice gentle. "And you know what else I know?"

"What?"

"Ben is a lucky guy."

Aiden's eyes hold mine. They are vivid blue, the color of sky. Warm, and serious, and looking at mine like Ben used to. I pull my hand and my eyes away.

"Kyla, listen. You see how important MIA is now, don't you? What we do. Find people or what happened to them, good or bad. For people like you, who can't go on with their lives until they know."

I nod. "I get it."

"I'm not going to put pressure on you today, but think some more about it, all right? Think about reporting yourself found. To help somebody like we are helping you."

There is a wave of panic inside just to hear him say it. I could do it: report Lucy Connor found. But what would it mean? She doesn't exist anymore, apart from a few shaky fragments of dreams.

"Come on," Aiden says. "Best get you home."

We walk back along the footpath, and Aiden opens the side door of the van. "Sorry, but it's safer if you travel in the back."

"It's fine," I say. Climb in, settle myself, then shift closer to the window once the door is shut.

I want to know the way.

29

A SURPRISE WAITS WHEN I OPEN THE FRONT DOOR. DAD, ON the sofa, feet up; Amy next to him, chattering about her week. Mum reading a book on a chair. Three sets of eyes swivel and stare.

Mum shuts her book. Frowns. "That was a long walk."

"Sorry, I—"

"Give her a chance to come in and say hello," Dad says. "I haven't seen her for a week." He holds out his hand and I walk over; he takes mine and pulls me closer, kisses my cheek.

"Sit down, join us," he says, and I perch on the other end of the sofa next to Amy.

"Where did you go?" Mum asks.

Dad shakes his head. "Can't the poor girl go for an afternoon walk without getting the third degree?"

Mum frowns, and there is *atmosphere*: waves of disturbed emotion in the air so real, I can almost reach out and touch them.

"You haven't been on footpaths on your own, have you?" she says.

"No," I answer truthfully. Not today. The only footpath I ventured down was with Aiden.

"It's not safe. They haven't caught whoever attacked Wayne Best yet," she continues. "You need to be careful, and—"

"Now, Sandra," Dad says. "She says she wasn't on footpaths."

Amy and I both look at him, eyes wide in surprise. Mum visibly bristles, as if she is a hedgehog and her spines are sticking out everywhere. Dad, on *my* side? And Mum, her face a picture of suspicion. She doesn't trust me.

I venture in. "Honestly, no. I just went along to the hall and back. On the road." I'd calculated in my mind how far that was and the time I was gone, and it was about right.

"I thought you said you had homework and just needed a short walk to clear your head?"

"I wasn't going to go that far. But it is such a nice day . . ." And my voice trails away. Even to me that doesn't sound convincing.

"Don't neglect your homework," Dad says. Something else lurks behind his eyes.

"I should go up now," I say, and start getting to my feet.

The set of Mum's face says this isn't over.

"Wait a moment," Dad says. "Now we're all here, we can have a family meeting about AMD." I look at him blankly. "Armstrong Memorial Day," he says.

"It's up to both of you," Mum says. "If you want to come."

Dad snorts. "Of course they're coming." He turns to Amy and me. "It's a huge celebration this year: twenty-five years since the assassinations, and thirty years of the Central Coalition in power. It's at Chequers. The prime minister's country house," he adds, looking at me.

"What is happening?" I ask.

Mum answers. "First up, the usual ceremony inside Chequers, live on TV like every year. That is family only, so just all of us and a film crew. Sympathy of the nation, speech from grieving daughter, blah blah blah."

Dad raises an eyebrow at her tone.

She continues. "And then, as a special celebration this year, the prime minister will be there for a second televised ceremony on the grounds of Chequers, to be held at the exact time the treaty was signed to form the Central Coalition thirty years ago. Government officials and the rich and famous will all be there to celebrate. After that there will be a long and boring dinner."

Government officials . . . Lorders.

"You need to come for the ceremonies, really," Mum says, regret in her voice.

"It's an honor!" Dad adds.

"But you can skip the dinner if you want to," Mum says. A look on her face suggests that would be wise. She still holds me in her gaze, some uncertainty hiding behind her bland look.

"Can I be excused? Homework," I say.

"Go on, then," Dad says.

I start up the stairs. What is up with these two? Mum is full of suspicion, Dad is chilled. Have they had a body swap?

And further joy: Lorder ceremonies, ones I have to go to.

Lorder ceremonies. Ones very hard to get into, unless you are in the family. This family. I stop at the top of the stairs, frozen in place by the *clink* of puzzle pieces clicking together in my brain.

Nico said I must stay in my life for a while longer; that I have a vital role to play. Is this it? Something to do with Armstrong Memorial Day?

Concerted attacks, Nico said. What better day to choose? The Lorders will be on high alert, but I can get in. I'll be there!

I force my feet to take the last few steps, go into my room. Pull the door shut.

Before any of this goes down, I have to warn Ben. Get him away safe so Coulson can't take any anger at me out on him. I hold Ben's face, inside, as I saw him today. He *is* alive. My tears earlier were misplaced. Okay, so I didn't get to talk to him, touch him, feel he still breathes, that blood pumps from his heart through his body. But I saw him. He lives. For now, that is enough.

I am grateful to Aiden for finding him, but he couldn't be more wrong than to think I will get involved with MIA. He thinks I'm torn between reporting myself found on MIA and doing nothing. If he only knew I am in a much more dangerous place: caught between Lorders and Free UK.

What next?

It is a waiting game, Aiden said. Wait until he finds out more about Ben and his situation, how to get me to him safely.

But I can't wait long. Coulson hinted Ben is alive, so that much of what he said is true. He also hinted he won't stay that way unless I do as he wants. But he doesn't know I know where he is.

In the meantime . . . Nico must think I'm on his side. Coulson must think I'm on his. Neither can find out what I do for the other.

It is like two high-speed trains, hurtling toward each other, getting closer and closer to disaster.

Late that night, Nico's com buzzes from its hiding place under my Levo. Awake in an instant, I fumble for the button in the dark.

"Yes?" I whisper.

"Okay to talk?"

"Quietly."

"The RTC attack will be tomorrow. But there is one condition if you go."

"What is that?"

"Rain, you must do exactly what Katran says. Do you promise?"

He'll love that. But what choice do I have? I promise, then listen to Nico's precise instructions.

Train number one leaves the station.

30

HOLLY LEANS A BICYCLE AGAINST THE TREE. WALKS TOWARD the door.

"Not sure this is a good idea." I breathe the words near Katran's ear. He grunts, says nothing. His face says he doesn't like it, either. The plan is Nico's, and it was easy to see when Katran told us the details earlier that Nico's interference in his group rankled. Much like my presence.

This Lorder building is out of the way as you'd expect for what happens inside it; no neighbors, yet just a few miles off a main road— good transport links. There is one black van parked out front now. Surveillance had said Monday's a good day for this. Other days there are more "deliveries": Slateds to be terminated.

Before Holly reaches the door, a Lorder guard steps out.

"Hi!" she says. Smiles too wide. She shouldn't look that happy to see a Lorder.

"What are you doing here?"

"Sorry, I'm lost. Could you tell me how to get to the farmer's market?"

Stupid story. You'd have to be a total idiot to have turned down this unmarked road and past all the DO NOT ENTER signs, and not the next one with all the signs to the market.

He says nothing, walks closer, face impassive. One eye on her and one scanning the woods around. Instinctively, I pull myself lower in the scrub, though I know we are deep in shadows, well hidden from view. His hand reaches for a com at his belt.

Holly does a sudden spin kick, knocks his hand away from the com. I tense to spring forward to help her, but Katran grabs my wrist. "Wait," he hisses. "Until the others come out."

There are spy cameras all over the front. By now inside they'd see the guard tussling with one slight girl. He soon has Holly immobilized, a grip tight around her neck.

The door opens. Another Lorder comes out.

"Report."

"She says she's lost, then kicks me."

"I don't like it. Check the area."

"My hands are full."

He shrugs. "So empty them."

He moves one hand to Holly's chin, another on her shoulder. *No!* I tense to spring forward, but Katran holds me in an iron grip.

A sudden violent twist.

The Lorder lets her go; she falls to the ground.

Her body twitches, then lies still: neck broken. Black horror inside quickly fills with rage. I glare at Katran, ready to lash out, but his face is filled with pain. When he sees me looking, it hardens to a mask. The look is gone.

One Lorder speaks into a com—to someone in the house? Then two of them step out. One heads toward Tori and her waiting knives, the other in our direction.

Katran releases his grip on my arm. Gestures for me to stay out of it, dark revenge on his face.

But then the Lorders stop, step back. There are vehicle sounds coming up the road. No. A van?

It pulls in front of the building.

Katran shakes his head slightly. "Too many targets," he whispers.

And I stare at him, disbelieving. Pull back? Now? After what happened to Holly?

Two Lorders get out of the front of the van, confer with the others. Glance at Holly's body on the ground. One pulls the van side door open.

A boy springs out, takes a swing at the Lorder, his face white. Slated: I can hear his Levo from here before he collapses on the ground. There is a scream inside the van. A girl is pulled out; she tries to reach for the boy.

"Do something!" I hiss. Katran's face twists in indecision. My fingers curl around my knife.

"Stay here," he breathes. "Don't break your promise!" He hits his com to give the order to attack. He and the others run forward.

It's a blur of motion, cries. Blows. Part of me is screaming to run after them, to be in it, to strike at the Lorders. Another part is holding me still, sick inside at what is happening, eyes clenched shut. What is the use of me? Why bring me here to do nothing? I force my eyes open.

One of the Lorders breaks free, runs for it headlong into the woods and straight at my hiding spot.

I crouch in a fighting stance, knock his feet out from under him. He's winded. My knife is in my hand, there are seconds when I could use it, stab him—I don't. He swings at my arm, the knife falls from my hand and he has one of his own. He smiles.

Then there is a loud *whack*—Katran has kicked him in the back of the head. He falls. Moves no more, blood on the back of his head. Katran bolts back to the house.

I stagger to my feet. There is *red* in his hair, so much red, and there is a rushing, roaring sound in my ears. I stagger away. Later someone calls the all clear, and I don't know how long I've been standing, still, unable to open my eyes or move away; almost in a trance. A blood red trance.

But something penetrates: There is screaming. A girl, still screaming. The Slated one? The buzz of her Levo is loud and grates deep inside my skull.

She needs help.

I fight the fog, force my feet to walk through the trees. Fix my eyes on the girl and not on what lies on the ground. I slip an arm over her shoulders. "It's okay. Just close your eyes. Don't look around you; blank it from your mind. Breathe in and out. You can do it." Her Levo is at 3.4: too low.

She shakes her head, eyes still wide and staring. Then Tori is there. "She needs Happy Juice; they must have some!" Tori says, and we help the girl inside the door.

Katran has a doctor in a death grip.

"Happy Juice—where?" Tori demands.

Katran eases his grip. The doctor gasps for air, points at a cupboard. At a gesture from Katran, the doctor pulls a syringe out of a drawer. Hands it to Katran. "It's illegal to use it on that one. Not that you'd care."

Katran turns toward her, but the girl holds out her hands. "No, you mustn't; no." Her hands are protective in front of her belly. "You can't. The baby." She's pregnant?

I look at the doctor. "It'll kill the child if you use it," he says.

Her Levo vibrates again. "3.2," I say.

The doctor shrugs. "She's dying, anyhow. What difference does it make?"

Tori punches him, hard, in the face. "Give it to her!" she says to Katran.

"We can't force her." Katran kneels next to her, takes her hand. "What do you want us to do?" he says. Her eyes are wide, panicked. Like a deer that wants to bolt into the woods but is caught, a leg held in a trap.

"No. No drugs," she says, her words clear.

He hands the syringe to Tori. "She says no."

It happens. Her levels drop that bit more. Her body arches with seizures. She cries out, her body twisting in pain.

"Give her the Happy Juice! The baby will die anyway if she does," Tori says.

"It's too late for that now, and we haven't got anything stronger here," the doctor says. "That is more painful than our way." He reaches back to the cupboard, a different drawer, and holds up another syringe. "Give her a full shot of this and it will be over quickly."

"She said no drugs," Katran says, voice barely controlled.

I hold her. She doesn't know where she is anymore, but her face is a rictus of agony. Her body arches one last time: rigid, then limp.

Gone.

Tori looks at the doctor, then at the knife in her hands. "Let me?" she says to Katran. "Slowly."

Katran shakes his head. Takes the second syringe from the doctor's hand. "No. Give him what he uses on others." He hands it to Tori.

Katran holds the doctor; realization on his face now, he struggles. "You can't do this. It's murder."

"What about what you do here? What do you call that?" Tori says.

"Laws are there for a reason. That one—if she had the baby, what then? Either she'd die from seizures in labor or we give her drugs to stop that and the baby dies. She broke her contract getting in that condition. Contract breakers over sixteen have their second chance terminated according to law. It is there when they sign!"

"Like we have any choice but to sign," I spit out, and hold my wrist in the air. His eyes go wide when he takes in my Levo. "They could have taken her Levo off so the baby could live, so they could both live!"

He shakes his head. "What then? Every Slated girl in the country would get pregnant on purpose to get out of her sentence."

Tori smiles at the syringe still in her hand. "So. You say a full dose of this is a quick death. What about half a dose?"

The horror that crosses the doctor's face answers the question well enough.

Tori moves toward him, but I can't stay, I can't watch. The spinning is back, everything going gray. I stumble out of the building. Past bodies I try not to look at, but there, at the periphery of my vision, they register. Blood. Dead. No more.

I reach the trees, loop an arm around one, and vomit on the ground. There are screams from the building behind me.

I struggle to clear my mind, to process what I learned. A Levo would kill a Slated in labor; the drugs to stop this would kill the child before it could be born. Is this the real reason why Amy and Jazz aren't supposed to ever be alone together? Why I wasn't meant to be alone with Ben? I didn't know. Did that girl?

Lorders Slated her, and now, no matter what we could do, she died. She looked older than Amy. How close was she to twenty-one and freedom? I open my hand. Inside of it, a ring I'd slipped off her finger at the end: a silver band. There is carving on the inside: *Emily & David 4ever*. Was he the Slated boy with her? They're together forever now. I clench my fingers around the ring, tight.

Emily. I'll remember her. I'll remember this moment.

Including Holly, three of us dead, and the Slated boy and girl. Five Lorders and one doctor. One termination center out of action: Katran sets the place on fire before we go. We melt into the woods in pairs to run to pick-up points, me and Katran together.

"You idiot," he hisses as we run. "What did you think you were doing, running at that Lorder with a knife in your hand? I told you to hide."

"You told me to stay where I was! I did. He ran straight at me."

He shakes his head in disgust. "If I wasn't babysitting you for Nico, maybe we wouldn't have lost three."

"What? You were *babysitting* me?"

"You heard me. What are you playing at? Look. I know you want to help, but you're useless. You're a danger to have around."

"What about Holly?"

"What about her?"

"She shouldn't have gone in on her own."

"She volunteered. Drawing them out of the house was the best strategy." He looks uncomfortable.

She had something to prove to Nico after breaking the rules, and she's proved it. Permanently.

We stay silent the rest of the way. What happened? I wanted to kill that Lorder. The knife was in my hand; the opportunity, there. But the mere thought of using it, pushing the blade in, cutting into skin, veins, and muscle . . . I froze. I couldn't do it.

If Katran hadn't come running back, I'd be dead.

My fists clench. What was all the training I did with Nico and the Owls for? I know so many ways to end life.

I hold Emily's face in my mind. She refused Happy Juice that could have saved her, for what? Now she and her baby are both dead. And Holly: neck snapped. The other two in her cell whose names I didn't even know.

Lorders did that.

Next time I have a weapon in my hand and a Lorder in front of me, I won't fail.

31

"WOULD YOU HAVE DONE THAT, WHAT THAT GIRL DID?" TORI asks. She inspects her knife as we walk the last steps to the house. She obviously didn't have problems using it.

"It was pointless. She didn't save her baby."

"But maybe she couldn't live, knowing that her decision is what killed it? Like, if I'd been there when Ben died, and didn't do everything I could to save him, I couldn't live with that."

I look at her carefully out of the corner of my eye. Does she know something about Ben? No. She's just relating what happened to that girl to herself, to the one she'd do anything to save. I sigh.

Tori slips an arm around my shoulders. "At least they won't be terminating anyone else there, not for a long while. Wasn't that brilliant today?"

"From what I could see of it." Which was more than enough.

Tori glances ahead; Katran, leading the way now, is almost out of sight. She lowers her voice. "It's not fair. Talk to Katran, make him see you have to be in on the action next time. But you were still part of it, and we *did* something." She raises her voice again. "We showed them, didn't we?" The others around us shout a ragged cheer.

Nico steps out of the house as we walk up to it. The afternoon over, he is back from school. Where I should have been. He glances around, sees who is missing. "Did they die a good death?" he asks Katran.

"Yes."

Holly's brother bounds out of the house behind Nico. Not allowed on this venture today; not trained enough, Nico had said. "Where's Holly?" he asks.

No one answers. Katran holds his shoulder while he shakes. We stand together; a minute of silence stretches out in slow seconds.

Nico looks up and nods; everyone starts to walk away. Katran with his arm around Holly's brother now, speaking in a low voice into his ear. Changed, and gentle, like the Katran of my dream, who comforted me when I was scared. Did that really happen? No matter how crazy it seems, something inside says *yes*.

"It's good to see you two getting along," Nico says, gesturing to Tori and me, next to each other, arms linked.

"Why wouldn't we?" Tori asks.

"It isn't often two girls who shared the same boyfriend can be friends."

Tori stares at me, eyes wide. Pushes me away. "Ben?" she whispers. I look back at her, shrug helplessly. What can I say? She turns tail and marches away into the trees.

Nico smiles. "A word," he says, pointing at me, and walks into the house. I stand there a moment, too stunned to react.

"Come!" he calls.

I follow him through to the windowless room he has taken as office. Candles cast flickering light on damp walls.

"Why did you do that?" I ask, unable to stop myself.

"What?"

"Tell Tori about me and Ben."

"Rain, you know how we must work in a group: total honesty. Nothing hidden between us. Lorders lie; we tell the truth."

"Truth is freedom, freedom is truth," I say, words from the past tumbling out from some hidden place inside.

He smiles. "Just so. Now tell me: How do you feel about what we must do after the attack today?" His face is mild, but his eyes are watchful.

I banish the red of blood from my mind and clench Emily's cold ring in my pocket. Focus on what the Lorders did to her, do to others like her all the time. We must stop them. Resolve hardens inside.

"I'm on the right side. Our side."

"Good. Soon there will be other work to do." He smiles, touches one hand to my cheek, and I am flooded with the warm glow of being in his favor.

"I'm in."

"I never had any doubt," he says, but he *so* did. "What is it?" he asks, alert as ever to any changes flitting across my face.

"It is just . . . I don't really understand. Why you even want me involved. What can I do?"

"You're one of us," he says. "No matter what happened to you when you were taken, or who you were after you were Slated, you will always be one of us. But more, you are important to me."

He says no more, slips an arm around my shoulders. The glow becomes more. I belong here, with Free UK: This is who I am. What I must do. But what is that, exactly?

"What is happening?"

"Soon, Rain; soon."

Disappointment must reflect on my face. "You don't trust me," I say.

"I do." He hesitates; smiles. "I can tell you this: Soon there will be concerted attacks, in London, other major targets."

"What were we doing today, then? That wasn't coordinated with anything."

He smiles again. "Clever, Rain. We don't want to pull in our activities now. They must think it is business as usual, not know we are leading up to something big. And we have identified individual targets as well."

My stomach twists. "Assassinations?"

"Don't be squeamish." His voice is cold. "You know what this government has done, is doing, to people like you. To Tori. Think of what happened to her. There will be kidnappings as well, high profile, in a variety of sectors at once. We'll get some attention in the right places."

"What about the hospital attack? It is heavily protected and guarded. It would take resources, and . . ." I stop, realization sinking in. "A diversion?"

"Just so. We'll leak plans of a proposed attack at the hospital, but this time, when they are ready for us there, we will be elsewhere."

Elsewhere . . . elsewhen. "Armstrong Memorial Day." I say it as a statement, not a question. "At Chequers. That is the place and the day things will start, isn't it?"

He stays silent.

"My family will be there."

"We are your family." A mild reproach. I flush.

"Nico, you don't understand. Mum isn't pro-Lorder; at least, not anymore."

"No?"

"No! They Slated her son." And I tell Nico about Robert, with guilt at confidences broken, but I have to make him see. "She tried to find out what happened to him; she's not one of them."

"Yet if she doesn't support us, her feelings about the Lorders are not relevant. She can be a martyr for our cause." He puts a hand on my chin, tilts my face up. The horror must be in my eyes. "Rain, I know this is hard. But you must be strong. We have to strike at the Lorders where it hurts the most. She is a symbol for their cause—she allows this. No matter her feelings on it, she is a Lorder tool."

I clench Emily's ring in my pocket.

I must be strong.

He kisses my forehead. "That is enough for your curiosity. Time for you to get back home before you are missed."

"Why can't I stay here?" I say, without planning to say it—but yes, why? Because when I'm here, with Nico, and even Katran, I belong. I believe in their plans: *our plans.*

He puts a warm hand on each of my shoulders. "Stay strong a little longer, all right? We need you on the inside. You can't disappear from that life, not yet. Go on, Rain," he says, giving me a little push toward the door. I walk through it. Leaving Nico's presence, it feels as if the temperature drops.

Tori isn't in sight, but Katran is back. He follows me as I head through the trees.

"I don't need an escort, you know. I remember how to get there."

Katran ignores my words, continues to follow.

"Did you hear me?" I turn and face him at the bikes.

He smirks. "I did, oh special girl, but this is an order from above. To see you safely home."

"I won't tell. Go slink behind some rocks and take a nap instead."

He ignores me and extracts our bikes from their hiding place, and we set off, Katran in front. Going much too fast for the need for quiet, but that was always him, wasn't it? More guts than sense, Nico used to say in the early days, but eased off when he saw Katran was always just within an edge of control. Close to the precipice, never going over. But soon I am exhilarated by speed, by remembering past times and using it to not remember all that happened today, and I don't care about the risk.

It takes me back to other days. With an edge of danger. Slips of memory come and go, make me feel alive; tantalize, then are gone.

And I don't understand. I study Katran, ahead. Who is he, really? Who was he to me all those years ago? Questions burn and tumble inside.

The hide a few miles from home appears in the distance. Katran slows, stops, turns his bike on the path to take off back the other way.

"Wait a minute," I say, then hesitate. "I want to ask you something."

"What, can't find your way home after all?"

I scowl, clench my fists; why even bother. "Why are you such a jerk sometimes?"

"Do you really want to know?" There's anger behind his question.

I turn away, yank my bike through the trees to the hide, and conceal it. Katran stays, watches, probably checking I do it right. I pull the tarp and camo over it and start marching up the path.

"Come back. I'm sorry," he says.

Katran, apologizing? I'm so stunned, I stop, turn back. He's off his bike now, and I walk up to him. Challenge is in his eyes, and I face him, unflinching. But with his dark eyes staring into mine, the words are gone.

"Well?" he says finally.

I swallow. "My memories are a little . . . messed up. Can I ask you about something? From years ago."

"Fire away."

I cross my arms. "I had these really bad dreams. Nightmares. I still get them." I sigh, stare at the ground. Not wanting to say it out loud, but needing to find out what he knows at the same time. "Being chased. Running, on sand, absolutely terrified. And . . ." I look up. "You used to wake me, hold me when I was scared." I say it, don't ask it, because somehow I know it's true.

And there, in his eyes: confirmation. He turns, the angry red of the jagged scar on his right cheek hidden. Sometimes, like now, when he isn't angry to match the scar, you can see a different person. The one who had an arm around Holly's brother.

The one who held me at night years ago.

"Thanks," I say.

"It's okay." He looks embarrassed. "We used to be friends, you and I. Things . . . changed."

"Why?"

"You changed."

"I don't understand."

"I don't really understand, myself." He sighs. "When you first came to train with us, you were different. You were scared, cried a lot. You didn't want to be there, not like the rest of us. But every now and then, you changed. Into this angry, crazy girl: Nico's puppet, dancing on his strings. And it was something to do with Nico and this doctor who took you away, sometimes for days. Each time you came back you changed more often, until the girl I first knew almost never appeared."

A doctor? A flash in my mind: a special sort of doctor, not the kind who mends bones or cures illnesses. I was afraid of him, so afraid. I try to push it away, but his face and then his name swing into view. *Doctor Craig.* In that dream I had, the doctor who said I would be sick.

"And Nico told us when you were this changed person to treat you like one of us, and to ignore you when you were the other one. Bit by bit the other went, until the only time she came back was when you had nightmares."

My head aches, pounds. Two people, like Nico said. Lucy and Rain. They split me into two people . . . That doctor? I feel sick. I turn away, but Katran follows. Turns me and holds my shoulders in his hands so I can't look away.

"Listen to me. Nico is up to something with you, and it started years ago. I don't get it and I don't like it. Don't let him use you. You don't belong with us; you never did. Run while you still have the chance."

I shake my head. "No," I say, faint, then, "No." Stronger. "You just want me out of the way. You're jealous of me and Nico. Of how important I am to him and the cause."

He laughs, anger behind it. "Yeah, sure; that's it." He turns away, gets on his bike.

I start to walk off.

"Wait," he says, and I pause. "Listen to me, Rain. I believe in what we are doing. That ours is *the* way, the only way, to get rid of the Lorders, to free ourselves. Make our lives better. But it doesn't have to be your fight. Not when you don't even know who you are. How can you make a choice? Try to get your memories back where they should be. Don't block them out."

I watch him disappear up the path, shaking with confusion. Anger, and fear. Memories lurk at the edges, threaten to overwhelm, but I don't want them. I push them away.

Somehow I stumble back to the house, let myself in, and slip upstairs in silence. Curl up on my bed.

It is late afternoon; no one will be home for an hour. I need to shower, change, look ordinary by the time anyone gets in, but my thoughts are in turmoil.

Try to remember?

But of what Katran said, about how I was those years ago, there is little trace. It is like a song I half recognize, can whistle along to the tune but don't know the words.

I thought my confusion, and how my memories come and go, was because I was Slated. But according to Katran, it started long before the Lorders got their hands on me.

I try to concentrate. Nico said he protected me from Slating, that I was split into two people. But how did he do that? I know he made Lucy be right-handed, and that Rain hid inside when the Lorders got me. They Slated me as if I were right-handed. Lucy is gone, and the memories that were Rain remained after I was Slated, hidden inside, waiting for the right trigger to let them out.

That is what Nico wanted to happen. But that isn't the whole story. Some wisps of Lucy and her memories—her dreams, fears—still remain. Buried deep. A squirm in my gut says Nico wouldn't be happy if he knew it. He was wary when I mentioned Lucy, surprised I even knew who she was.

And then I'm angry, so angry, at Katran. I'd been sure earlier of being in Free UK and part of it all: to *belong* to them. So that I belonged somewhere, and knew who I was. Katran spoiled everything.

Now all that is left is confusion.

That there is something wrong with my memory is an understatement.

Is it just down to choice? Forget Kyla and her life, and be with Free UK. Do it completely, not holding anything back. I grip Emily's ring so tight in my hand, it forms a round circle in my skin.

But I don't want to forget Ben. I focus on his face, holding it clear in my mind, but it's not enough. Never enough. I get out my sketch pad and pencil and draw him over and over. *Concentrate.* I hold on to the look in his eyes, the way he stands. The way he runs. Katran defies the natural world as he moves through it. Ben is part of it.

Ben is part of me.

I long to see him, to touch him. When I was with him, I always knew who I was. Together, we can work out what to do.

Aiden said he would get in touch once he found a way to get to Ben that was safe, but it can't wait.

I can't wait.

32

HEAVY FROST GLISTENS ON GRASS IN THE MOONLIGHT. I shiver in equal parts with cold and excitement as I slip quietly through our sleeping village to the footpath. I hope I'm right, that Ben will be there. Maybe it is too cold, too dark this time of year for an early morning run?

Once I get to the trail bike, I wish I'd thought to wear gloves. The cold makes my hands numb and clumsy as I work out how to get into the hide in the dark. I finally pull the bike out and start up the canal path.

Once past familiar territory, I struggle to pay attention, to find my way from the map I'd memorized, when all inside is *Ben*. Now and then I have to put my flashlight on when the way is unclear, worried I'll go wrong in the dark.

At one point miles from home, I stop and take Emily's ring from my pocket. I can't keep it; it is too dangerous. What if someone sees it? I kiss it and try to throw it into a deep part of the canal. To let it disappear into the muddy bottom. But I just can't bring myself to let it go. I climb a tree instead. Slip it around a twig not visible from below. My eyes note the place, the bend in the canal. One day, I'll come back for it.

Miles on again, something niggles, pulls me out of my concentration. Something not right. Faint, distant behind me, too far away to be certain; whispers of sound. Very like another bike.

I stop, pull mine into the trees, and creep back the way I came; slow, quiet, stealth. Shadowing the path rather than on it, and—

There.

A figure waits on the path. On a bike. There is the faint flash of a tracker on the handlebars: What he tracks is stationary. Indecision plays across his face. Stay a safe distance, or go on to see why it has stopped?

I step out in front of Katran.

He jumps. Guilt crosses his face, then is gone.

"Hi," I say.

"Hi."

"So, do you want to tell me, or should I guess?" I say, and he shrugs, doesn't answer. "There is a tracker on the bike. You're following me, checking up on me."

Katran flushes enough that even in this light I can see.

"There is a tracker on the bike, yes. But it isn't like that. They all have trackers, for safety, yeah?"

"But you were monitoring it."

"Nico told me to."

Nico: There is a flash of fear, inside. "Does he know?"

"Not yet. Where are you going?"

I stay silent.

"Well, wherever it is, I'm coming with you."

I stalk back up the path. Maybe I can ditch the bike before we get too close, and slip away. Or maybe I can find the tracker and take it off.

But Katran, busted now, is staying close.

When we get to my bike, I turn to him. "Please don't follow me. Wait here if you want to. I won't be long, and we can go back together."

"No."

"I don't need a babysitter!"

"Yes, you do."

I sigh, cornered; no choice but to tell him. "You know how you told me to remember who I am? Not to let go of things." He waits. "I'm going to see Ben."

"What? The one Tori keeps going on about?"

"She hasn't got things right. He and I were . . . close."

"But I thought he was dead."

I shake my head. "He's alive, and I'm going to see him."

"He's been in touch?"

"No. He doesn't know I'm coming. He may not even be there today; it's just a hunch."

"But how—"

"Don't ask how I found him. I won't tell you. But now you see why you can't come with me?"

Katran's face has so much emotion—worry and hurt, warring with anger—that before I know I am even moving, I am right up to him, a hand on his arm. "Katran? Are you all right?"

"No." He sighs, ruffles his hair back with one hand. "Look. I'll follow behind, stay out of sight. I'll have your back in case anything goes wrong. That is the best I can do. All right?"

And it is so obviously against his better judgment, so much more than I could have expected of him, that I smile. "All right."

I get on my bike, take the next few turns, and my memory has served me correctly: It is the right way. The sky is still dark when we reach the stretch I'm sure Ben will run near his school. We hide our bikes and wait in the trees, watching.

The darkness gives way to a dim lightening in the sky, bit by bit.

No sign of him. My throat is tightening, and I'm just about to turn to Katran and say, sorry, I must have gotten it wrong, when he grabs my arm.

"Look," he breathes. Points up the hill from the path. A lone figure runs down it, the light behind him. I squint, unsure, and then—yes. It's him! The smile is wide on my face, and my feet are scrabbling out of the woods and chasing down the path after his retreating figure.

Ben can run. Can he ever. I push the speed more and more. He must hear something, turns his head slightly to see who is behind him—then turns forward and keeps going.

Perhaps he can't tell it's me in this light. I push faster. "Wait up," I call softly. "Ben, wait."

His pace slows, then becomes a walk.

I reach him.

"Yes?" he says.

I smile widely into his eyes, brown with golden glints. I grab his hand. He looks down at our hands. Half smiles.

The details start to penetrate. Something isn't right.

"Ben?"

"Sorry. You've confused me with somebody else."

"No I haven't." And I cling to his hand.

He shakes his head, pulls his hand away. "Sorry, I'm not Ben. If you'll excuse me, I've only got a short time to finish my run." And he takes off. Runs away. Leaves me standing, watching him go, watching him run, and every movement he makes is *my Ben*. Tears begin to leak out of my eyes.

He doesn't know who I am.

He doesn't remember anything.

My stomach twists. He's been re-Slated. It's the only answer. But he is seventeen. They're not supposed to do that unless you are under sixteen. Why would they break their own rule for Ben?

He doesn't know who I am.

I'm shaking, still standing on the path. Ben may turn and come back this way. With that thought, I stumble into the trees and wait. Soon he appears in the distance. I watch as he runs closer, his usual graceful gait, then past in a blur back up the hill.

There are sounds in the woods behind me, but I stand still, watch Ben disappear into the light of the sunrise above.

"Rain?" A low voice: Katran.

I don't turn, unwilling for him to see the tears on my face, unable to stop them. A warm hand touches my arm, pulls me around.

"What is it?"

I shake my head, unable to speak. He hesitates, reaches a hand for my shoulder. He pulls me closer, his arms stiff at first, then softening. And I sob, tell him that Ben doesn't know who I am anymore.

Finally he pushes me away and looks in my eyes. "You've got to pull yourself together, and do it now. We've got to get out of here. It's getting too light; more people may come."

He pulls me back through the woods to our bikes, and we head down the canal path. The cold air on my face stings my eyes, making it hard to see, while three words go over and over in my mind. They still don't feel any more real.

Ben is gone.

Even though I was Slated, I got some of my memories back because of what Nico did. But Ben won't. It doesn't work that way. It is like I never existed to him. Nothing that happened between us ever happened to him. He doesn't know any of it.

Ben is gone.

My tears have stopped; all I am, is empty. There is nothing. No hope. No way out.

We get to the hide, and I just stand there while Katran stuffs my bike in.

"What were you thinking, going there?" He's shaking his head; the usual Katran is back.

I stay silent. He pushes my shoulder, a challenge.

"You tell Nico and the rest of us that you support Free UK, then you do something like this. Risky, Rain. What if I hadn't been there to drag you away and you got caught? They'd get things out of you. They have ways. You'd have them come down on all of us."

Something twists and hardens inside. "The Lorders took Ben from me once. Now they've done it again. He's gone. That's it. I'm done now. I'll do anything to get back at them."

"You look like you mean it. Is this your one thing?"

"What do you mean?"

"The thing that finally pushes you over the edge. So you truly *are* capable of anything."

I shrug, but everything inside is shifting, realigning. Emily's ring, now hiding up an unmarked tree, was enough. And Ben, too: *Yes.* I'm so far over the edge, there is no way back. "What was your one thing?"

He grabs my hand, touches it to his cheek—the scar on it—then pushes me away.

"Don't you remember? This. When I was ten, my older sister was missing. Hiding. She'd gotten in some trouble, nothing too serious, but you know what Lorders are like."

He suddenly twists around, pulls me with my back against him, an arm around my neck. "One held me like this," he whispers. He raises his other hand to my cheek, just under my eye. "We were by our boathouse. He took my dad's diving knife, and he dug the point in, here." He traces his finger down my cheek, the path of his scar. "By the time he got to here, I told them where she was. We never saw her again."

He pushes me away. The diving knife: a katran. The name he chose so he can never forget. The knife he still carries now. *I remember.*

I hold my cheek. He'd not hurt me, but I can still feel his finger on my skin, tracing the path of a knife. I stare at him in horror. "It wasn't your fault. You were a child!"

"Maybe so. But that is why I would die before I'd ever betray anyone again. I won't tell Nico what you did today. And I won't tell Tori about Ben, either. Now go. Get back home before you are missed."

"Katran?"

"Yes?"

"Thanks."

He stares back. "I accept you want to be with us. But you have to know your limitations."

"What do you mean?"

He shakes his head. "Another time." He hesitates, then touches his hand to my cheek. "I'm sorry about Ben."

It is nearly getting ready for school time when I jog up our street, too late to sneak in the back way, thankful I'd left a just-in-case note. One that said, *Out for a run.*

No point in being quiet this time.

I open the front door. "Hello, I'm back," I yell.

Mum peeks out from the kitchen as I bend to unlace my shoes.

"Wasn't it too cold for that this morning?"

"Cold is good for running!" I say, trying to force my voice to be light. Failing.

She walks out into the hall as I chuck my shoes in the closet.

"What's wrong?" she asks, and her eyes look like they have concern, real and genuine. I'd so like to believe it is true. To fall into her arms and tell her about Ben. But I can't. Neither can I deny what she can so obviously see on my face. My red eyes.

"Just thinking of Ben. I couldn't sleep, so I went running."

She puts a hand on my shoulder, gives it a squeeze. Pushes me to the stairs. "Go. Have a shower and warm up. I think a cooked breakfast this morning after all that."

33

SINCE YESTERDAY MORNING, IT IS AS IF THE WORLD IN sympathy has been dipped into a deep chill. The temperature staying near freezing all day, and much lower at night. That and Ben have kept me numb, going through the motions of school, home, and in between, almost without awareness. Minutes ticking past in a strange way where I can stare out the window, blank, and look up a moment later to find hours have passed. I even did my Shakespeare homework for English to have something, anything, to occupy my mind. A poor effort, but that is one less thing to get in trouble over. At least until they read it, because it's pretty bad. Though Nico or Coulson may have made my English homework irrelevant by then.

And tonight, it is Group.

Running usually makes me feel better, more myself. Whoever that is. But as my feet thud up the road, I'm not sure this was a good idea. All it does is make me remember running to Group with Ben.

We used to run to overcome our Levos. All those happy brain chemicals from excessive exercising—endorphins—made it possible to think, to talk about unpleasant things without our levels dropping. But it was so much more than that: Ben loved to run. Even more than I did. It was part of who he was.

My feet falter, I almost stumble: Running is *still* part of who Ben is.

I slow to a walk. What does this mean? Something has been niggling away at me behind the grief, and that is it. I'd guessed Ben would run in that place in the morning because I know him so well. He did. That means part of him is still there.

I force myself to remember every moment of yesterday morning, examine it. Something I'd been trying to avoid. He didn't know who I was, so I'd assumed he'd been re-Slated. There wasn't a new Levo in sight, but his sleeves were too long to tell. They would have hidden it.

But something isn't right. If he had been redone, he'd have been like a new Slated, wouldn't he? All joy and big dopey grins. It hasn't been that long. And he wasn't like that at all. If anything, he was less that way than he used to be. Whatever has happened to him, it isn't that. This is something else.

I walk along the icy road, deep in thought, barely noticing the grip of the cold now that I've stopped running. Now and then lights come up bright behind me, then are gone, as cars and a van sweep past.

As I round a corner, the van is pulled in at the side of the road.

Some part of my brain notes: a white van.

BEST BUILDERS painted down the side.

Run!

The thought barely forms when hands reach out from shadows at the side of the road and grab my arm.

My instant reaction is to spin and kick, but car lights come the other way. He lets go of me as light sweeps over us and confirms the only conclusion: It is Wayne.

Wayne, but he has changed. His face, never a picture, is worse. An angry scar runs from his eye into his scalp, hair missing around it that isn't growing back.

"Pretty, ain't I?" he says, reading my face.

"What do you want?" I say, stalling. Reminding myself that he doesn't remember—that is what Amy said was going around at the doctor's office. He has traumatic amnesia. He doesn't remember who beat him up. Unless seeing me brings it back?

Another car passes.

"I think you know."

Every instinct screams, *Run, get away!* "Tell me," I say.

He raises his eyebrows, and one, trapped by the scar, looks like it splits in half. "Just this: Keep looking over your shoulder, honey, because one day, somewhere lonely, I'll be there."

He winks, and I realize one eye is false; it looks the wrong way.

"Later," he says. Walks back to his van. Gets in, starts the engine, and drives up the road. Gives the horn a double tap—*toot toot*—before he disappears from sight.

My knees are shaking so much, I have to stop and lean against a tree. I look at my hands: so much damage they caused. Nico's training brought out in danger. It was self-defense, yes, but all I can see is the blood. His head soaked with blood. I breathe in and out, fight not to be sick.

And Wayne *remembers*. He knows it was me who did that to him, yet he hasn't told the authorities. He wants to deal with me himself.

I shiver and start moving again, walking, then running. Let's face it: Terrifying as he is, Wayne isn't the worst bogeyman in my closet. There are so many threats to look for over my shoulder, I should install a rearview mirror to keep them all in sight.

The bright lights and smiles of Group don't lift the chill. I'm still shivering when Mum picks me up at the end.

"See? I told you it was too cold to run. You should listen to your mother."

• • •

Honk, honk! *Car horns are loud in my ears. But the traffic is stopped. They're not going anywhere, and I yell at the bus driver: Move, do something! I know what's going to happen, but he can't hear me.*

There is a whistling noise, a flash, a BANG that rattles into my bones, sends me sprawling, but there is no way to get away. The side of the bus is splintered, folded in on itself.

There is screaming from inside, bloody hands beat on windows. Flames lick the back of the bus.

A pause. Another whistle, flash, explosion.

Opposite the bus, a sign hangs on a pole, half dislodged—from some stray bit of shrapnel? The building behind untouched.

The sign says LONDON LORDER OFFICES.

Heart beating wildly, eyes finally open, I'm shaking: a blanket in my mouth to stop a scream.

A Free UK attack gone wrong. A face floats into view: Doctor Craig. Why? What has he got to do with this?

Katran would do *anything* to strike at the Lorders. So would I! Determination clenches tight, inside. *But not that.* I couldn't do that.

Something went wrong when that bus was hit—it was a mistake.

Was I there? Everything says yes—the details, the sounds, the smells—so real, so clear.

I've had this dream a few times before. In one version, Mum's son, Robert, and his girlfriend were on the bus. But it happened over six years ago: I was ten years old! I couldn't have been there; it doesn't make sense. I wasn't even with Katran and the Owls until I was fourteen.

Yet I must have done things like this in the past. That must be why the details are so real, so clear. Then, when I was one of the Owls, I would do *anything* to strike at the Lorders. I was strong.

I will be strong again.

I *can* do anything.

34

NICO DRAWS ME INTO HIS SCHOOL OFFICE THE NEXT DAY AT lunch. Locks the door behind us.

"I have a job for you," he says, and holds up a small envelope. "Plant this someplace your mum will find it, where no one else will see. But not until tomorrow afternoon."

I reach out my hand, grasp the envelope.

"Aren't you going to ask what it is?"

I hesitate, shake my head. "No. Because you were right."

"I'm always right, but about what in particular?" His face quirks.

"About Mum. She is a Lorder tool. No matter her private leanings, if she is a willing symbol for them, she is a target for us."

Nico's eyes glow warm. He smiles. "But you were also right."

"I was?"

"In telling me about her son, Robert. There is a chance we can use this. If we can get her to come out publicly on our side—even better."

I look down at the envelope in my hand. "And this?"

"You could say it is an invitation."

A sealed invitation, I notice as I hide it away in my bag for delivery tomorrow.

In classes, I turn things over in my mind. So after all my hardened resolutions—my commitment to do *anything*—has Nico found a way out for me? He cares. He doesn't want to hurt me, he believed me when I said Mum doesn't support the Lorders. He's finding another way.

At the end of the day, Jazz drives Amy and me to Mac's—a visit planned earlier this week. I'd forgotten it with everything else. The promised meeting with Aiden so he can update me on Ben.

When Jazz and Amy go for a walk, I find Aiden in the back room.

He doesn't say a word, just looks at me with his intense blue eyes, until I blink, turn away. "What is it?" I ask.

"I didn't want to leave this. I wanted to tell you straightaway. Yet now that you're in front of me, it's hard."

"Has something happened to Ben?" I say, panic suddenly filling inside.

"No. Not as far as I know. But I've been looking into the boarding school he's at. It doesn't exist."

"What do you mean? We saw it."

"It is physically there. But if you look at the usual places schools exist, it doesn't. It isn't in any of the county or country educational databases. There is no information on it in any official channels."

That stress on *official*. "What about unofficial?"

He hesitates. "This is more guesswork and rumor than anything else."

"Go on."

"All right. There may be some connection between that school and Lorders. You know how we saw agents at the training field? That wasn't just some weird coincidence. They have a presence in that school."

"There are Lorders in my school sometimes, too. They go to assembly and seem to have an office there."

"Not like that. They are always about the place, and not just a few of them. The rumor is that there are some sort of experiments and training happening there, something new. And the students: There is something different about them as a group. They're not your average mix. All of them, fit, healthy, tall. Athletic or with other skills that make them stand out."

"What are you saying?"

"I don't really know. We're curious to find out more if we can. But one thing I do know: It is far too dangerous for you to see Ben."

I cross my arms and stare into space. Aiden pulls me close, a comforting arm across my shoulders. "You don't seem as upset as I expected you to be."

So many secrets; when is it right to share? I slump forward, head in hands, and sigh. "There is a reason for that."

"What is it?"

I straighten and face Aiden. Face the truth.

"I've already been to see him."

"You *what*?"

"You know that canal we crossed in the van near the training field? I saw it out the back window. And somehow, I just knew: The Ben I knew would run there, early in the mornings. And he does."

Aiden's jaw drops. "Are you completely crazy?"

"Nothing happened to me, did it?"

"That isn't the point." And Aiden looks angry, really angry. "I told you to wait until we found out more."

"You're not my boss," I snap, then regret it. "I'm sorry. I couldn't wait."

He pauses, gathers himself. Studies my face. "I take it this wasn't a happy reunion, then," he says.

"No. He didn't know me. Not at all. At the time I thought he must have been re-Slated, even though he is too old."

"At the time? What did you think after?"

"I don't know. It wasn't right for that. For a start, I still knew him, what he is like, didn't I? That he'd run there in the morning. And he wasn't like a new Slated. Not all smiley and dopey. He was more . . . distant. Not like a Slated at all."

"Interesting. Did he have a Levo?"

"His sleeves were too long to tell. What do you make of it?"

"Well, a few things: He isn't a prisoner there, is he? He is trusted to come and go, or he wouldn't be running in the early morning alone."

True. I cling on to that bit of good news.

"And they are doing something else. Not Slating. Or at least, not as we know it. But to what purpose?" He grips my hands, stares into my eyes. "Promise me, Kyla, that you will keep away from him. For now, at least. I'll see what else we can find out."

"But—"

"No buts. It is far too dangerous to go there with that degree of Lorder presence. I don't want anything to happen to you. Neither would the Ben we knew."

Ben: subject of some unknown Lorder experiment. He doesn't re- member me. At least he seemed fit, well. Not Slated-happy, but not miserable. Despite Coulson's threat, they're not likely to do anything to him because of me, are they? No matter how cruel, Lorders are rational. They won't ruin an experiment just to get at me. He doesn't know I know where Ben is; he could just tell me some other tale and expect me to believe it. But there is nothing to gain by going to see him again. He still won't know me.

"All right," I say. "I promise."

But no matter that logic tells me Ben is safe, at least for now, everything inside screams in fear for him. Who knows what is happening or is going to happen to him there?

Dr. Lysander might know, or be able to find out. I'm meeting her tomorrow, our usual hospital appointment. But will she tell me?

35

THE SAME LORDER STANDS GUARD OUTSIDE DR. LYSANDER'S office while I wait. He stares straight ahead, expression blank. Whatever possessed him to wink at me the last time has clearly gone.

"Come," Dr. Lysander calls, and I escape inside, shut the door.

She watches me walk across the room, sit down. Her hands are folded in front of her, the computer shut. Something is up. *Danger.*

I swallow.

"Good morning, Kyla," she says finally. "How are you today?"

"Fine. And you?"

She pauses. "I'm well, thank you. But I realized something after our last meeting. We've been playing cat and mouse, you and I."

"Am I the cat or the mouse?" I quip, before sense can stop me.

"You should be the mouse, but sometimes I'm not so sure. I want some answers, Kyla."

"I have questions, too."

Annoyance wars with curiosity on her face. "All right," she says at last. "You ask one, and I will answer it; then it will be your turn. Deal?"

"Deal," I say, though caution says it would be better for her to go first. I search for the words.

"Well?"

"You remember Ben: Ben Nix. My friend," I say, and she inclines her head slightly. "I want to know what happened to him. Where he is now."

"I've already told you, I don't know."

"You knew he cut off his Levo; you said so. You must know something."

"You knew also, and I never asked you about that. But as far as what happened to him afterward, I looked at the time. That information wasn't on our system." She sighs. "Look, I'll prove it, all right?"

She opens her computer. "Come around and you shall see with your own eyes. Surname Nix, did you say?"

I nod. She taps *Ben Nix* into the search box.

No results.

"Perhaps he was a Benjamin." She tries that: no results.

"I don't understand." She frowns, then her face clears. "He will be in your notes. Yes. I cross-referenced him under your friends and family listings." She switches screens. "Yes, here is his number." She taps at the screen again.

No results.

Her face flickers between anger and something else. She closes the computer.

"What is it?" I ask.

She sits back, takes her glasses off, rubs her eyes. She looks different without them—they are harsh, heavy black frames. Her eyes without the lens magnification look tired, more human. She puts them back on.

"He must have been deleted."

"What does that mean? Is he . . ."

"Is he dead? I don't know. Merely dying isn't enough to delete you from these records, Kyla. Even I haven't got clearance to delete a record from the system. No one at the hospital can, not even the Board.

I can create new patient files, update them, edit them, but not delete them. It is against every rule. Yet it is like he never existed."

"Who could do that?"

"Nameless faces, with . . ." She stops. "Are you the cat, am I the mouse? Enough of your questions. You can see I have answered you, as much as I can, and told you things I should not. It is your turn. Tell me: Have you had any more memories come back?" She leans forward, face still carefully detached, but behind it is eagerness, curiosity.

There is part of me that longs to tell her everything. She could see what has happened to me, explain it. But *danger*. No one can know. I'm on the Lorder radar: Who knows if they listen?

And my eyes are looking, searching about the room. There could be listening devices in here, hidden anywhere.

"What is it?"

"Not here. I can't talk about it here. I don't feel safe."

"I can assure you, this room is not monitored. It would be a complete breach of doctor-patient confidentiality."

"Is that a bigger rule to break than deleting a patient record?"

She half opens her mouth, closes it again. Thinks a moment.

She writes on a slip of paper, then hands it across: *Meet me 9 Tuesday morning,* it says. A bridle path near my school is marked on a rough map sketched underneath.

With so many reasons to say no, I clutch the paper in my hand. Nod.

"Can you ride?" she asks.

"Yes," I say, the word out before I even know if it's true. And it is. There is a flash of memory, horses running across a field. Jumping a low fence: like flying!

"What is it, Kyla?"

"I remember," I whisper. "A horse. Black and white. We could fly!"

And her eyes hunger to know, to know everything. To see what went wrong inside my head.

But if her curiosity is satisfied, what then?

Once home from the hospital, I stare at Nico's envelope in my room, willing it to reveal its secrets.

I could open it; see what's inside. I shove it in my pocket and head downstairs.

"I'm going to Cam's," I announce, put shoes on, and open the door.

I step out, pause, and stick my head back in. "Mum?" I call.

"What?" She comes into the hall.

"This was stuck in the door. It's got your name on it." I hold out Nico's envelope, not hidden where Mum could find it alone as instructed. But I have to know. What is in it, what is her reaction?

She frowns, takes it. Tears it open and pulls out a sheet of paper. Scans it, and her eyes widen. A sharp intake of breath.

"What is it?"

"Nothing important," she lies, and shoves it in her pocket.

I stare back at her, disbelieving, and for a second her eyes relent; there is indecision there. She is on the verge of telling me something, whether the truth or some other story. There are so many secrets between us. Will she open up? If she does, will I?

Rat-a-tat-tat.

We both jump.

Mum opens the door. "Cam, hi. Come in."

He steps in, looks between us as if he senses something is up.

"Great minds think alike," I say. "I was just about to come over to see if you want to go for a walk."

"Sure," Cam says. "But first I've got a question. What should I wear to this thing on AMD?" Mum and I both look at him, surprised, and he looks between us. "Uh-oh, he didn't tell you, did he?"

"Who? Tell us what?" I ask.

"Your dad. He asked if I want to come along to this ceremony thing with you, so I can take you home before the dinner."

My eyes widen with alarm; I fight not to show it. No, Cam! Don't be there. Who knows what will happen?

"But if you don't want me to come . . ."

Mum jumps in. "No, of course we do, Cam. That's a good idea! Just didn't know, that's all. Suit and tie needed, I'm afraid."

I make the right sort of sounds, and try to make it convincing. While thinking what can I say to make him *not* come, once we're alone.

"Time we head out for a walk," I say. "Before it gets dark."

"Cam, a question before you go," Mum says. "Have you seen anybody out front of our house today?"

His eyes flick to me, back to her. "Don't think so. Just Kyla coming out, then going back in a moment ago. Why?"

"No reason. Go on, you two."

We walk up the footpath above the village. I look at Cam sideways. "You don't want to come to this stupid ceremony at Chequers."

"Sure I do! A chance to get all dressed up and rub shoulders with the great and the good. What's not to like?"

"It's going to be *really* boring."

"Probably!" He grins, and winks. "But you'll be there."

"Cut the lines, bonehead. It'll be speeches, politicians. Lorders everywhere. If there were any way I could get out of it, I would."

"That is why I'm going. So I can whisk you away after. So no buts."

We reach the top lookout, and with Cam there, demons are exorcised. He does a Tarzan impression, swinging off the side of a tree, and I laugh, standing in late afternoon sunshine. The sun is low in the sky; soon it will be dark. I shiver.

"Come on, we best start back," I say, and he follows as I head down the path.

"So," he says. "Are you going to tell me what's going on with you? It's obvious *something* is on your mind."

"Nothing."

"Don't take me for an idiot."

"I don't," I say. Shrug, hesitate. "It's just the usual."

"The usual and mysterious?"

"Pretty much."

He holds my hand on the way down. Says good-bye out front. Adds, in a low voice, that if I ever need a friend to talk to, he is there.

But I can't put him in danger like that.

36

NICO PULLS INTO THE BACK OF A PUB. WE GET OUT OF HIS car, and he knocks on the back door; it opens. We walk through a kitchen, then connecting rooms. The building is old, very—thatched roof, uneven floors, strange nooks and crannies in higgledy rooms. There are faint voices coming from the front of the building. A back room with a few mismatched tables and chairs is empty. There is another door at the back of it: Nico opens it to reveal a small storage room.

"In you get," he says.

"Thanks for letting me come."

He smiles. "This is something you have set in motion. What happens in this meeting will affect you. I thought you should listen in. Now, in. Be quiet." He glances at his watch. "If things go to plan, it won't be long."

He shuts the door; there is a grating in it I can just peer through. Perhaps ten minutes later the man who let us in the back door comes in, carrying a tray of tea things. Behind him is Mum.

She sits down across from Nico. Pale, hands fluttering until she knots them together. Her eyes look this way and that, even at the door where I'm hiding, and I involuntarily shrink back despite knowing she can't see into this dark room.

"Tea?" Nico says.

"Where is he?" she says.

He pours cups of tea, puts one in front of her. Saying nothing, and I can see her fighting to not ask again. Failing.

"Where is my son?" Ah . . . Robert. That is the carrot he used to get her here. "You said he'd be here!" She starts to stand.

"I said come if you want to see your son again. I didn't say he would be here."

She pauses, eyes guarded. She lowers herself back into her chair.

"Well?" she says.

"We know where he is."

"I've been trying to find him for years."

He raises an eyebrow. "We may have sources you cannot access."

"Who are you, exactly?"

"I think you know."

"I guess, but I want to hear you say it."

Nico's lips quirk. He's amused. He is playing with her, and some part of me wants to rip the door open and yell at both of them to just say what they are thinking.

She does just that. "You killed my parents; you bombed my son's bus."

He shakes his head slightly. "I'm not old enough to have done the former, and that isn't quite what happened to the latter."

"Oh?"

"You know what happened to Robert." A statement, not a question.

"I have sources, too."

"And?"

She sighs. "The official version of events is that he was killed in the bus bombing, but he was seen alive and well soon after. He must have been Slated."

"You do realize that if you see him, he won't even know who you are."

She doesn't answer; her shoulders are slumped. Of course she knows that.

"Think about what has been done to you," Nico says. "What is done to countless mothers and fathers."

"To their children," she whispers.

"You have a chance to do something about it."

"Your ways are not mine."

He inclines his head. "I'm not suggesting they are. But there is something you *can* do. Help future parents and children not go through what you have gone through. Make no mistake, the Lorders are behind it all. If not for them, we'd have no reason to be here."

"I'm listening."

"Armstrong Memorial Day. When you give your speech, at Chequers. It is televised live?"

"Yes. It is every year. But—"

"Tell the whole country about your son. Your Robert. Begin with the usual, the tragic loss of your parents. Then mention Robert was also killed by terrorist bombs—then tell the truth about what happened to him. That the Lorders break their own laws. If you take the secrecy away—if the people know what really goes on—they'll stop it."

She shakes her head. "It'll never work. The Lorders will cut the transmission."

"I have sources. I can assure you, this broadcast is truly live. There is no delay. You'll be able to get it out fast enough if you are clever how you say it."

"And then?"

"You are someone the people will believe. It will be the beginning of the end for the Lorders. And we'll take you to Robert."

My stomach is in knots. What will she decide? What will Nico do if it isn't what he wants?

But then, as she starts to say something, he silences her with a raised hand. "You need to think about this, about what to do. Don't decide now. Go."

She gets up from the table, walks to the door. I'm gripped by fear that he isn't really going to let her go, that his paranoia will kick in and he'll be convinced she is going to shop him to the Lorders. It is only when she's gone that I can breathe again. I'm not sure where she stands; she might even be the one who betrayed me to the Lorders, a possibility Nico knows nothing of. How could he know what she might do now?

A slow minute counts down before Nico stands, opens my door. "Come. We should get out of here."

Out through the back door, into his car. Down a side road and another, several quick turns. He watches, but no one follows.

"We'll head to the house. We need to talk," he says.

"Do you really know where Robert is?"

"Not yet, but we will." He glances sideways. "You know her better than I. What do you think she will do?"

"Honestly? I'm not sure."

"Neither am I," he admits, and I'm surprised. It's unusual for Nico to admit uncertainty. "But there will be a plan B, have no fear."

He drives the rest of the way in silence.

• • •

When we arrive at the house in the woods, he draws me into his office through a wall of curious eyes. Katran is there, and the others. Tori looks through me as if I am not of notice.

"Sit," Nico says, and shuts the office door. We are alone. He pulls the other chair opposite mine, tilts my face up so we are eye to eye. "There is something we need to talk about. Rain, I understand you've been to see Ben."

"What?" I half jump out of the chair, the shock of betrayal deep. After all he said about why he wouldn't, Katran told him?

"Now, Rain, this was a very foolish thing to do." He pushes me back in the chair, holding on to my hand as if to keep me there. His face is set, and a tremor of fear runs through my body. He raises his other hand before I can speak. "Wait. You shouldn't have done it; it was dangerous. You risk us all if you get caught. You know that. But I do understand."

"You do?"

"Of course. I know what it is like to love, to lose that which you love." And his eyes are full of sympathy. "Tell me, Rain," he says. "What happened when you spoke to Ben?" And his eyes, so familiar and so alien at once, hold mine, soothe, draw me out. "Tell me," he repeats.

I swallow. "It was awful. He didn't know me, didn't remember me at all! I don't know what has happened to him, and—"

"I do."

I stop. "You do what?"

"Know what happened to him."

He pauses. "Be strong, Rain. That so-called school where Ben is staying isn't a school. At least, not what you think of by that. It is a

241

Lorder training center. They have been experimenting with different procedures. Like Slating, but less drastic. Useful so subjects keep initiative and ability, yet remain under control." He takes both my hands in his again. "Believe me when I say, I'm sorry. But Ben is lost to you forever."

"No." I shake my head, tears threatening behind my eyes.

"He is training to be the enemy: a Lorder agent."

And I am unable to take it in. Aiden hinted as much, I realize, without spelling it out. But Ben, a Lorder? No. He couldn't. He wouldn't.

I grow cold with understanding. After what has been done to him, he isn't who he was. He isn't making the decision.

Deep shuddering sobs start working their way up, and I'm struggling to keep some composure in front of Nico, to save it for later, but he pulls me against his shoulder. Tears spill out.

There is a knock on the door. "Wait," he says to me.

He leaves, shuts it behind him.

I drop my head in my hands. Somehow, I already knew. I was avoiding the truth. And here is another, one I will face: Katran told Nico I went to see Ben; he must have. How else could he know? But he said he wouldn't!

The pain and tears turn into anger, then rage. Katran said I couldn't make this decision, but he was wrong. It is mine alone. The Lorders must be stopped, at any cost. Any sacrifice.

Before my memories started to come back, I could never have joined Free UK. As just Kyla I could never face their methods, no matter their aims. But now I can. I can forget that Kyla hates violence, forget her fear, that she ever even existed. Just like I forgot Lucy. But I'll never forget Ben.

Yes! Keep the pain. Use it to focus.

By the time Nico opens the door again, rage has obliterated all other feelings but the desire for revenge.

He sits down. "Where were we? Ah, yes. There is something else we need to discuss. Katran and I had a few words earlier today. About you."

"What?" Has he been telling more of my secrets? I clench my fists.

"He was very careful to say you are on our side."

"I am!"

"But he also expressed concerns. He feels you're too . . . fragile, to be of use."

"That isn't true! I'll do anything."

"Will you, Rain?" Nico leans back, doubt on his face. He holds up one hand, a gesture that says, *Be quiet.* I bite my lip. "Here is the problem I have. Katran thinks you are a liability. I generally trust his opinion."

Again, the shock, the betrayal. There Katran was, reminding me how we used to be friends, that he was the one who held me when I was scared. Being all nice about Ben. *Used to be friends* is right.

"Yet . . ." Nico shrugs. "As much as I want to believe in you, Rain, there is something else. Are you a danger to us?"

"What do you mean?"

"Your actions without thought of consequences." Again his hand is held up, demanding silence. "Like Tori—a risk I've grown fond of now, but still a risk. And going to see Ben. What if you'd been captured? Would you have been able to keep us secret?"

"Yes," I answer, instantly and without thought. I never told Coulson anything about them he didn't already know, did I?

Nico, alert as always to any nuances of thought or feeling, sees. "Tell me, Rain. Is there some other risk you have exposed us to?"

But I can't tell him about Coulson: It is too late.

"Rain?" An impatient voice, one that doesn't wait. "Tell me what you haven't, and do it now. What is the risk."

Switch and hit. "When I got my memories back, I was attacked, and had to defend myself. He . . . survived, and remembers it."

"Name," he says flatly.

"Wayne Best." The words come out slow and quiet, as if reluctant to be heard. Was this handing out a death sentence? Yet so many who die don't deserve it; Wayne is far down the list of humanity, as far as I'm concerned.

"Why didn't you tell me this before?" He shakes his head. "How can I really trust you?"

"I will do anything to prove myself."

"Will you?" He sighs. Turns suddenly and moves close, a hand on each of the arms of my chair, stares intently into my eyes. "Think, Rain. What can you do for us? What can you give us, that says you really *will* do anything. So I know I can trust you."

I scramble through my mind for something, anything, that will prove to him where my loyalties lie. Images and faces spin through, and then—

My eyes widen as one face holds still.

"You've got something. Tell me," he says, with a voice that commands. A flash of another time, another place: a brick. Fingers. I flinch, inside. He must be obeyed.

Words are dragged from inside, slow, each one a fresh, new hurt. A line drawn. A choice made. "I can give you Dr. Lysander."

As I leave, uncertainty and fear fight with the glow inside at gaining Nico's trust.

All it took was offering up Dr. Lysander.

I grit my teeth. She deserves it. It is all because of her: Slating was her evil invention, if you can call it that. Everything is her fault. Ben's fate is her doing, indirect though it may be.

Nico nods at Katran, who gets up as I walk to the door.

I flush. "I can get myself home," I say, but Katran follows me out. As he does, I see there is a car by the back of the house, and a man, smoking and leaning against it. He turns as if to hide himself. A quick glimpse of an average face, average build, yet somehow familiar. How?

We walk the short way through the woods to the bikes. I ignore Katran, take off, but the anger grows the farther we go. We're not even halfway there when I slow, gesture to stop. I almost throw my bike to the ground.

"What's with you?" he says.

"You told Nico!"

"Told him what?"

"That I went to see Ben."

His face registers surprise, and hurt. "I said I wouldn't. I didn't."

"Then how does he know?"

"Nico knows!" he says, our old saying, but the shrug and smile are missing.

I shake my head, unable to see how it's possible. Yet . . . that familiar face by the house; it comes to me now. Was he Aiden's van driver? Maybe that is how Nico knows; maybe it wasn't Katran. But there is still all the rest.

"How could you talk to Nico about me behind my back, tell him I am a liability?" I say the words through clenched teeth, my hands curling into fists at my sides. "I'm a better shot than you! Just as good with knives, and—"

"You are, Rain. There is no doubting your skills. Against unmoving targets, you are the best."

"What do you mean?"

"Don't you remember?"

"What?"

He rolls his eyes skyward. "I'll show you."

He pulls a knife out of a sheath, hidden along his side, and holds it up so it glints silver in the watery late afternoon light. Not just any knife—*the knife*. The diving knife a Lorder used to cut his face all those years ago. He rolls up one sleeve, touches the blade to his inner arm.

"What are you doing? Stop!"

But it's too late: He drags it along his skin. The blade bites in; it wells up red. Not just drops, but an actual trickle, a line of red that runs down his arm to his hand. I hate blood. Hate it. The smell, the feel, the taste. I start gagging, back away, but can't tear my eyes from the red. A few drops fall from his arm, seem to hang in midair, then splash to the ground, and my stomach starts heaving. I breathe in and out, hard, bent over, my vision starting to waver, trying not to be sick.

Katran reaches for me, and I flinch. He sighs, takes out a hanky, wipes his arm and holds it.

"It's just a little nick. I'm fine. See?" I turn back and all evidence of the red is hidden, out of sight, and my breathing starts to come easier.

"Do you see now, Rain?" he says, voice low. "Why you can't be with us. You're a danger, a risk to us all. If you react like that to a few drops of blood, what do you think bombs and bullets do? You could fall to pieces at any time. If I have to babysit you, others are at risk."

"I don't understand. I *can* remember attacks, and blood." I swallow, and force myself to focus: loud noises. Screaming, people running. But details are fuzzy: I don't remember what I did. I must have hurt people, then made myself forget so the details aren't clear. Inside I shy away. Could I really kill anybody? Have I?

"What is Nico playing at," Katran muses, almost talking to himself. "He must see this is impossible. Why does he want you involved? Why is it so important to him?"

Then, as if he remembers I'm still here, he turns back. Takes my hands in his. "Rain, just promise me. Think about it. Think about what happened today, and before, and every time you see blood. Think about it, and remember." He pauses, his eyes intent on mine. Unwavering, and I want to look away, but I can't.

Without thought, I reach up, trail my fingers across the scar on his face with a sense of wonder. I've done this before.

He yanks away as if my fingers burn his skin. Gets back on his bike, and I follow. The rest of the way home my mind spins: Is what he says true? Am I a total failure as a terrorist?

Everything inside screams *no*. It is what I'm good at; all the things Nico taught us. I fought to be the best at everything we did, and I often was.

This makes no sense. If what Katran says is true, why would Nico even want me to be involved? Tracking me down couldn't have been easy. And I'd always wondered how he found me after I was Slated. If that van driver is his plant in MIA, that may be how. And that must be how he knows I went to see Ben. My memory may fail in some ways, but I do remember this: Katran never lies. If he had done it, he would say so.

Why would Nico go to such an effort to find me if I'm so useless?

He couldn't have known ahead of time that I'd be placed with Mum. Who she is. And I am meeting with Dr. Lysander, but he couldn't have guessed that would be possible.

I grit my teeth. Okay, blood is beyond gross, fair enough, but I'll overcome it, by sheer force of will. If Nico believes in me, I can do it.

I must do it.

Anyhow, getting Dr. Lysander for Free UK has got to be worth something. A whole lot of somethings.

Late that night, I try. A sharp kitchen knife, a shaking hand: just one drop of blood. But I can't do it, I can't. I throw the knife across the room and it sticks in the wall.

37

"KYLA! WAIT." CAM'S VOICE CALLS OUT BEHIND ME IN THE most colossal case of bad timing.

I consider ignoring him, but he is as likely as not to give chase if I do. I turn on my heels. "Yes?"

"Aren't you going to class?"

"Of course."

"You're walking the wrong way."

Students stream past us in all directions, racing to the first class of Tuesday morning. Providing cover that will soon be gone.

I concentrate. Smile. "I've got some homework to drop off first. Art project," I say, picking a subject I know he doesn't take. "I'll see you later," I lie, and hurry on, but he walks along with me. I curse internally.

"Is everything all right?" he asks.

"Just fine. How're things with you?"

He shrugs. His face isn't swollen anymore from that Lorder's back-hander; the purple bruises have faded to brown, but still have a way to go. The hit he took standing up for me. I thaw a little inside. Poor Cam. Will the Lorders go after him once they find out I've ignored their deal? I should warn him.

No time, not now.

I stop. Smile again. "Sorry, I've got to run, or I won't make it back. See you later?"

"All right," he says.

I bolt up the path and go straight for the art building across the grass in case he watches. Then I shrug inside. Why would he? Still, I don't deviate until I'm at the door, then dash around the building. I'm just in time out the side gate to follow behind some agriculture students going to the school allotments. To the casual observer, I'm catching up to my class. But once out of sight of the school grounds, I drop back and hit the footpath, then dash up the road.

I should be hurrying, but my feet begin to slow. She wants to talk to me today, to find out my secrets. She is going to learn the biggest of them all, isn't she?

My stomach feels sick. Nerves?

Or guilt.

No! She is part of this whole Lorder system, Slating and everything that goes with it: Emily. And Ben. I can't feel sorry for her. I can't.

I won't. I have to show them all: Katran, Nico, Tori, and the rest. That I am part of their fight against the Lorders. It is my fight, too.

The bridle path is rutted tracks of mud and slows my progress. She is waiting, and I see her before she sees me. Her horse is beautiful, and that isn't all: There is another, and on it, the same Lorder who guards her at the hospital.

I groan. Nico said she would probably have someone with her. I'm supposed to try to separate them, then signal when they should come.

I wave as I walk up the bridle path. The Lorder's eyes widen when he sees me: I am a surprise? Good. Dr. Lysander says a few words, and he seems to argue with her, then nods. Gets off his horse as I walk up.

"Glorious day, isn't it?" She grins, and she looks different. Her dark hair, loose with fine streaks of gray, hangs down her back. Her riding clothes look more *her* than the white coat I've never seen her without before. The heavy glasses are gone; contact lenses, or are they a prop? "You did mean it when you said you could ride?"

"Yes."

"Agent Lewinski has kindly offered you his horse, but says we may only walk and not let him out of sight. Do you need help?" I shake my head. My foot barely reaches the stirrup, but I manage: up!

My horse shifts on his feet, and I get the feel of him, the saddle. Blinking again at the memories, swift and sharp. Horses, but where, when? Eyes closed, I am some other place and time. There are no details; it is more a feeling than anything else. Of joy! Speed. A certainty that I am safe, that nothing could ever happen to me, so long as . . . what? Childish knowledge that knows nothing of the world.

"Are you all right, Kyla?"

I jump, look around me, back to here and now. "Yes, fine. Who is this?" I say, stroking his mane.

"Jericho," she says. "And this is my Heathcliff." She pats the neck of her horse; he stamps and snorts.

We start walking up the path. Her guard hangs back as requested, but looks unhappy about it. I can sense a large report filed on me coming soon, and I'm sure it will fly straight to Coulson. I shake myself internally. It will hardly matter after today, will it?

Gradually we start to walk a little faster. I urge Jericho with my knees, to put distance between the Lorder guard and us before I call Katran.

She glances at me sideways. "That missing hospital record of your friend Ben? Not the only one," she says, voice low. "A little checking, and there are others. Gaps in the records. And worse."

"What?"

"There are missing doctors, too," she says, her face a picture of horror.

Inside, I snort. A doctor going missing is far more worrying to her than a hundred Slateds, I bet.

"What does it mean?" I ask, but wonder: Could the missing doctors be at that so-called school of Ben's?

She hesitates. "I can only guess at the moment, and my guesses are all unpleasant."

I stare back at her and finally ask the questions that have plagued my curiosity for a while. "Why do you tell me these things? Why haven't you turned me in, when you suspect I'm remembering things? Why have you met me here? I don't understand."

"Partly, I am curious. And I want to know what went wrong with you, so I can stop it from happening again."

"And?"

She hesitates, shakes her head. "Such sentimentality on my part. You remind me of a girl I knew in school, long ago," she says, and sadness crosses her face.

"What happened to her?"

"She got caught up in the riots. There were no other options then; she was executed." She looks back. "Enough of your questions and the past. He is far enough behind us, Kyla, to truly put you at ease. It is your turn. Tell me now as you said you would do so. What do you remember? Why do you remember?"

I could push the com at my wrist to signal Katran and end this conversation before it starts. Yet . . . her eyes. So curious. The one thing I can do for her is answer her questions truthfully. Maybe she can make sense of things I cannot. Or is it more that some part of me is programmed to answer her, and can't easily stop doing so? Nico would be furious, but he isn't here to listen.

"I remember strange things: sights, sounds, feelings. People and places; unconnected, connected. It is hard to even explain. Like when I got on this horse. Feeling him move brought all these associations and feelings of another time, but I don't know where or when."

"Fascinating," she says. "Every scan and test you had before you left the hospital said everything was as it should be."

"It hadn't started yet then, not really. Other than some dreams. When I left the hospital, things began to come back. At first just small things, in bits and pieces."

"And then?"

I hesitate. And then, Wayne. "I had a fright. And they came back in a huge rush. And this?" I point at my Levo. "Useless now." I give it a twist to demonstrate.

"I don't understand how that could be possible."

"I don't understand it completely, either. But there are a few things I do know. I was born left-handed, not right. Free UK gave me some sort of training, conditioning. I don't really know what. But it's almost like it made me two people, my memories split between them: one right-handed and one left-handed. When I was Slated, they thought I was right-handed because I was being that person. The other was hidden away inside."

"Interesting. Extreme pressure of circumstances can sometimes cause a dissociative identity disorder. Essentially, a fracking of self into layers," she says. Her eyes turn inward, musing. "It is theoretically possible to induce such a personality fracture, such that one personality keeps the memories the other discards. But only by extreme methods: deliberate trauma or abuse of a nature so severe that fracking is the only way for the self to survive."

Her words send shivers down my back. What trauma would be enough to achieve this? What was the brick Nico held that did this to me?

"But, Kyla, I don't understand. Why would this be done to anyone?"

"So part of me could survive Slating."

Her eyes meet mine in round O's of shock. Little wheels are spinning behind them as she thinks it through, the implications. "There have long been arguments on this; it was felt to be impossible." Something else registers on her face, in her eyes. "Kyla, why were you Slated?" she asks gently.

"Lorders caught me. Wasn't it in my records?"

"Your records state you were captured in a terrorist attack. They list you as a Jane Doe: identity unknown." As she says the words, one eyebrow goes up, skeptical.

"A Jane Doe?" I say, stunned. "Isn't everyone DNA tested at birth?"

"They are according to law. But sometimes babies are born in quiet places, to parents who keep out of the way, and they slip through the cracks."

My mind is spinning with this information. Is it really possible the Lorders didn't know who I was? Even though I was reported missing on MIA? I can't believe they don't monitor that illegal website. But maybe it explains something else. "If they didn't know who I was, how would they know my age, whether they could Slate me or not?"

"Simple cell testing reveals age very accurately, Kyla, and was conducted according to law. You were under sixteen when you were Slated."

"But I wasn't. I was sixteen. I know I was; I remember my birthday."

"You must be mistaken. Those tests are foolproof. But enough diversions: Back to my question, Kyla. *Why* were you Slated?" she asks again, and I am confused by the question.

"I don't know. I don't remember what happened."

Her eyes move, focus behind us, and widen. I turn in time to see her Lorder guard grappled to the ground by Katran. But I haven't called them in yet. I'd meant for us to leave him behind first. What is happening? And then she is off the other way, urging her horse to a gallop, and I curse. Distracted by her questions! I should have grabbed her, done something, anything.

But before I can follow, she stops. Pulls Heathcliff up sharp. Holds out her hands in a gesture of surrender. Why? And then I see two Free UK ahead with weapons trained on Heathcliff. She won't risk her horse.

There is a sound behind: a choke, a gurgle. I turn. Katran has the Lorder with one arm pinned behind his back, but then he releases him, pushes him away. He wipes his knife on the grass as the Lorder makes a slow crumple to the ground.

Red.

Not just a drop of red like I'd tried last night. A sheet of red. His throat is a curtain of blood that pulses with his heart. His body twitches on the ground, then lies still, just as I fall from my horse.

38

MY MOUTH TASTES SOUR, FULL OF GRAVEL, AND ALL IS darkness. I am lying down, on something soft. Head full of fuzzy cotton. Where . . . what? My eyes open. Everything is a blur that as I blink becomes clear.

A small room, a shut door. One square window, barred. And I'm not alone: Dr. Lysander stands a few feet away, looking out through the bars.

I sit up.

She turns at the movement. "All right, Kyla?" she asks, voice quiet, calm.

Confusion is thick. "What happened?" I say, and my voice sounds wrong.

"You might know better than I. But maybe not. You appear to be locked up in here with me."

I sit up. My mouth tastes awful. My clothes are a mess. Mud, and worse. Vomit?

The smell makes my stomach twist, and I breathe in and out, slow, until it passes.

"Is there any water?" I ask.

"No." She bangs on the door. "Hello, out there! We require some water," she says. Her voice has its usual note of quiet authority, one that may not work here.

There is a murmur through the door; time passes. Then a voice: "Stand away from the door."

It opens: Tori peers in. "It stinks in here." She wrinkles her perfect nose, looks at me. "You stink!" Past her, Katran is sitting in a chair, alert, weapon in hands. I recognize Nico's office. So we are where I thought, but why am I . . . ?

A wave of fear grips me inside. Perhaps Nico found out about Coulson, and thinks I am a traitor.

Katran shakes his head slightly as Tori gives Dr. Lysander a bottle of water. His eyes say, *Be quiet. Wait.*

"Let me go," I try. But instead of demanding, my voice sounds weak, a plaintive whimper.

Tori laughs. "I don't think so," she says, and leaves, locks the door, looking far too pleased with the situation.

Dr. Lysander has a small drink, then passes me the bottle. "You have the rest. You will be dehydrated after that." And she gestures at the mess I'm in.

I drink some, then dampen the cleanest corner I can find of my sleeve to wipe my face. As far as the rest of me, there is no hope. I sigh. My head throbs. What happened? I try to focus, to think, but all is a fuzzy mess.

"I used to think you'd make a good doctor, Kyla, but I see I was mistaken. Have you always had a phobia of blood?"

"I don't! I . . ." And I stop. With her saying the word, it floods back. All I can see is her Lorder guard, and *red red red* . . .

A curtain of blood. Tears are rising in my eyes now, and I'm shaking. All that blood. Forget it, put it away, banish it—

But Katran said I mustn't forget, I must remember, I—

Katran. He killed him. Cut his throat and did it in front of me in a way that almost said, *Watch this.* Why did he kill him? Why that gruesome way?

A phobia of blood makes a failed terrorist.

"Can you get over a phobia?" I ask.

"Of course. It isn't easy. The most successful way is systematic de-sensitization: facing the thing you fear in a controlled environment until it begins to lose its power to terrify. Such as putting a person who fears spiders in their company more and more while teaching them to relax. Witness a few dozen more murders, and you should be just fine."

Desensitization. A word that echoes, deep inside, until the world is spinning and I am *back*. Flashes of images, like an old-style 3-D horror film where things of terror jump out at you again and again. No peace. Explosions, screaming, blood. I wrap my arms around my head, curl up into a ball, some distant part aware that Dr. Lysander is calling my name, that her hand is on my shoulder. I'm shaking and fighting it, clenching eyes shut but it is all still there. A whistle; a flash; an explosion. A bus full of children. Screaming, bloody hands beating against glass windows. And then, it all happens again. It runs over and over.

On a loop. On . . . replay? With realization, the images twist and morph into something flat. A movie screen. Me, in a chair, unable to move. Not reality. All those horrible things. I was never there, but forced to watch: an attempt to *desensitize*. One that never worked.

I uncurl, open my eyes. Maybe . . . I never killed anyone. Maybe, I couldn't.

Time passes. I avoid Dr. Lysander's eyes. She must know everything is my fault. Yet she doesn't do or say anything. She is pulled into herself, calm, contained. Watchful and waiting.

And then—sounds of a car.

Soon there are voices on the other side of the door, and my skin goes cold. Nico's voice. Only he could have said to lock me up. Why?

Minutes pass, and then our door is unlocked by Nico himself. A very cheerful-looking Nico.

"Ah, hello there. Dr. Lysander, I presume? Would you like to step through? It is time for some afternoon tea."

He holds the door, smiles, as if inviting a guest. She pauses, steps through, and Nico turns to chuck the keys in a desk drawer. I think I am ignored, but after Nico asks her to take a seat, he turns back to me.

"And what have we here?" He wrinkles his nose. "Oh, dear child. Perhaps . . . yes. I think before you join us you must get cleaned up a little."

He turns to Tori. "Take her out for a wash and find her some clean clothes, please, then bring her back."

She yanks me out the door and around the side of the house, and I'm thinking, *Run?* But there are others. Guards, guns in hand: Katran is outside now, as well as two more. Courtesy of Dr. Lysander's presence, no doubt.

"Wait," Tori says. She goes around the back and I hear water splashing. She returns with a bucket in her hands and dumps it over my head, an icy shock of cold water. I cough and sputter. She stands back, considering. "No, not good enough." Another bucketful follows. She leaves me there, shivering, and goes back in the house. Returns moments later.

"Put these on," she instructs, and tosses jeans and a hoodie at me. I look up, and the guards are watching. Then Katran coughs with a pointed look and they turn away. I shuck my clothes fast. Shivering, numb. Head light. When I bend to pull the jeans on, it spins so I almost hit the ground. I pull the hoodie over my head, shaking violently as I struggle to get my arms in the sleeves, until Tori gives it an impatient tug. The other guards still look away. Not Katran: His eyes lock on mine, calm, steady, saying something. What?

"Come on," Tori says, kicking my clothes out of the way with distaste. "Nico waits." She smiles, and my flesh crawls as I follow her into the house. It is only marginally warmer than outside, and I shake with cold and fear.

There is an extra chair now in Nico's office.

"Ah, there you are," he says. "Sit down, Kyla."

Tori lingers in the door.

"Go!" he says, and she jumps back through the door and shuts it behind her, but not before I see the look on her face: serious annoyance.

"Tea, Kyla?" Nico asks, teapot in one hand.

"Y-y-y-yes, please," I say. Teeth chattering despite attempts to control it.

"Ah, poor thing. We don't have hot water here, I am afraid," he says to Dr. Lysander. "Still, we make do as best we can."

He pours a cup and passes it to me, and I wrap my hands tight around it, concentrate on the heat absorbing into them.

Nico leaves the room but returns seconds later, blanket in hands, and drapes it over my shoulders. "Can't have you freezing to death before we decide what to do with you."

Dr. Lysander is sitting, legs crossed, a cup of tea in one hand. Still in her day-off clothes, of course, but she is back in hospital mode as much as if she had on her white jacket. Observing and calm.

"Perhaps it is time you told me what is going on?" she asks Nico, one eyebrow up as if gently interrogating an errant patient.

"Let's have a cookie first." He opens a box and holds it to me, but I shake my head, stomach empty but unable to contemplate anything beyond the tea clenched in my hands.

Finally Nico finishes his tea and handful of chocolate cookies. Sits back in his chair.

"You may have heard of Free UK? You will perhaps be more familiar with the Lorder name for us: AGT," he says.

She inclines her head. "Now and then."

"You have been honored today with an invitation to help our cause. To overthrow the evil Lorders that stifle and choke our youth and everything else in this great country."

She raises an eyebrow.

He looks at me. "Take this poor child, for example. Look at her, shivering. Lost and alone. The government Slates her, makes her incapable of judging her friends from her enemies. She can't think for herself. So easy to turn and manipulate to whatever purpose. Generally Lorders' purposes, but we can do so as well. What next for her? What does this country give as a future?"

Part of me, some small sliver of defiance inside, jumps and rages and screams. Is this what he thinks, what he has done? Twisted me to his purposes, and now sees me for as useless as I am, something to discard? But more of me is numb, cold. Aware that interrupting Nico could be the last thing I ever do.

"Strange questions you ask of me," Dr. Lysander says. "Her future? By having her take part today you have extinguished it like blowing out a match."

"Might as well end it now, then," Nico says, and opens a drawer in his desk. He pulls out a pistol. Checks the barrel. Smiles. Raises it casually, flicks the safety off. Points it at my head.

Terror, hot and real, fills me inside. Yet . . . no. Nico would never shoot me in here. He doesn't like mess. He'd have me dragged out in the woods and shot if that were his plan.

"Don't," Dr. Lysander gasps. "Please."

He raises an eyebrow in surprise, half frowns. "Why not?"

She seems rattled by the question. "I am a doctor, sworn to protect life. She is my patient."

He half smiles. "No. That isn't it, is it, Dr. Lysander? It is apparent, all over your face. You actually care. I can see it. This miscreant," he says, and smiles at me fondly like a favored puppy who makes messes but you still love, "is like the child you never had.

"You care, as do I. And that, Dr. Lysander, is what this is all about." He lowers the gun. "You may go now, Kyla."

"What . . . ?"

He opens the drawer again, replaces the pistol, and draws out something else. "Here." He throws my school ID across the desk. "I saw to it that you were in all of your classes. Get going, or you'll be late home and need excuses."

I stand, confused and uncertain, looking from Nico to Dr. Lysander. Her composure cracked then, just that bit when Nico had the gun. She hasn't got a blood phobia. I'm sure she's seen worse than gunshot wounds, though maybe not inflicted at close range in front of her.

I step to the door, reeling with the discovery: *She cares.*

"Why, Kyla? Ask yourself why," Dr. Lysander says softly as I step through, shut the door behind me.

All of this, today, was Nico playing a game with her. That is what it is about.

Nico and his games, games within games. Hidden meanings and manipulations. He is a master, and there is something he wants from Dr. Lysander, that much I can work out.

But somehow I think she is his match.

Tori is lying back on one of the bedrolls on the floor, hands behind her head. Laughing.

"What's with you?" I say.

"You should have seen your face! 'Let me go,'" she mimics, a plaintive tragic whisper.

"You enjoyed that way too much."

She sits up. "Maybe. But I had a grudge to settle. You and Ben," she says. "But now we're even. Friends again?" She holds out her hand, but I ignore her, stomp out of the building. Her laughter follows behind.

I walk into the woods, suddenly afraid letting me go was the act. That Nico really does mean to kill me where I won't make a mess. That he'll send them after me. But just Katran follows, gun not in sight. Not that he'd need it if those were his instructions.

"Rain?" he says. I don't answer. "Is this the silent treatment, then?" he asks a moment later.

I shrug.

"What specifically are you pissed off at?"

"I'm too cold, too tired, too empty, to even take a stab at it," I say, then cringe at my choice of words. I slump against a tree.

"I couldn't tell you," he says. "I'm sorry."

"Couldn't tell me which bit? That it was an ambush, not waiting for my signal? That I was being taken prisoner, too? That being a prisoner was all just pretend? What?"

"Any of it. If you'd known, Nico would have been able to tell. You know what he's like."

I shrug, but I do. He sees all.

"You must know I would never have gone along with it if it was for real."

"Really? After what you did today, I think you could do anything."

The pain in Katran's eyes is real. He reaches a hand for mine, but

I flinch, pull back. That hand held a knife, pulled it across a throat. Ended a life.

"Did you have to kill him?" I ask.

"Rain, he was a Lorder. The enemy. Aside from the fact he saw us and could identify you, yes: I had to kill him. We are fighting a war. People die." He shrugs, and there is nothing in his eyes that says he regrets it, or felt a life end. Just pushed him away as his blood spilled on the ground, like so much rubbish.

My throat twists again. "Take me home," I whisper.

"Come on."

We have to double, since my bike is by my house. He puts me on the bike behind him. We sit close and I'm greedy for his warmth, but the space between us might as well be to the moon.

When we get to the junction of this path and the one behind my house, he stops. I get off, walk away, saying nothing.

That night, a hot bath and dinner cannot dispel the cold inside. Covers wrapped tight around and the radiator all the way up in my room, and still I shiver. The day flits around my mind, in and out of order, again and again. I so want to banish it all, go back, forget it, yet—

If I do, how can I go forward? I have to remember, have to work out *why*. Have to stare at fear and see what stares back.

With so many things fighting for attention, one thing repeats, again and again: Dr. Lysander's *why*. She doesn't waste words or thoughts; she says what is important. It flies around in my mind looking for a place to settle. I start to fall asleep, so tired, body and mind swaying in a rhythm, like running, or being on the back of a horse galloping over fields, jumping fences.

Why . . . ?

. . .

I scream again and again.

Until my door opens, light spills in from the hall.

"Sweetie, what is it?" Daddy sits on the side of my bed.

At first I just cry. And then I point. Down.

"What is it?"

"I heard something. There is something there," I whisper.

"Where?"

"Under my bed."

"Oh, dear. I better take a look."

"Be careful!"

"Don't worry, I will be." He finds our monster-hunting flashlight in my cupboard, switches it on. He bends down, shines it under the bed, swings it back and forth. Looks up again.

"I checked very carefully. No monsters."

"But I heard it! I did."

"There is nothing there, I promise." He sits back on his heels, still on the floor, thoughtful look on his face.

"You know, the best way to be sure is to look for yourself." I shake my head, but bit by bit he persuades me out from under the covers.

"Look, Lucy. Then you'll know for sure. Face your fear, and it won't be so scary."

I tremble, kneel down, and shine the light under the bed. A few shoes, a missing book.

No monsters in sight.

39

IT IS STILL DARK WHEN I WAKE. I HUG THE DREAM CLOSE, try to hold on to how Lucy felt with her dad. I know who he is, though his face is never clear in these dreams. To Lucy, the child I was all those years ago, there were no monsters her daddy couldn't deal with. A memory, or just some made-up fantasy? No. Everything in me says it is real. But the more awake I become, the more it slips away.

Yet if I *try* to remember anything about Lucy, I can't. I know some things, facts: her birthday, just weeks ago, being one. No matter what Dr. Lysander said about cell testing for age, I know they must have gotten it wrong: My birthday is November third. But feelings, or faces? Nothing.

Lucy is meant to be gone forever. In Dr. Lysander's terms, I was fracked into layers—Lucy and Rain—and Rain hid inside when Lucy was Slated. So what of these dreams?

And then there is Dr. Lysander's *why*. I force myself to think back over yesterday and all we said. Before, on the horses, I told her my secrets. As I know them. The thing she seized on then was *why was I Slated?*

Is this the same *why* she called out as I left?

I pull at strands of memory, try to follow them, but like tangled wool all is in confused knots. Lorders Slated me because they caught me: simple. I have no memory of that at all. Slated away or banished in a place I can't find, either way makes no difference. I don't know what happened.

But maybe she doesn't mean her question that way, not the specifics of events. Maybe, she means what led me to that place.

Well, Nico did, of course. If I weren't with Free UK I'd never have been Slated. But we all take that risk: Whatever the case in the past, this time, I chose this cause. Chose to ignore Coulson's deal and oppose the Lorders.

Yet there is something in Dr. Lysander's *why* that aches deep inside like a rotten tooth. One you know must be pulled, but you can't bring yourself to go to the dentist.

And worse: Even there, in Nico's custody and the worst possible danger, danger she was in because of me, was she still trying to help me?

Downstairs, a surprise: Mum and Dad having breakfast together.

"You're early this morning," Mum says.

"Yep. Woke up and couldn't get back to sleep."

I pour myself some tea, sit down. Amy wanders in later, squeals with delight and gives Dad a hug. She is like Lucy and her dad, and inside there is a swirl of jealousy. Amy found a family with her assigned parents after Slating. She is really close to Dad in particular. With me, he has always been weird: sometimes so friendly, sometimes cold and threatening.

Something niggles, something about Dad and Amy. Mum bustles about the kitchen looking everywhere but in Dad's eyes. Dad makes all the right noises in reply to Amy's tales, but his eyes are on me.

Watching, assessing. Curious, even, but holding back, and that isn't like him.

There is a little *click* inside. Maybe I got things wrong.

Upstairs I knock on Amy's door, go in as she hunts around, stuffing things in her school bag.

"Amy, you know that day you found my drawings. Of the hospital and stuff. Did you tell Dad about it?"

A flash of guilt crosses her face. "Sorry, he called, and yeah, I told him. He'd asked me to look out for you and make sure you didn't get in any trouble. Did he give you a hard time about it?"

"No, no; it's fine," I say, not wanting her to run back to him. "What about Mum? Did you tell her?"

She frowns. "No, I don't think so. Why?"

"Nothing. Don't worry about it."

I wander back to my room and brush my hair, staring unseeing into the mirror.

Well. I had that so wrong. I thought it couldn't be him; he wasn't even here. I didn't bank on Amy spilling over the phone.

So, it was Dad who went to the Lorders. It was because of him that Cam and I were picked up that day.

Poor Mum. I want to rush downstairs and give her a hug, apologize for how I've been shutting her out. But it's too late for that. Lines have been drawn. Dr. Lysander is a captive because of me, and her guard is dead. I can't let Mum into my life, not anymore. I've chosen my path with Free UK, and there is no turning back.

If I could be so wrong about Mum, what else could I have gotten wrong?

Why was I Slated?

"Amy, Kyla," Mum yells up the stairs. "Jazz is here."

As we drive out of the village, there is a line of traffic. We inch along, and eventually reach the reason. There is an ambulance, a few Lorders. The road is blocked one way, a Lorder directing traffic, and we wait our turn to get past. There is a sheet thrown over something on the ground. And a burned-out white van smashed into a tree.

I go cold inside. Because I know what it says, I can just make out the remains of BEST BUILDERS painted down the side of it.

I slip into Nico's office at lunch. He locks the door.

"Rain!" He grins as if ecstatic to see me there, and gathers me in for a hug. I don't hug back.

He lets go. "Ah. Are you upset about yesterday's little charade? Sorry about that, Rain. All for the cause, yes? Sit," he says, and pushes me into a chair. "It's my last day in this place."

"In school?" I ask, surprised.

"Too many plans afoot to spend time here." He winks. "Between us, tonight I will have a family emergency that takes me away."

"How is Dr. Lysander?" I ask, unable to stop myself. "What will happen to her?"

"She is a fascinating woman," Nico says. "Such strength of character."

He says nothing else. Maybe he couldn't get whatever he wants from her. Has he done something to her?

He must see it on my face. "Rain, remember: She is the enemy. Though she is quite safe, for now. But enough of her: We need to talk about what is happening at Chequers. If your adopted mother doesn't do what is right and tell the truth, what then?"

"You said there is another plan. What is it?"

"You, dear one, are plan B."

"What do you mean?"

"Either she tells the world the truth, or she dies. And it has to be on that broadcast, live to the country."

I stare back at him, stunned. "I'm plan B . . . me? I have to do it?"

"There is no other way. Only you and your family will be present at that ceremony. And you go together in a state car, like the prime minister; they aren't security screened. You are the only one who can get a weapon in."

I start to panic. Me, kill someone? Not just anyone . . . but Mum?

"Nico, I—"

"You are the only one who can do this, Rain. The only one who can stop the Lorders. Freedom is there, in your hands: Take it!"

"But I—"

"Don't worry. You won't let me down." He says it with complete assurance, his eyes boring into mine. Eyes that must be obeyed. If Nico says I must do this, that I can do this, it must be so.

Lurking somewhere inside me still, behind the horror: What brought me here today? The *why* behind everything.

"Can I ask a question?" I say, barely daring, but somehow the words come out. "Will you answer it with the truth?"

He holds himself still. "You imply I don't always answer with the truth," he says, a dangerous note in his voice. "You should know better by now. I may not answer every idle curiosity, but when I do, it is always the truth."

Yet Nico's truths are not the same as other people's all the time.

But then he smiles. "You, dear girl, after giving us yesterday's prize, may ask the question of your choice, and I will answer." He sits on the edge of his chair, alert. "Go on."

I swallow. "Why was I Slated?"

"You know why."

"Do I?"

"Or, at least, you knew why. Think. See if you can work it out," he says. "We protected part of you from Slating, didn't we? Your memories are coming back more and more."

And another question slips into view in my mind, as if it had always been there: Why prepare me for Slating unless I was always meant to be Slated? Was this Dr. Lysander's real *why*? My eyes widen with shock.

"What is it?" he asks.

"I was always going to be Slated. It wasn't just a risk, or bad luck I was caught, or any of those things."

He inclines his head. "Bravo, Rain; you remember."

I recoil, shock and horror overcoming fear enough that I don't take them from my face.

"But why?"

"We needed to show the Lorders that they can fail, that we can get around them. That anywhere, anytime, when they least expect it, they are vulnerable."

"But how could you do that to me?"

"Now, Rain, you agreed to this plan. As did your parents. They gave you to us for the cause, for this purpose."

"No," I whisper. "No. They wouldn't."

"They did. Your real dad was in Free UK. He knew there was no future in a country led by Lorders for his child, or any other." His face is full of compassion. "It is the truth you asked for today, and there it is."

I close my eyes, shut out Nico's face and words, and hold on to last night's dream. That man wouldn't do such a thing. He wouldn't hand his daughter over to Nico. Never.

I open them again, this time careful to hide disbelief.

Nico puts a hand on each shoulder. "You made this choice. It is the right choice. You know, firsthand, that Lorders and their Slating must be stopped."

"They must be stopped," I whisper, and I don't have to fake conviction. Truth is freedom; freedom is truth.

"You won't let me down." He leans down, kisses my forehead. "And don't forget what they've done to Ben." A wave of fresh pain rolls through with his name. So much has been crowding inside me that he has been pushed out a little.

"Ben was on our side, too, you know," Nico says. "He'd want you to fight this fight for him."

Nico ushers me out of his office. His words only really sink in as I walk away, out of the building and into a gray November day.

Ben was on the side of Free UK? Nico could only know this if he'd been recruiting Ben.

My hands turn to rigid fists at my sides. I'd always wondered another *why*. Why had Ben suddenly decided to cut off his Levo and thought about joining Free UK in the first place? There could only be one answer: Nico.

He's recruited others from our school, but why Ben? A Slated isn't an ideal recruit: They're not good at keeping secrets and they've got definite issues with violence. Ben could only have been targeted because of me.

• • •

Late that night, there is no sleep. Not for me. Waves of rage pass through my body, a rush of molten metal pulsing through my heart, my veins, at all Nico has done to me. To Ben. A rage that has nowhere to go, and so it grows.

But at the end of it all is still the Lorders. They and their Slating are still the ultimate enemy: It is still them that led me to this moment. They Slated Ben, and took him away. They are still the target. Nico will keep.

I jump with a buzz at my wrist: Nico's com, as if he is listening in on my thoughts and waiting for the right moment. I consider not answering, but press the button. "Yes?" I say, voice low.

"It's Katran. Meet me by your bike in an hour." It clicks off.

40

I SLIP INTO THE DARK SHADOWS BEHIND OUR HOUSE, THEN up the footpath. Too many mysteries make the miles go fast, walking with a head full of questions and half answers.

What is this meeting about? Maybe Nico decided I am too big a risk and sent Katran to eliminate me along with it. My stomach twists to think what Katran did, and has done, and what it makes him: a spiller of blood. A casual murderer.

But years ago, it was Katran who held me in the night when dreams made me cry in terror. Katran, who believes with all he is that what he is doing is the way to overcome the Lorders and make our world a better place.

I'm so lost in thought I almost walk straight into him.

"Hi," I say.

"Watch where you're going," he hisses. "And try to be quiet; I heard you coming a mile off."

"Liar. What's up?"

"Nico sent me."

At his name the anger flares up again, and I clench my fists tight. "Why?"

"He wants me to give you this, but I don't want to give it to you." He reaches into his pocket, and a small gun glistens in his hand in the moonlight. He's going to kill me. I take a step back.

He laughs. "You should see your face. You idiot. It's for Nico's plan

B, so you can kill your mother. But who are you kidding? You'll never be able to do it. Give it up. Run while you still have the chance."

I hold out my hand, willing it to stay steady.

He holds it up as if to pull the trigger. "See here, Rain? You pull this. Close range. Single shot. The damage this can do: destroying tissues, muscle. Blood, Rain: a shower of red, warm blood. It'll spatter all over you."

My stomach twisting, I fight to not imagine what he describes. To keep my hand steady.

He curses under his breath, and the anger on his face changes to something softer. "Rain, please. Think this through. If you manage to pull the trigger, what is going to happen to you? You'll be dead in seconds."

"Give it to me. Do it now."

He drops it into my hand. Shakes his head. Shows me how it works, properly this time—small, single barrel; a holder that straps around the arm to keep it hidden. Special plastic design that should pass general detectors. Close range only. No problem as I'll be right next to Mum, ready if she doesn't give her speech the way Nico wants.

"Nico also wants me to check you are still with us. What has him worried?"

"I figured a few things out, and foolishly spoke to him about it."

"Oh? Like what?"

"Can you answer a question first?"

"You can ask. Can't say that I'll answer."

"How did the Lorders get me? What happened that ended with me being Slated."

Katran goes still, and I start to think he won't answer. Then he sighs, runs his fingers through his hair as he always does when troubled. How can I remember little things like that and not the big things?

"Honestly? I don't know. There was a raid on a Lorder weapons storage site, but I wasn't there. I was supposed to be, but at the last minute Nico sent me off on a stupid errand. I was so angry! Then, when I got back . . ." He shakes his head. "I heard it was an ambush. Somehow they knew we were going to be there. Three killed. You and a few others who were underage taken, presumed Slated. I wasn't there to protect you! Until I met you here, days ago, that was all I knew of what happened to you."

I stare at him, shocked. So many lives wasted. "It wasn't your fault. Besides, what could you have done if you had been there, but get killed?"

"Maybe. I don't know," he says. But Katran has always seemed invincible, like if he had been there things could have turned out different. Is that why he was sent someplace else?

"It wasn't your fault, but I know whose it was."

"The Lorders."

"They did the dirty work, but who set it up?"

"What do you mean?"

"Listen. The thing I worked out today is that I was always meant to be Slated. It wasn't some random act of bad luck that I got caught. I was prepared for it, and it was always in Nico's plans."

"No. No way. Even if that could be true, not with all the others there. No!"

"Well, he couldn't just hand me over to the Lorders and say, 'Here you go, please Slate this girl we've been experimenting on,' could he?"

Katran's fists curl. "If it's true, I'll kill him."

"It's true. He told me so. But what about Free UK and all you've fought for?"

His eyes are wild. "How can I just keep on as if I never knew this? How can I ever trust him again?"

"Simple: Don't trust him. I don't. But that doesn't change what we're working for: the same thing Nico wants. To overthrow the Lorders." I hear myself say the words, hating myself for defending Nico when what happened to me, what happened to Ben, lies at his feet. And to think I'd blamed Aiden when Nico was behind Ben's actions all along. But it was still Lorders who Slated Ben; Lorders who did whatever has been done to him now. "But when the Lorders are gone . . ." I say, and shrug. *After is another time.* Nico won't get away with it. Not now that Katran knows.

"When they're gone . . ." Katran says, and in his eyes, I see Nico's death.

"Do you think it can really happen? Can we win against the Lorders?"

"Yes. We're going to do it this time. We're organized like never before."

"Really?"

"There is so much in place. There will be coordinated attacks all over the country. Key assassinations, too, and all at the exact moment the treaty was signed that began the Central Coalition and their grip on this country. But we still need general support. Without it . . ." He shrugs.

Without it we will ultimately fail.

"We need Mum's speech, for her to tell the truth. But if she doesn't? What then?"

He spins me around, a hand on each shoulder. Eyes intent on

mine. "Nico says plan B. Cut the heart out of the Lorders by killing their hero's daughter. Show that no one is safe, that they are vulnerable everywhere. But don't do it, Rain. Save yourself."

I swallow. "I have to. The Lorders have to go. Remembering things, what Nico has done, doesn't change that."

Katran's dark eyes plead with me to change my mind. Without thought my hand reaches up like it did before, to lightly touch the scar on his face. His *why*. This time he doesn't pull away.

"Katran, you were right, what you said the other day: I need to know what happened to me, and why. Everything."

"Do you really mean it?"

"Yes. Nico said my parents gave me to him. That they and I agreed to have this done to me. I want to know. I *need* to know the truth."

"I've got something for you," he says. "But only if you are sure. Do you want to remember, no matter what?"

"Yes. I'm sure."

He reaches into his shirt, pulls on a bit of leather thong around his neck. When he pulls it out from under his clothes, I see there is something hanging on it.

"What is it?"

He pulls it over his neck and hands it to me. "This is something you gave me, years ago."

The light is faint, and I feel it with my fingers: still warm from his skin, a carved piece of wood, a few centimeters long. A rook. My fingers remember it, and not just as any rook, but *the* rook. My rook. Daddy's. I gasp.

"Do you remember it?"

"I think so. Something from my childhood. I don't understand. Why did I give it to you?"

"Your nightmares were so bad. You said even though you didn't want to lose any more pieces of yourself, you couldn't take that one anymore. You had to let it go, to forget it. Somehow it is tied up with this rook. You asked me to get rid of it for you because you couldn't bear to do it. But I've always kept it, Rain. To keep part of who you were with me. Maybe it will help you remember."

I stare in wonder at Katran. Something of me, next to his heart? "Thanks," I say, and I slip it around my neck, under my clothes. A dread I cannot identify steals over me to feel it against my skin.

"Time to go," he says, but he doesn't move, and neither do I.

"Take care tomorrow," I say. "Fight the good fight." Echoes of Nico whisper in my ears—*die the good death*. A shiver goes up my spine.

"We'll be all right, you and I," he says. Slow, uncertain, he holds out his hands. The violent hands of a killer; gentle hands, that comfort and protect. I move toward him, and he holds me against him. His heart beats mad in his chest. "Go," he says in my ear, and gives me a little push away. "Try to be quiet this time."

I walk off, and moments later hear the faint sounds of his bike.

Back in bed I hold the rook tight. Are my hands the hands of a killer, too? Why is the rook so important? All I know of it is a happy dream memory, playing chess with my dad.

We run. He holds my hand tight, like he will never let it go again.

But my legs are failing, my breath in such great gasps that my chest will surely burst, but still I can't get enough air. Sand slips under my feet, and still I run.

Until I fall. I trip, sprawl, and land on the beach hard, winded. No strength, nothing left.

"Go!" I push him away, but he turns, holds me.

"Never forget," he says. "Never forget who you are!"

And terror is closer. I can hear it, but I can't look. He shields me but I twist and shield him, and my eyes are clenched shut tight. I can't look, I can't.

An echo inside of another time, another place. Midnight terrors, and a gentle voice: Go on and look, Lucy. Face what scares you, and it will lose its power.

I open my eyes. But this time, it isn't like under the bed. This fear is real.

Terror stares back. Wide, pale blue eyes gleam with death, and triumph.

I jump bolt upright in bed, heart thumping a painful beat against my ribs. Terror so real and strong the lights must come on, blankets pulled up to my chin, yet still I shake. Never in all the replays of that nightmare have I dared to open my eyes and see what chases me.

Only one man has eyes like that.

Nico.

I curse the fear that woke me, so close to knowing . . . *What?*

Who was with me? What happened next?

41

"HOW DO I LOOK?" CAM DOES A MODEL TWIRL IN HIS SUIT. Mr. Casual looks surprisingly good in a jacket and tie, but other things are on my mind.

I frown. "Your tie's crooked. Stay home, Cam. You don't want to come today." My eyes plead with him.

He straightens his tie in our hall mirror, faces me. "What's up, Kyla?" he asks. "Tell me."

"Nothing. But this will be boring as hell. You don't have to come; run while you can."

He looks thoughtful, as if he can see there is something that I'm trying to hide. Half opens his mouth to say something else when Dad comes in from the living room.

"Aren't you two a picture," he says.

I'd worn what I was told, without comment. A deep green dress—swishy, silky stuff—luckily with long sleeves. Fits well. Stupid shoes with heels—not my footwear of choice on any day, but today speed might be useful, and if so, they'll have to come off. The cold feel of something round and deadly against my skin, strapped inside my arm.

"Isn't your mother ready yet?"

"I'll go see," I say, and climb the stairs. Knock on their bedroom door. "Mum?"

"Come in," she says.

"Are you all right?"

She shrugs, dabbing powder on her face. "I hate these ceremonies."

"Why? It honors your parents, grieves their loss to you and the country." I parrot the official line on Armstrong Memorial Day. Watch her closely.

"I miss them both so much. But today, here, I am a puppet on a string. This isn't about my parents, or me. It's about *them*."

"Lorders?"

Her eyebrow quirks; she nods.

"Maybe it's time to cut the strings."

She stares back. "Maybe," she finally says, and sighs. "If only it were that simple."

"Can't you just tell how you feel. Tell the truth. Isn't that always the right thing to do?"

"Knowing what is right and wrong isn't the end of it, Kyla. I've lived my life like this: Cut the crap, cut the politics, keep out of it. Look after the people I care about who are here, now. Like you." She touches my cheek and a knife of pain twists, deep inside. "If only everybody did that."

"Maybe, sometimes, here and now aren't as important as doing what is right. Maybe the people you care about will understand." And I know I'm pushing it, that she'll start to wonder. But I can't *not* say it.

She stares back at me. "Maybe."

"Car's here," Dad calls from below.

"Come on," she says. "Time to dance."

Cam walks us to our car. "It's not too late to change your mind," I say to him.

"Not a chance! I'll see you there."

Our limo is a state car, like Nico said it would be. Flags on the hood. A Lorder motorcycle escort in front and behind. Dad is in happy mode as we set out, chatting with Amy. Mum is silent; her eyes are tired, drawn. A face that hasn't slept well. A face that is grappling with decision.

Inside everything is pleading to her silently: *Tell the truth. Do it! Don't make me kill you.*

We near the gates to Chequers, and next to the entrance is a black van. Lorder security. A wave of fear clenches inside: Perhaps it ends here. They will haul me in, search me, find the gun and take me into custody. Surely Coulson would never let me through these doors without making sure, not when he suspects what is true. Not when he doesn't know if I'll stick to our bargain.

But then, like Nico said it would, our limo and escort sweep past the guards and straight through the lodge gates. Down Victory Drive, a gravel lane that sweeps around a lawn with a broken statue.

"See that?" Dad says. "Statue of the Greek goddess of health. Broken by vandals in the riots. They were found, brought here, and executed at the sight of their desecration; it is left as it was to remind us what we fought for."

Executed, there: on the grass. For knocking over a statue? Lorders do these things. Resolve grows hard and cold inside.

We pull in front of the main doors. Guards open them, and we step through and into a stone hall. We follow an official to the Great Hall inside, and I catch my breath. The ceiling is so far above and the space huge, our footsteps small as we walk across it. Massive paintings hang on the walls, portraits of dead people watching on. A crackling fire burns in a white fireplace, two armchairs arranged to one side of it. Cameras and microphone set up show the speech will be here.

An official goes through the order of the day. First, at 1:10 P.M., the moment the bomb went off killing her parents, Mum's live televised speech. Only immediate family will be in attendance: Dad, Amy, me. Then our friends and family—Cam included—will be allowed in, and we'll have tea. Second, and new this year to commemorate twenty-five years since the assassinations, the current prime minister addresses the nation and a select crowd of dignitaries. This will be in the grounds of Chequers, us alongside him, at exactly four P.M., the precise moment the treaty that ended the riots was signed thirty years ago. Then I'm leaving with Cam while Mum and Dad stay for the endless reception and then, later, dinner. Amy, crazy girl, chose to stay for that as well.

But things will never move beyond *first,* will they? One way or the other.

I stare up at the ceiling, so high above. Would a gunshot echo?

"Impressive, isn't it?" Mum says. "Yet it still felt like home. I used to love staying here. There's a library so long you can play cricket in it."

"Did you?"

She winks. "I wasn't much of a reader back then."

We're called to our places. Mum in one chair, Dad in another. Amy and I are to stand behind Mum, a hand each resting on her chair. Lights are checked, then sound; I'm checking things of my own.

Lorders. They are everywhere, but not too close so they stay out of the screen shot. Not close enough to stop her speech if they think it is going wrong, but she'll only have seconds before transmission is cut. I search their faces, convinced Coulson will be here, that he'll stop this before it starts. But he's not.

A girl darts forward and dabs Mum's face with powder.

But if she doesn't give the speech we want, what then?

My head is light. I look up again and feel as if I'm floating above the room. Everything is crawling, each second—*tick, tock*—slowing.

If she doesn't give the speech we want, *then*: I must slip my hand in my sleeve, pull the gun out? No. I'm next to her, no aiming needed. Hand in sleeve, grasp the gun. Shoot her through the sleeve; they won't have a chance to see it, to stop me.

No. She'll tell the truth. She will.

If she does . . . what then? Lorders are still here. Transmission stopped. Will they arrest her? Shoot her? I blink.

Nico said no. They wouldn't dare; they'd have to do things legal and proper for a change. Everyone would be watching how she was dealt with. And that if what she said is proven true, there is no crime of treason. That he's finding Robert, and they'll prove it is true.

Unless they react without thought, shoot her to stop her words before the transmission is cut. My stomach twists. The country would see them in action, see them for what they really are.

But if she doesn't tell the truth . . . I try to reach for the cold resolve I felt earlier, hold it inside. Focus. Hand in sleeve; gun; shoot. I can do this. There will be blood. But not until I've done it, and what does it matter then if I flip out? With all the Lorders here I'll be dead before I have a chance. We'll both be dead.

"Kyla?" Amy pokes me in the side. "Smile."

I compose my face. They're counting down. A light comes on the camera, and then—

She begins.

"Twenty-five years ago today, there was a terrible tragedy with the deaths of William Adam M. Armstrong and his wife, Linea Jane Armstrong, at the hands of terrorists. Our nation lost its prime minister and his wife. I lost both my parents.

"There was no accident to the timing on this day. November twenty-sixth. Thirty years ago today, the treaties were signed in this very room to form our Central Coalition government. The government led by my father that ended the riots, that brought peace back to this country.

"I am here before you with my family now, and I ask myself what my dad would say if he were here. What he would do."

She pauses. There are little white cards clenched in her hands, held together. Not open.

I see the official behind the camera exchange a watchful look with another. She's not on the prepared speech anymore! Hope quickens inside.

"Dad was a man of principle. He believed what he did was right, and he fought to make this country a safe place for his children, and his children's children, at a time of chaos when that seemed an impossible dream. Yet he never knew his own grandson. A son I have also lost."

She really is going to do it. Without thought my hand reaches forward to her shoulder. Mum's hand reaches up, holds mine.

The official is whispering to a technician, listening, watchful.

"One of my beautiful daughters reminded me today of what is important: to do what is right. To tell the truth. But the truth to me is this: It is time to stop focusing on past tragedies. We can't go back, only forward. It is time for our country to focus on what is good, on what we can do for our children and our children's children."

The Lorders are alert; her words are getting close to the line now.

Her eyes flick to them. She turns around to Amy and me, smiles.

A Lorder moves toward the camera technicians.

Time is running out! *Say it now!* I plead inside. *Say what happened to Robert.*

She turns back and faces the camera. "Thank you," she says.

I'm frozen. That's all? It was in her eyes, that moment when she turned to Amy and me. She wasn't going to do or say anything to put us in danger. That was it. She still holds my hand, the hand that should be slipping up my sleeve now, reaching for the means to end her life. Mine as well.

An official steps up. We are in front of the camera next to him, still transmitting live. He thanks Mum, starts to explain the order of the day. And all the while I could let go of her hand. Reach inside my sleeve. There is time. The seconds are slowing down; each tick of the clock sounds further apart, each an eon of decision.

Think.

Cut the heart out of the Lorders. That is what Katran said; parroting Nico, without doubt. His words I recognize.

We need popular support: Katran again. But how could killing Mum, the daughter of the Lorder hero, achieve this? The hole in logic is gaping in front of me. It could have the opposite effect, swing opinion away from us. Surely Nico realizes this.

Nico says we must strike at the Lorders wherever and however we can: show their vulnerability . . . ?

No.

I push their words away. It is just me, alone, in this moment.

Here, now: I decide. I'm not who I was, or who Nico wants me to be. I almost gasp out loud when I realize:

Who I am is what I choose to do.

Just like Mum. Who she is, at her core, is made up of all the decisions she makes. She did what she thought was right: pushed the boundaries of what she said, but not too far. To protect us.

I can't do it.

I won't do it.

The camera light goes out. Too late. It is too late for her to say what she should have said.

Too late for me to do what I never could.

"Are you all right, Kyla?" Mum says. "You look pale."

"I've got a headache," I say truthfully. People have spilled into the Great Hall now for tea and cakes. A few familiar faces, but many more that are not. And Lorders, everywhere: watchful eyes that will take more notice of Mum now.

Everything is shifting, shaking inside. She couldn't do anything to put us in danger, no matter what she thought. I couldn't hurt her, either. All this feeling: Is it a trap? The ties that tangle our loyalties, Nico would say. He was wrong about me. I couldn't do it.

"Go if you want," Mum says. "You don't need to stay for the second ceremony. You only really needed to be here for the first one, the family photo op." She rolls her eyes. She beckons to Cam. "Why don't you two go now?"

"Sure," he says. "This suit is itchy. Come on, Kyla."

We are told to follow an official: down hallways, out a door. Across a lawn to the parking lot with Cam's car.

As we walk, thoughts tumble inside. What happens now? Nico said the Free UK attacks were timed to go with Mum's speech that the Lorders Slated her son, or her death. Neither happened. Is it all off?

Nico will be livid at my failure. I sigh. Not just angry; lethal. I'm dead.

Maybe Katran will try to stop him. But—

Katran. He said the attacks were timed for when the treaty was signed: the second ceremony. Nico said for the first. Did I hear one of them wrong? I frown to myself. No, I'm sure I didn't. What did Katran say? Attacks and assassinations timed together, at the second ceremony. It takes place at four P.M.

Assassinations . . . does that include Dr. Lysander? Pain twists inside.

We've reached Cam's car now and get in. An official signals us to wait. Another state limo is coming up the drive, motorbikes in front and behind. It stops, and the door is held open; we catch a glimpse of untidy blond hair before security flank the prime minister, hiding him from sight. They walk up the steps and into Chequers. Once the door shuts, we get the signal to go.

"You've missed your chance to meet the prime minister," Cam says as we head down the drive and out the gate. I don't answer. "What's wrong?" he asks.

I shake my head, close my eyes, lean back against the seat. Dr. Lysander has been pushed out of my thoughts by everything else. Or maybe I was avoiding thinking what would happen to her.

All along, even when I didn't understand what she was doing, she has protected me. To the point of falsifying hospital records. She has broken rule after rule to tell me what I needed to know. And the biggest of them all in meeting me outside of the hospital. Nico said that to her, I am the child she never had. Yes, she is part of the whole Lorder regime that I hate. But because of me, her guard is dead and she is a prisoner.

Dr. Lysander is part of my family in the ways that count. She, like Mum, would protect me if she could. Mum's words earlier, at home: *look after the people you care about, who are here, now.*

I glance at my watch: 2:20.

"Kyla?"

"Cam? Do you remember when you said if there was anything you could do to help, you'd do it?"

"Of course."

"Can you drive home really fast so I can change? Then drop me off someplace else. But the really important bit is, no questions asked."

He grins and hits the accelerator.

Racing up the stairs at home, I kick off my heels and unzip the dress as I go. I chuck the dress on my bedroom floor, yank on jeans, a dark top. I hate the feel of Nico's gun on my skin, but leave it strapped to my arm. I might need it. I start racing for the door, then pause.

Nico's com. It might be a tracker as well as a com, and I don't want him to know where I'm going. I pause, fiddle under my Levo to try to find a release on it. Curse, about to give up, when my nail finally finds an edge. A pinch and it is off. I chuck it in a drawer of clothes and sprint downstairs.

Cam is already at his car, changed as well. "That was quick," he says. "Is there some kind of emergency?"

"No questions, remember?" I say, then relent. "You could say I've just got to help a friend."

I give him directions as we go, all the while wondering: What am I doing? Do I dare? Can I oppose Nico?

Yes.

For too long I've been pulled one way, then another, between who I was, and who I am. But who do I want to be?

Who I am now and what I do, now, will be decided by me, and me alone.

There are so many big questions: political ones. The sort embroiling Katran and Nico. The Lorders are wrong, so wrong, but is cutting their throats one at a time any sort of answer? I'd convinced myself that Nico was right; that, as Rain, I'd already made this choice, long ago; that we should use any means necessary. But I was wrong. It isn't my answer.

I direct Cam down the single track road, the way Nico had taken me the first time, and then feel a sudden constriction of fear: What if he comes this way today? But it is too late to turn back.

"Stop here," I say finally. "You'll have to reverse back a bit before you can turn around."

"Here? Are you sure?" Cam peers out at the overhanging trees.

"Yes. Here. Thanks."

"Isn't it about time you told me what is really going on?" He pauses, peers closer at my face. "Hallelujah! You actually *are* going to tell me something, aren't you?"

"One thing," I say. "You know those Lorders we were introduced to the other day? They might be pissed off at me, and I really hope that it doesn't extend to you. I just wanted to warn you. I'm sorry."

"Pissed off Lorders I like, though not in my immediate vicinity. But if they're going to be that way anyhow, let me come with you. Maybe I can help."

"No."

He sighs. "Are you sure you'll be all right?"

"Positive," I lie, hand on the car door, poised to run if he tries to follow.

"Good luck," he says.

"Bye now, Cam," I say, and get out, slip into the trees. I linger out of sight to be sure he goes. He reverses back up the lane, disappears from sight.

That felt *wrong*. Why, I can't quite work out. Did he give up too easily? I listen until the engine sounds fade away and are gone.

Cam is one of the worst of many points of guilt in all of this. It isn't his fault he came to the Lorders' attention; it was purely because of me. I hope, so hard, nothing will come back to bite him. If today works, if Dr. Lysander escapes, Coulson will know soon enough what I've been up to. I can't imagine he'll be too happy about it.

42

AT KATRAN'S HIDE, WHERE BIKES WERE HIDDEN THE FIRST time I came this way, the tarp is lower than I hoped. I pull it back to be sure, and sigh: no bikes here today. They must all be at the house: I'll have to walk. Fast.

The air is damp and heavy, still, wet. The sky is darkening. I think I hear muffled sounds, someone or something hidden inside it. Imagination on overtime, I keep turning, sure I've heard a distant twig snap or something in the trees. But if I double back, silent and careful, nothing is there.

As I walk, I consider the weak point of the plan: Who is guarding Dr. Lysander? If Katran has things straight with the four P.M. attacks, everyone who can be should be deployed; it may be just one guard outside her locked door. How do I get them out of the house and distracted enough to free Dr. Lysander? I have no illusions on an all-out battle: The only way I could really hurt anyone is in self-defense. Like with Wayne. I wince inside: I can't feel sorry, exactly, that he is dead. It may be at Nico's hands, but it is still another death that is my fault.

Focus.

If Nico is at the house, I'm in real trouble. He shouldn't be; he should be coordinating the attacks.

Unless he is the one to kill Dr. Lysander at four P.M.

You could always back out, run away. Hide.

No. It is time I faced up to the trouble I've caused. I hurry up the path, half walking, half running. One eye on my watch: 3:15 now, and I go faster, examining and rejecting plans on the way. There are too many unknowns.

I reach the place the bikes are stashed near the house—nearly there. Again overcome by a feeling of being watched, so strong, I stop, hold my breath, and listen, but can hear nothing. The only movement is a hawk circling overhead, eye on some prey far below. Fear and imagination, that is all.

Silent, I slip through trees around the house, under cover, out of sight. No cars: Nico isn't here! The relief is so strong I sag against a tree. As much as I try to keep up the pretense that I could stand up to him, could I? Really? Apart from the usual hold he has on everyone, there is another on me, until recently buried so far down I didn't know it. He is my terror. The black stuff of nightmares.

There is a movement at the door; I scrunch down. A dark-haired figure steps out, chucks remains of a cup out on the ground and goes back inside: Tori. She is the guard? And perhaps executioner as well.

Otherwise the house still looks abandoned, empty. My eyes can search out the little details that say otherwise only because they know where to look. I see and avoid the tiny trip wire that encircles it, hidden in the undergrowth, a warning system for those inside.

Yet—something still feels *wrong*.

A silence, not from the house, but around me, as if the trees hold their breath. Birds are silent. The wind itself, and—

I retrace my steps. There is a slight *crack,* left. I spin around, foot up for a looping kick, but pull it back at the last second.

"Cam? What the hell are you doing here?" I say in a fierce whisper, and pull him back into the trees.

He grins. "I couldn't let you go without making sure you were all right. What's going on?"

"Don't look so pleased with yourself. This isn't a game!" And I am angry: at myself for taking the easy way, letting him drive me; at him, for following; at myself again for not catching him at it sooner.

He pulls the smile away, but it stays in his eyes. "Sorry, miss."

"Go back the way you came, and do it now."

"No way. I'm not leaving. You might as well let me help you. What is it? You said you were helping a friend, yet if it is your friend in there, you are very careful to circle their house, check it out, be quiet. Shall I go knock on the door and see if they're in?" He takes one step forward, and I grab his shoulder, pull him back again.

"You're really not going to leave quietly, are you?"

"No," he says, and this time there is a serious determination in his eyes, one that was there all along behind the jokes.

"Cam, you don't know what you're getting into."

"So tell me."

I sigh, pull him farther back into the trees. Trapped.

"It's like this: There is someone locked in the house, and I want to bust them out."

"A jailbreak. Good, I like it."

"I'm hoping there is only one guard."

"Right." He drops into a crouch, fists up. "Want me to take him out for you?"

I roll my eyes. "It's a her, and shut up and let me think."

He stays quiet. I need to distract Tori thoroughly. A fight is one way, but there is another: Ben. I sigh inside. All these points of guilt that need to be dealt with in this effort to do what is right. I have to tell her Ben is still alive. That should be enough to get her attention away from her guard duties.

"Okay, how about this," I say. "I'll go in, get her to come out for a talk. I'll walk her around the side of the house. You slip in the house, unlock the door, and get the prisoner out." I explain to him the layout inside, where the key is in Nico's desk drawer. Hoping that Tori doesn't grab it when she comes out.

"Yep, got it," he says. "No problemo."

I shake my head. There could be all sorts of problems.

I get Cam to hide around the side of the house, away from the door so she won't see him when we come out. "I'll go back around so I come out of the trees at the right place, in case she watches the paths. So give it a few minutes."

As I cut back through the woods, careful still not to make a sound, something niggles inside. This still feels so *wrong*. He shouldn't be here, but it is more than that. *How* is he here?

I stop in my tracks and consider the doubt twisting inside. I'd been so busy being angry and trying to work out how to get him to go, and then what to do when he wouldn't, that I didn't focus on the one crucial thing.

How did he follow me? He would have been well behind. He drove far enough back up the road that I couldn't hear his car anymore, then would have had to double back on the road and into the woods. How did he know which way to go? I was going at speed—how did he even keep up?

I cross my arms when it hits me: Either he is a master at following and running silently, or, far more likely, he hung back because somehow, there is a tracker on me. I don't understand this; it doesn't fit. Cam?

I slip back to his position, quiet and careful. Maybe he was just lucky, went the right way and stumbled onto the bike path. Once you get far enough in, it is marked enough to follow without too much difficulty.

Not likely.

He is still where I left him, waiting, as instructed. I creep closer, quiet. His back is to me; he is leaning over, doing something with his hands. There is a faint metallic *click.* He turns slightly, and I see the gun in his hand, the deadly expression on his face.

Cam? With a gun?

The shock is so great that I get stupid, shift back on my feet. He turns to the noise, sees me, and there is no choice now but attack. I spin a kick at his wrist. The gun flies through the air.

"Who *are* you?" I manage to spit out.

No answer. But now there is a knife in his hand. He dives, feints to one side. I roll, but not fast enough; there is pressure, a cut, into my shoulder. And I remember the gun strapped to my arm, fumble to get it out, but he dives again and there is another slash of heat at my side, a deeper one. The hell with diversion; I need help. I stumble back into the hidden trip wire and collapse.

Cam walks up and smiles, but it isn't in his eyes, and this isn't the Cam I thought I knew.

"Who are you? What are you?" I whisper again, pressing my hands to my side, and there is red and sticky wet on my fingers. The world spins. His image splits into four or five Cams, suddenly ugly, changed.

Facing me, he is turned away from the house. He doesn't see Tori appear around the side of it, or the gun in her hand. Indecision on her face, bad shot that she is. She creeps close and hits him with it, hard, in the back of his head.

There is a sickening *thud*. He turns, then tumbles facedown to the ground.

She walks around and kicks him over, but he stays still. "Who is this?" She turns to me, finally notices I'm bleeding, not moving. Rushes over.

Some part of my mind notes that Nico would be *so* unimpressed with her. Not checking for other attackers, or covering Cam in case he can get up, or anything.

I groan, the beginnings of a plan forming. "I'm dying," I whisper, though I doubt it. Messy, but superficial cuts; blood is doing its usual thing and almost making me pass out, but not from the wounds. But Tori doesn't know that.

Freaked, she looks. No illusions I'm her favorite person, but she knows Nico wants me, for whatever reason.

"Tori," I whisper. "Doctor, I need a doctor now, it's the only way . . ." My voice trails away, and my eyes close. I slump back in the best form of imitating unconsciousness I can muster, then peek between my lashes. To her credit, she gives Cam an experimental kick to check he is neutralized before running back into the house.

I breathe in, out, in, out; forcing myself to ignore the red seeping from my shoulder, at my side. I test my limbs, but just a little movement and everything spins sickeningly. Not good enough. I curse inside.

A moment later, Dr. Lysander appears in the door. She runs over to me, Tori behind her, gun trained on her back.

She crouches down, checking, pulling at my clothes. Dr. Lysander must realize I shouldn't be unconscious just from this. She is between Tori and me, blocking Tori's view. I open my eyes and wink. Her eyes widen.

"I need a tourniquet, now," she says. "Get me a first aid kit!"

Tori hesitates.

"Go! Get it, or she'll die."

Tori scampers into the house. I sit up. "Run," I say, and point. "Straight through there is a path; go left when it branches."

"Not without you."

"Go! Do it. I can't; I'm half blood-tranced."

"No." She pulls me to my feet. My legs wobble underneath me, but she puts a determined arm around my waist, and we start to hobble into the woods.

Then Tori bursts out of the house. Drops the first aid kit and dives for her gun.

But before she can reach it there is a loud *bang,* and wood splinters over our heads. "The next one won't be in a tree," a voice says. A voice that makes me tremble.

We stop. Turn around.

And there is Nico, gun pointed at my head. "Now. Would somebody like to tell me what the hell is going on here?"

43

"I'M FEELING RATHER ANGRY," NICO SAYS. HIS EYES AND voice are ice; not just cold, but glacial. "Someone must pay.

"You." He glances at Tori while still holding his gun trained directly on me. "You did one right thing, at least. Calling me. I was nearly here anyhow, so came up quietly to see what the emergency was, and what do I find? You let our prisoner out," he says to Tori.

He turns and trains his gun on her.

She blanches. "No, Nico; no, I—"

"You deny that you unlocked the door?"

"No, but—"

"It was my fault," I say.

He spins back to face me. "And who is that?" He gestures at Cam, bleeding and still on the ground.

"Just someone from school; but I don't know. Something else, too. He followed me. He shouldn't have been able to do it."

"You let someone follow you *here*?" He shakes his head in disgust. "Such stupidity I am surrounded by! Who shall pay?" He sighs. He cocks the gun at me, and Dr. Lysander steps forward and raises a hand, about to say something, but I pull her back.

He pulls the trigger; it rings out loud in the woods. Over our heads again.

I stand frozen. Fear. Shock. Eyes turned as far as they can be from Cam, from blood on the back of his head, from my blood also, but I cannot collapse now, I can't. Breathing deeply, blanking it from my mind. Holding it away, to one side, so *now* can be dealt with.

"And you, Rain. Such deceit; it wounds me. Why aren't you at Chequers right now where you should be?"

"I couldn't do it. I couldn't hurt her, of all people. She's done nothing to deserve getting shot."

He shakes his head. "Stupid girl. If she'd made her speech as we wanted, that would have been icing on the cake. But you needed *to be there* at four! You idiot." He is shaking with fury.

Yet . . . why did I need to be there at four? The seconds are ticking along. It is 3:50 P.M. now. What was going to happen there at four? I'm confused. I was supposed to kill her at the first ceremony, inside.

Unless he always knew I wouldn't be able to do it.

The rage in Nico's eyes is absolute. "After all I've done for you." He shakes his head. Steadies the gun again. "I should do this, right now, but I will not. There is a reason, you know," he says conversationally. "You must live to die another day. Your death can still have such impact! It would have been the perfect occasion for it today. But no matter. Another time. If we have to drug you up and prop you up, we'll see to it you are on film and screen forevermore: the angelic-looking little blond Slated girl who kills people, and takes her own life."

I shake my head, not understanding. Too horrified to move, too scared to speak.

"Of course. It makes sense now," Dr. Lysander says. "You want to publicly prove a Slated can be violent, to strike at all the Lorders are doing in one swoop. But what about all the Slateds? What would happen to them?"

Realization seeps through my numb fear. "The Lorders would see us all as a risk. They wouldn't know who might turn. What would they do about it?"

"Any atrocities the Lorders commit further our cause. Give us more supporters. Tori," he barks. "Lock these two up together."

She stands there, staring at him. Confusion on her face. "But what will happen to all the Slateds?"

He rolls his eyes. Raises his gun and points it at her. Then her eyes focus behind him; I see it as he does. There is a split second where he wonders if she is misdirecting him, but before he can decide his gun flies through the air, kicked out of his hand. By Katran.

"You bastard," Katran snarls. Nico feints, spins around, and knocks Katran off his feet.

"Tori!" Nico shouts. "Choose sides."

Tori picks up Nico's gun, stares at it in her hand.

She looks to me and then back at the gun. I walk over, feet still faltering but stronger now. "Give it to me," I say. Hold out my hand.

Nico and Katran grapple on the ground. There is a flash of silver and Katran cries out: Nico has sliced into his arm with a hidden knife. Nico scrambles to his feet, knife out. Lunging. Katran rolls away and pulls out his knife. Gets to his feet.

"Ben is alive!" Nico yells. "She knows it."

Tori's face contorts. She raises the gun. I dive and a shot ricochets behind me.

Dr. Lysander is frozen. "Run," I scream at her, and this time she does, into the trees, me following behind, my muscles working again enough to stumble along but not keep up. Crying inside with each step with fear for Katran. Nico can't win that fight. Can he?

But then there are new sounds: shouts. Feet thudding.

I look back, and there, through the trees: Lorders. Half a dozen of them at least, converging on the house on foot.

RUN.

"Stop," a voice says in front. A voice I know.

And I do just that. Instead of diving, attacking, anything, I just stop.

Facing me is Coulson.

"You could have made things much easier on yourself if you'd just *told me* what was happening here. Luckily young Cam called us in and tracked you here."

"Tracked me? How?"

He taps his forehead, half smiles. An unnatural movement of his facial muscles. A gun has appeared in his hands and is pointed at my head.

After everything, is this it? There are shouts, fighting, and noise behind us that gradually fade away until all there is, is here, and now. My eyes and his. My legs are jelly. I half fall to my knees.

"Let me go," I whisper.

"I can't do that."

"Please."

He shakes his head. What happens beyond us is still dim, a distant other place, unconnected to this moment. Yet some persistent sound intrudes, nears. Until—

Coulson steadies the gun in both hands and pulls the trigger.

44

INSTEAD OF BEING THROWN BACK, PINNED BY A BULLET TO A swift death, instead of this, there is a thud and cry behind. I spin around.

"Katran?"

His hands are clutching his chest. *Red red red* spreading out as he falls to the ground, and inside I'm spinning, everything going gray, about to disappear and take me from this new horror, and—

No. I fight inside as much, as strong, as I can. *NO.* I crawl to him, take his hand, wrap my arms around him. His body shudders, and *red red red . . .*

"Sorry, I'm sorry, I'm sorry," I'm saying over and over, and his eyes are mirrors of the shock in mine. Katran is invincible; we can't believe *this.* Then—a slight shake to his head, his eyes change, he tries to speak but coughs, and there is more blood, more seeping red. The words won't come, but his eyes speak. *Love's eyes.* "No, Katran, no. Don't go!" I say, shocked but knowing the truth of how he feels at the same time. How he has always felt, and the anger he hid his feelings behind. The anger that tried to push me away, away from Nico and Free UK. To keep me safe.

His eyes go blank, his body stops shuddering.

No.

NO NO NO and I'm screaming inside and outside, and then, all at once, I am *remembering*. Another place and time, too like this to hide from any longer. One I never want to go to, but get dragged back to, again and again.

THEN

I didn't know him at first. Not with my eyes.

The changes were marked, his face so forgotten. Consciously, at least. Yet something almost *chimed* inside: a confusion of terror and longing, tangled together. I didn't understand, but stared whenever I could.

He was there, at that place, delivering food and other supplies. But not just a delivery person; he was one of them, that was plain. I saw him through the bars at my window, talking with the guards. From the room that was mine and had been two years now.

Once a week he'd come, stay one night in the building next door, and then be gone. One day, he saw me looking out the window, and something crossed his face. Some marked desperation, in a flash replaced by a gentleness that didn't belong. I dived back in my room, shaken and confused.

Every week he came he'd have a special look for me if he found my eyes. A kind look in a place without them.

He started bringing a bottle and other things for the guards, slipping them out of his coat and into theirs. Then one week, most of the guards got very ill. Food poisoning, but no one else got sick. And he stayed the week, filling in, and I saw him more, not just through my window. He was there when I was coming and going to sessions with Doctor Craig; to weapons training under watch of the cold one with the strange eyes who led the guards.

Then one day he slipped something in my hand. I almost cried out:

a slip of paper. A note. I tucked it away, read it later. *Lucy, I know I look different: I'm in disguise. But it is me: it's Daddy. We'll get you out of here, and I'll take you home as soon as I can work out how. I love you.*

And I tore it up into as many little pieces as made it dust. I don't have a family anymore. Doctor Craig has said so, over and over. And even if he is my dad—my thoughts tripped over themselves to even think the label in my thoughts—*he* gave me away. He didn't want me.

I didn't believe in him in my mind, but some other part of me did, and I'd catch myself: hoping, feeling. Things Doctor Craig didn't like, like remembering things I must forget.

Then one night I was asleep, and then, somehow, the one who gave me the note was in my room. Talking in a low voice with such sadness of other times, other places. And it made me want to cry out, to scream. Get the guards and make his voice stop and go away and never be heard again. But I didn't.

He was making plans. We'd go next week. But I shook my head no; scared of what, I don't know. Of leaving a place I hated? Confusion and longing mixed in together. Then he held out his hand. In it, a small bit of carved wood, like a castle.

When I tucked it into my left hand, there was something, some memory. And all at once others tumbled inside.

"Daddy?" I whispered, and he smiled with such joy.

He took the rook back. "I better keep this safe for now, so no one sees it. But if you find it tucked hidden on your window ledge, that is the night we go. Be ready."

And every night, I checked. Then finally it was there: hidden against the side and a bar where it could not be seen, only felt and rescued by small fingers.

That night the house was quiet when he unlocked my door and

took my hand. "Quiet," he breathed, and we slunk down the hall and out the door. But what of the guards? None were there, but as we crept down the side of the house I saw feet sticking out behind a hedge.

He whispered in my ear of a boat waiting at the beach, that we had to be quick to get the tide. We crept through the outer dunes that led to the sea when it happened. A distant noise. Voices.

"Time to run, Lucy."

And we ran. He held my hand, and we ran and ran. There were voices, sounds behind us, getting closer. "Faster!" he said, and we ran.

Over and over my feet pounded on sand that slipped and gave way.

Then I tripped, fell. He tried to pull me to my feet, but exhaustion, terror, fixed me to the spot. "I can't," I cried.

"Never forget," he said. "Never forget who you are!"

And they are on us. I'm grabbed, pulled away. Daddy is pushed back down on the sand.

The cold one smiles, raises a gun.

"Lucy, close your eyes," Daddy says. "Don't look." His voice calm, reassuring.

I stare at the gun. *No. He is just scaring him like he does me all the time. He won't do it, he won't.*

Will he?

"Look away, Lucy," Daddy says, but my eyes are open wide, and as if something controls them other than me, they are caught, trembling, unable to look away or do anything else.

Moments combine and spread out, a flash in succession and all at once. The deafening noise. The rook clenched tight in my hand. The red that spreads out from one place until there is more and more of it, and still I can't look away. The hands that hold me back let go, and I run to him just in time for his eyes to hold mine before they close forever.

Seeing what scares you for what it is does not lessen the terror. It still has the power to break your heart, over and over again.

45

MOVEMENT. DIMLY PERCEIVED, BUT IGNORED. UNTIL IT stops and a thump of my head against something hard forces me back to *now,* to my body, to consciousness. I open my eyes, struggle to sit up. Unsure how much time has passed.

I'm on the ground near the house. I feel my arm; the gun that was strapped there is gone. A Lorder with a gun of his own stands close by, pivots toward me when I move, watchful.

Coulson is barking at other Lorders who disappear into the woods, hunting somebody. Who?

Tori is held by a Lorder, one arm pinned behind her back suggesting she's been giving trouble. Cam is sitting up, facing away. A medic is checking his head. Dr. Lysander is here also, speaking to Coulson. Katran is—and I swallow—dead: I count him on a list of those whose whereabouts need listing, but shy away from any thought of the gaping loss. Of my part in it.

The only one unaccounted for is Nico. He got away?

Nico runs, and they chase. If caught, will he be shot in the woods like my father on the beach? Like Katran. Both pains are so huge they threaten to take over, engulf me, so all there is, is pain. One current, one years ago but forgotten. Both fresh as today.

Later.

Dr. Lysander catches sight of where I've been dumped. She leaves Coulson in midsentence and hurries over.

She kneels down, touching, checking, pulling at my clothes. "Where are you hurt?" And I can't answer, can't speak. Where don't I hurt? But then I realize it is all the fresh blood on my clothes that has her attention. Katran's blood.

"Not all my blood," I manage, a whisper.

Coulson walks over, skirting past a few bodies on the ground. Bodies dressed in Lorder black.

"I've told them you got me out, hadn't called them in yet for my safety," Dr. Lysander says, her voice low and hurried.

Everything is remote. Cam was part of the Lorders he claimed to hate? *He betrayed you,* a voice whispers inside, but even that is something for later. I can't deal with anything beyond the fact of my father's death.

And Katran: Coulson killed him. Given a chance, Katran would have killed any of these Lorders without thought. And them likewise. Nico kills even his own to further the cause of killing them. "What does it all mean? What is it for?"

"Hush," Dr. Lysander says, and I realize the last thing I'd said out loud.

"And there she is," Coulson says. "Will she live?" he asks her.

"I expect so. She needs some stitches."

His cold eyes sweep across me, assessing. "I understand we owe Dr. Lysander's safety to your actions. We will investigate further, and see what has happened here. But tell me now: Who is the one who has eluded us?"

What loyalty do I have to the man who murdered my father?

None.

"Nico. Nicholas. Surname unknown."

Coulson pauses, a glint in his eyes. "He is known to us."

He nods at the Lorder whose gun is trained on me. "She is free to go. For now." He turns to me. "I'll be in touch."

Tori's face contorts with fury. She lunges, a sudden movement that surprises her guard. She breaks free and is almost on me before being dragged back.

"Traitor!" she screams. "Kyla, or Rain, or whoever you are, I'll get you. I'll hunt you down and gut you with my knife." She is dragged away, thrown in the back of a Lorder van. But not before I see the hate in her eyes.

46

COULSON HAS ONE OF THE LORDERS DRIVE ME HOME AFTER
a stop at a local hospital for stitches. In one of their black vans, but
this time, sitting in the front. Distaste is all over his face at the state of
me, but I don't care. Too much *caring* screams inside.

It is late evening now. Dark. As we go down the main road of our
village, I wonder absently if curtains twitch in kitchens and bedroom
windows at the sight of a Lorder van going by?

It pulls in front of our house. Dad's car is here. The front door
springs open: Mum.

"Get out," the Lorder says, voice flat.

I open the van door, step down. Start walking stiffly to the house
as he pulls away.

"Oh my God," Mum says. "What has happened to you? What have
they done?" I sway on my feet, and she tries to grab me.

I shrug her off. "I'm fine," I say, the biggest lie of all, and walk in
the front door.

Amy's shocked face appears from the kitchen. Silent.

Dad walks over from the lounge, and looks me up and down.
Smiles. Claps his hands: once, twice, again; slow and deliberate. He
knows; somehow, he knows. *Lorder,* my mind processes. Not just an
informer, but one of them.

Mum looks between him and me.

"Kyla?" she asks uncertainly. "What has happened?"

But I stare at Dad. "You didn't just report me to the Lorders. You're one of them."

He doesn't answer; his eyes shift uneasily to Mum, and back again.

"Doesn't matter," I say, realization sinking in. Cam was here, worming his way into my life before I even made that drawing of the hospital. They were keeping their eyes on me *anyhow*, like Coulson said. All Dad did by reporting me and getting us hauled in was tip me off that I was watched. "You're a small fish, aren't you? They didn't even tell you what was really going on in your own home. Then when you finally noticed something, they told you to shut up and keep out of it."

His mouth starts to open, then shuts again.

"Kyla?" Mum says again, but I can't talk anymore, not now.

"Excuse me," I manage. "I need to clean up." I walk up the stairs. Lock the bathroom door. Strip and chuck my clothes covered in a bit of my and more of Katran's blood into the garbage bin. Moving stiff, slow, like a puppet. Not quite in control of my body with so much control required elsewhere. To stop myself from curling into a ball in the corner and screaming, over and over.

Blood washes away; I know this. Soon I'm clean, skin soft and smooth. A few new scars on the way, courtesy of Cam. Half a dozen stitches in my shoulder, more on my side. Painkillers still in my system to help me go on, but they do nothing for the real damage, inside.

But I'm never forgetting anything, ever again. No matter what it is, or how bad it hurts. Nico and that doctor—Doctor Craig—in that place I didn't even remember properly until this afternoon: They taught me ways to forget, to hide. And my missing years, between Lucy disappearing at age ten and Rain taking over at fourteen? That is where I was. With them, being forced to split down the middle, so that part could be hidden behind a wall in my mind and survive Slating.

And the brick, big enough to smash me in two: now I know what it was. Watching Nico kill my father. When Katran died in my arms, it brought it all back.

In my room I get into pajamas and wrap a blanket tight around myself. There is a light knock at the door.

Amy peeks in. "Want some company?" she asks, hesitant. I shrug. She comes in, and Sebastian follows. He jumps up on the bed, climbs into my lap. Amy gets up next to me. Puts an arm around my shoulders. I wince and move her hand so it isn't on my stitches, then droop against her.

There are echoes of voices downstairs. Heated voices.

"They sent me upstairs," Amy says.

"Oh?"

"I'm sorry."

"What for?"

"For telling Dad about your drawing. Mum got him to admit he reported it. I can't believe it." Amy's face is a picture of shock.

"What else did he say?" I ask, my voice sounding dim and distant to my ears, like I'm talking underwater.

"Stuff I can't believe. That you've been some sort of double agent for the Lorders. Mental."

"Yeah. Mental," I whisper.

"Do you want to talk about it?"

I shake my head and instead of asking twenty questions like I expect, she seems almost relieved, says nothing else. But she stays, warm and solid, next to me.

There is a sudden slam of a door downstairs. A car starts out front, squeals up the road, and is gone. There is a long pause, then footsteps on the stairs. The door opens and Mum stands there, quiet, taking in the two of us and the cat snuggled up together.

"What a good idea," she says, and manages to slot herself in by my other side. A tight squeeze.

I must drift to sleep. Hours later when I wake, the room is dark, and the only one still with me is the cat.

The numb blankness is seeping away, leaving nothing but pain behind. I cry for the little girl I was who I can't even remember apart from the fact that she loved her dad. I cry for him and all he did to try to rescue her, no matter how she ended up there in the first place. I cry that I failed him, utterly: *Never forget who you are,* he said, and I did. I cry for Katran, whose flaws were obvious, but whose caring was not. When he could have run, gotten away like Nico, he came back for me. Trying to save me led to his death.

And I cry for myself, who I am now. Where is my place in this world?

A LORDER COMES FOR ME DAYS LATER. ANOTHER BLACK VAN out front early in the morning, and I suppress the urge to run, to hide. Where am I going to go? And I wonder if it's the back or the front of the van for me today. Have they worked out it was because of me that Dr. Lysander was a prisoner in the first place?

But the Lorder gets out and opens the passenger-side door, and off we go. *Take me to your leader*—a random thought I almost say out loud, and have to clamp down a hysterical giggle that works its way up my throat.

We drive on awhile. "Where are we going?" I try, but the driver stays silent.

In the outskirts of London we go through a secure, guarded gate, into an ugly concrete building with thick walls. Looks like it is meant to withstand angry citizens.

I follow him out of the van to an office door. He gestures, and I go in. I hear the click of a lock behind me.

There is a huge wooden desk, plush chairs. I stand, uncertain, then think, *Oh what the hell,* and give in to the urge to sit on the massive desk chair. It reclines and spins, and I'm giving it an experimental twirl around when the door opens.

Coulson.

Katran's killer. He stares at me and I stare back, unflinching on the outside, unwilling to let him see the pain, the fear. Inside all I see is his hands, the gun in them, Katran, and—

He narrows his eyes, and I spring out of the chair.

"Luckily for you I'm in a good mood today," he says, though his words and the fact that I'm still alive are all there are to show for it. His features are as expressionless and cold as always. "Sit, there," he barks, pointing at a chair opposite his desk, and I scramble to obey.

"We had an arrangement," he says. "You haven't done things in exactly the way I would have preferred, yet the result is satisfactory. Shortly we'll be transporting you to the hospital to have your Levo removed."

I look at the useless thing on my wrist. Wow. What a great prize. Of course, he doesn't know that my Levo is useless. He must think I've been on Happy Pills all this time to stop from going under.

"But there is one other thing you must do for us."

Everything twists and tumbles inside. "What is that?"

"If you see or hear anything of Nico, let us know."

If there is anyone I'd enjoy turning in to the Lorders, it is Nico, yet I'm filled with disbelief. "He's not been captured?"

A quirk of annoyance crosses his face. "No. But we have dismantled most of his evil little plans." His lips curl up in grim satisfaction. "Much of that because of you."

I flinch. Once I saw things clearly, I didn't want to be part of Free UK, part of their explosions and death. But dismantled Free UK plans mean captures, arrests. Slatings and death sentences. Because of me, the Lorder grip is stronger than ever.

My fault. And Nico, still on the loose, his plans in disarray, will blame me. "He'll come after me," I say in a small voice, hating myself for saying it, and like that: an unspoken *protect me* behind it. I don't want help from Lorders.

"We'll be keeping an eye on things."

But why haven't they always kept an eye on things? "There is something I don't understand," I start to say, then pause. He says nothing—permission to continue? "If you were watching me, why not on Armstrong Memorial Day? Why'd I just get in? No questions, no checks. Nothing."

Is there a flash of anger in his eyes? It is gone so quickly I can't be sure. "That is not your concern." There is a knock at the door. "Time for you to go to the hospital," he says.

"One more thing," I dare to say as I stand. "You said you'd tell me what happened to my friend. Ben Nix."

He looks up. "Oh, yes. Ben. Unfortunately, he died," he says, but there is nothing on his face that takes in *unfortunately*. At best, disinterest, distaste.

The ground feels unstable under me, my knees wobbling. No. It can't be. Can it?

I pause at the door, look back. "What happened?" I choke out.

"Seizures when his Levo was cut. Don't worry, that can't happen to you today, not at the hospital."

I stumble out after the Lorder driver, relief almost tripping me up. For one horrible moment, I thought something had happened to Ben in these last days since I saw him running at that school. But no, he said it happened when his Levo was cut off. He's lying.

Soon I'm in Dr. Lysander's office at New London Hospital.

"I'm sorry," I start with, but she raises her hand, wraps it around her ear, mouths, *Later*. She must have found out her room is bugged.

"Today we are removing your Levo. There are no significant risks having this done in the hospital." She drones on about this, that and the other, while my mind wanders.

I grip my Levo at my wrist. It has been there a long time. Ruled my life when I first had it: Too much misery or anger and it caused painful blackouts; more, and it could have killed me.

Yet . . . some part of me still misses that control. It made it impossible to really feel pain past a certain level. And when it's gone, what then? Realization floods in all at once.

"Come along now, Kyla," Dr. Lysander says, standing by the door. We leave her office.

"I don't want it to come off. Does it have to?"

"No. At least, I don't think so; I could check how prescriptive is this Lorder request. But why keep it?"

"Everyone will know. I can never be the person I was."

"After everything that has happened, could you go back to being her in any event?" she asks gently. We get to the elevator, and again she cups a hand about her ear, shakes her head. The elevator is bugged, too?

We go down several flights to a treatment floor. Nurses bustle about, with patients in wheelchairs or unconscious on gurneys.

She beckons me into a small office. A man typing on a screen looks up; she gestures, and he leaves.

"Now we can talk properly," she says, and sits down. "What worries you about the Levo going?"

"The only way I could get rid of it and not be taken by Lorders is if they did it. Everyone will know. They'll think I'm some sort of Lorder spy."

"This is probably true. Yet do you think they won't suspect that, anyhow?"

And I think of the Lorder vans coming and going at our house, and all the missing people linked to me, however unfairly. Watchful eyes and voices that whisper will put things together. I sigh. "You're probably right."

"There is another consideration," she says.

"What is that?"

"Nico. Sources tell me he hasn't been captured. As long as you have that Levo, you are a visible Slated. He could revive his plan to use you in an attack, to show the world a Slated can be violent. Without it, he cannot."

"No. I'd never do it. He can only use me if I forget what happened, and I'm holding on to every detail." Years ago I was forced to forget the pain of my father's death at Nico's hands: Think how differently things would have been if I'd remembered? I would never have fallen under his spell.

"Shall we get on with this, then?" she says.

"First, I have a question."

"Go on."

"I have some fragments of memories from before I was taken by Free UK. But I don't remember anything of my home before, my mother—nothing. Can I get these memories back?"

"There are a few possibilities. Memories you have consciously suppressed as part of Rain's life may be accessible, but to find them, you need the right triggers. This personality fracture they induced? I don't know how deep, how far it went. If the other half was Slated, it should be gone, yet . . ." And her voice trails off, her eyes inward looking, thinking, and I force myself to stay quiet, not interrupt.

"There may be a way to get those back also," she says finally. "Surgically reconnect the severed paths to make them accessible once again. It is theoretically possible, but has never been attempted to my knowledge."

"What? I thought Slated means gone forever." My mind is spinning. "What about Ben? Could you reconnect stuff in his brain?"

"Ben? I told you, Kyla, that we have no record of his location. As hard as it is to accept, even if he lives, he is lost to you."

Should I tell her? Even though so many in my life have proven they aren't what they seem, after everything, and against all logic, she is one I trust.

"He isn't."

"He isn't what?"

"Dead, or lost. I know where he is."

Dr. Lysander's shock is strong when I explain Ben's whereabouts, and how he is: no idea who I am, but not like a new Slated.

"This is very disturbing," she finally says. "Anything they do there is unsanctioned by the Medical Council. Unethical."

"Slating is ethical?"

She looks up sharp. "It is," she says, but on her face are traces of doubt. "Would you rather have faced a death sentence? Like my friend, all those years ago."

"How can I know? I don't remember!" The words are bitter. But I'm fixed on what she said before. "So you could change Ben back."

She shakes her head. "No. I don't know what has been done to him. It would be far too risky to even consider."

"Risky, but possible?"

"Theoretically, maybe. Now. We've been in here too long. Come along; let's get that Levo off."

Minutes later, it is gone, my wrist an empty expanse of skin, that is somehow *wrong*. Naked. Hospital removal was a simple matter of a machine, pushing some buttons, and watching it spring apart, undone.

I feel conspicuous, different.

As if a big flashing sign floats over my head: *See the Lorder spy!*

Back in her office, Dr. Lysander opens her computer, motions me over to look, but keeps talking about nothing and everything at the same time.

She goes into my records. My Levo number: 19418.

She pauses, consults a list on-screen that says *Inactive Numbers*. Changes my number to 18736.

I shake my head, not understanding.

On a slip of paper she writes a single word: *untraceable*.

It is only when I am halfway home in the Lorder van that I realize: If I'm untraceable now, that implies I was not before. All she did was change my number on the computer, the same number that was on my Levo. How could I have been traceable with that number without my Levo?

But there is something else. Something inside me: the chip in my brain that worked with my Levo. That is still there.

I feel sick inside when it hits me: Coulson, tapping on his head when I asked how Cam tracked me. The chip in my head, put in when I was Slated. They must be tracker chips. Like they use in dogs.

Now that Dr. Lysander has altered my records, changed my number, they can't use mine to find me anymore.

Untraceable.

48

"**You can't hide in the house forever,**" Mum says.

"I know."

She kisses my forehead, then marches out into the drizzle and cold to her car for work. Amy has already left for school with Jazz, and Mum's patience is wearing thin on my refusal to join them.

I retreat back to bed with a cup of tea, a place I've been spending a lot of time lately. I know she's right, but it's as if I'm in suspended animation. My stitches are out, wounds nearly healed, but inside, I'm processing things that happened, learning to live with loss, pain. Memories. A new experience for someone who was forced to forget.

And questions are niggling away inside. I used to think getting caught when I was with Free UK, getting Slated, was just bad luck. I found I was wrong. Nico engineered it. I've lost the ability to accept coincidences; there are too many of them in my life. I just happened to be placed after Slating with Sandra Armstrong, the daughter of the Lorder hero? I just happened to be a Jane Doe, someone who miraculously has no DNA records that can be traced? They just happened to make a mistake on cell tests with my date of birth, so Slated me even though I was over sixteen? The Lorders never noticed a girl who looked just like me on the MIA website and worked out who I was?

And all that happened on Armstrong Memorial Day: It isn't like Nico to have left so much to chance. And Coulson just overlooked having me monitored, searched, on that day of all days?

Behind all my unanswered questions, vague ideas and plans are forming in the background, and one Ben-shaped necessity. But it's almost as if I am gathering my strength, waiting for something. For what, I don't know.

Then it happens.

Bzzzz . . . bzzzz . . .

A slight noise, more a vibration, and without thought, I automatically reach for my wrist to where my Levo used to be.

Bzzzz . . . bzzzz . . .

My eyes fly open wide with shock. Nico's com; it mimics the buzz of a Levo. I stashed it in my room, tossed it in a drawer before dashing off to rescue Dr. Lysander. In case it was a tracker.

Bzzzz . . . bzzzz . . .

What do I do? I swallow. Better to know . . .

I fish it out of the bottom of the drawer where it lay hidden and forgotten all this time, and push the button.

"What?"

"Hello, Rain," a voice says, one I can never forget: Nico.

"That isn't my name. Not anymore."

"A rose by any other name would smell as sweet . . ."

"Cut the bull. I remember you killed my father."

"Ah. Was that the reason for the treachery, Rain?" His voice is cold. "No matter. We can begin again! All will be forgotten."

"Never. Anyhow, the Lorders had my Levo removed, so I'm of no use to you now, Nico. Come up with another plan."

I switch it off before he can reply, trembling. Will he accept my word, move on? Just let it go?

Not the Nico I know and hate.

And then I can't stand having anything of him here, in my room, in this house, for even a second longer. I rush to the open window and chuck the com out as far as I can. Once it leaves my hand I realize I'll have to find and destroy it another time. Stupid. I watch as it glints in the early light, arcs partway across the lawn. Rests near the oak tree.

I shut the window, turn back to bed, and—

BANG!

A wave of sound and something else pushes me across the room. I fall on the floor. Winded. Pain. I groan. Pull myself up, realize I'm covered in glass. Broken glass from the window. Stunned, confused. Smoke billows in, and I cough. What is happening?

I stagger to the window. The tree is on fire. What is left of it.

The same tree Nico's com rested near seconds earlier.

I stare, disbelieving. The com didn't double as a tracker, but as a bomb?

The shock of realization nearly knocks me from my feet. Nico insisting I couldn't let him down, then his anger that I wasn't at the second ceremony at Chequers. An outside ceremony, so no signal block like there would have been in the house. A ceremony where I would have been standing next to my family and the current Lorder prime minister. The great and the good all around, as Cam called them. Nico didn't just have a plan B; he had a plan C, too. Unknowingly, I was to be his suicide bomber. When they sifted through the rubble and found what was left of me to be the carrier of the bomb, with an AGT gun strapped to my arm, they'd have no doubt: a Slated who was beyond just *violent*. It would strike at all the Lorders do. Make all the Slateds a risk the Lorders couldn't tolerate.

Nico was going to kill all of us at that ceremony, but I ruined it by running off to rescue Dr. Lysander. No wonder he was so angry!

And now Nico has remote detonated it to kill me. Either he

believed me when I said my Levo was gone, or he decided revenge was more use to him than anything else he could do with me.

Or maybe he just called first, to make sure I had it on me.

A giggle starts working its way up my throat.

Settle!

But I can't help it, and soon I'm crouched on the floor, laughing, wincing at the pain the movement gives my cut back.

Nico thinks I'm dead. And I laugh harder.

And I'm *untraceable* by the Lorders. Thanks to Dr. Lysander.

Before the thought is fully formed, I'm on my feet, stuffing a few things in a bag. Hastily checking my back in the mirror: just minor cuts. Some blood, but that has lost the power to unnerve me it used to hold. I throw clothes on and clench my teeth when pulling a sweater over my head. Physical pain I can ignore. Quick, now.

Sebastian appears at the bedroom door, fur and tail completely fluffed out. That is one seriously freaked cat. There is a pang inside as I pick him up, give him a quick cuddle. "I wish I could take you with me, but I can't. Look after Mum and Amy."

Another pang: a note for Mum? No. I can't. Someone else may find it. I'll get word to her, somehow.

Sirens are starting up the road by the time I push through the back hedge and disappear up the canal path.

All those half-formed plans in my mind, the ones I might do one day?

One day, is now.

49

IT IS A LONG TRIP IN THE DARK WITHOUT ONE OF KATRAN'S trail bikes. On an ancient bicycle instead, bouncing around the canal and footpaths in the middle of the night. I'd allowed loads of time so it is still dark when I arrive.

Guilt, I'd felt, sneaking out without a word to Mac, after everything he's done for me, letting me hide out at his house while I work out what to do. Guilt, likewise, for borrowing his rickety bicycle without asking. But the thing I realized more and more was this: I couldn't make any steps forward, without taking one step back.

I stash the bicycle in the woods.

This time, it will be different. I will be different, having thought it through with care.

What if he doesn't come?

He will come. He has to. I can't accept any other possibility, even as the fear of it gnaws inside.

I stash the dark camo gear I wore over my clothes for the trip. Hat off; brush hair until it shines. A pale green running top, warm yet fitted, that Ben once said brings out the color of my eyes.

The sky is barely beginning to lighten as I warm up. A distant figure appears at the brow of the hill: Ben! I almost melt with relief. Shaking with so many emotions I can barely work out what they are, I run up the path. Fast. So that as he comes over the hill I am in full view.

He won't be able to resist trying to pass me. Will he?

But he won't be able to.

I hear him closing in behind, and bit by bit increase my pace so he almost, but can't quite, catch up. Feeling the strain, the effort. The joy of speed. I slip back slightly, and then it happens. We run side by side. That familiar skittering music of feet: his *thud-thud* and my shorter-legged beats in between. I glance up at his face just as he looks down at mine. He grins, wide, and is so much the Ben I knew that my feet falter, and he pulls ahead. But then he drops pace so I can keep up.

Finally we both slow, dropping to a walk.

He is laughing. "Brilliant run!" he says, and I smile. It feels as though I am lit up inside, and all I am is there to see, plain on my face. Like I used to be. It is so easy to forget, to pretend that nothing happened. That we are just Ben and Kyla. Friends, and then more, with uncomplicated lives, families. A possible future together. I ache to reach out, clasp his hand. Stop and pull him close, and—

But we're not those phantoms. Not anymore.

"You're that girl," he says, and I hold still. Does some part of him recognize, or feel who I am? *That girl*—no. He must remember the other time on this path. "The one who said she knew me," he says, confirming. "But I'd remember you."

"Would you?" I laugh. The sunrise is properly under way now. Warm light in a cold morning on our faces.

"I'm going to be late. We came too far," he says, and reverses direction. "Run back?"

"Not yet. We need to talk."

"Do we? What about?"

"Who are you?"

"Can't answer that. I'm on a secret mission." He says the words like he is kidding around, playing some game, but something is behind them. "Who are you?"

"I'm on a secret mission, too. But I can tell you a story. One that was."

"Go on," he says, still Ben in his eyes: curious, wanting to know everything I am inside, like he always did.

"Once upon a time, there was a Slated boy named Ben, who loved to run. He met a Slated girl with a few problems: Let's call her Kyla. But she loved to run, too. They became . . . friends. More than friends." I blush.

"Ben—that's what you called me the last time."

"Yes."

And I see the realization in his eyes. "I've got good taste in girls, even in fairy tales," he says, still light, teasing. Curious.

"But now is where it gets difficult." My smile falls away. "Listen, Ben, or whoever you are now. You've been re-Slated, or treated somehow to forget. I don't know how, or why. Don't believe what you are told. The old you fought to think for himself! He believed there could be a better way than the Lorders' way."

He stares into my eyes, something inside him thinking, considering, for a few heartbeats. Then the look is gone along with his smile. "This is indeed a fairy tale," he says. "Time for me to go now, dream girl." And he takes off running, back the way he came. I stop myself, just, from chasing after him, and slip into shadows under the trees. Fighting not to cry at the cold vacuum created by his absence.

I did the best I could. Did I achieve anything?

For a moment, there was something in his eyes, some trace of thought. I didn't imagine it! Have I planted a seed of doubt that will grow into something strong enough to withstand what has been done to him, what is being fed to him in that Lorder place?

I pull my dark clothes back over my running clothes and get on the bicycle to start the long ride back to Mac's. Thinking of what I said, what I could have said that was better, and—

When it hits me, I almost fall from the bike.

Dream girl, he called me. Has he been dreaming about me? Like I dream about the past, and lost memories. Am I still there, hiding, in his subconscious?

Somewhere inside is a glimmer, a feeling. It is warm and unfamiliar, and I hold on to it, hug it tight.

It is hope.

Late that night I'm at Mac's, sitting at his computer. Lucy's face—my face, from so many years ago—fills the screen on the MIA website. She was Missing in Action, but not any longer.

Aiden sits next to me.

"Are you sure you want to do this?" he asks, his dark blue eyes intent, and kind. Not pressing, even though I know how much he wants this.

"Yes," I say. And I am; so sure. Dad said *never forget who you are,* but I did. I failed him. There is only one thing I can do to try to fix it: I owe it to him to find out who Lucy was. Who I was. And there is no other way to find the missing bits of myself than this.

Who reported me missing? With my dad gone, is it the mother I cannot remember, or someone else? There is only one way to find out.

I take the mouse, and click the box: Lucy Connor is *found.*

Turn the page for a sneak peek
at the final book in the trilogy

SHATTERED

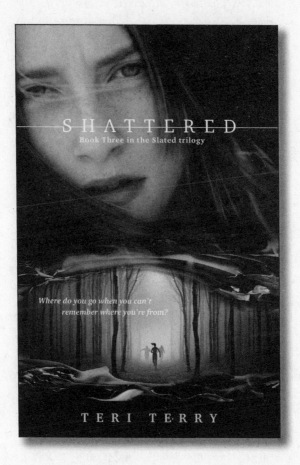

1

IT DOESN'T LOOK LIKE MUCH FROM THE OUTSIDE. BUT WHAT you get outside is often like that. People, especially, can be so different from what you can see that you'd never guess what goes on in their secret places. What they are capable of. In my case, what lurked within was so well hidden even I didn't know about it.

Aiden parks the car along the side of the run-down building. He glances at me. "Don't look so scared, Kyla."

"I'm not," I start to object, but then I glance at the road, and all at once, I am. "Lorders," I hiss, and scrunch down in the seat. A black van pulls in behind us, blocking us in. Leaden dread pools in my veins, holds me still and numb even as everything inside is screaming *run*. The fear takes me back: another time, another Lorder. Coulson. The gun in his hand, pointed at me, and then—

Bang!

Katran's blood. A sea of hot red that covered us both, and took my friend away forever. So like my father's death years ago that it wrenched up that most buried memory. Both dead. Both my fault.

Aiden puts a hand over mine, one worried eye on the mirror and the van, one on me. A door opens; someone steps out. Not dressed in Lorder black? A slight figure, a woman, hat pulled down low to shield her face. She walks to the door of the building. It opens from the inside, and she disappears through it.

"Look at me, Kyla," Aiden says, his voice calm, reassuring, and I tear my eyes away from the van behind us. "There is nothing to worry about; just don't draw their attention." He twists in the driver's seat, slips his arms around me and tries to pull me close, but I'm rigid with fear. "Play along," he says, and I force my body to relax into his. He murmurs into my hair, "Just giving them a reason why we were lingering. In case they're getting curious."

I breathe in slow. *They're not after me.* They'll go away now. *They're not after me.* And then I'm clinging to Aiden, and his arms wrap around me even tighter. There are vehicle sounds behind; tires crunch on gravel. And keep going.

"They're gone," Aiden says, but he doesn't let go. And the relief is so strong that I sag against him, bury my face in his chest. His heart beats fast, drumming a *thump-thump* of safety, warmth, and something *else*.

But this is wrong. He's not Ben.

My fear is replaced by embarrassment, then anger: anger at myself. I pull away. How could I be such a total wimp and let them get to me like that? How could I cling to Aiden just because I was scared? And I remember what he said on the way earlier: Lorders come here. Lorders, government officials, and their families. People with money and power who can make others look away and keep quiet. That woman is probably a Lorder's wife. She is probably here for the same reason as me. I flush.

Aiden's blue eyes are warm, concerned. "Are you sure you can pull this off, Kyla?"

"Yes. Of course I can. And I thought you weren't supposed to call me that anymore."

"It'd be easier if you'd make up your mind what your new name is going to be."

I don't say anything, because I sort of have, but I don't want to share it yet. I'm not sure he'll like it.

"Walk in like you own the place, and no one will look at you twice. It's all anonymous."

"Okay."

"Best get going before anyone else comes."

More Lorders?

I open the car door, step out. It is cold, a gray January day. The chill is reason enough for the scarf wrapped around my head, obscuring an identity that will soon change. I square my shoulders, walk to the door. It opens, and I step inside.

My eyes widen; my feet almost falter until I remember: *Walk like I own the place.* This shiny place, with enormous, plush chairs, soft music, and a smiling nurse? A guard stands discrete in the corner. The woman we saw come out of the Lorder van moments ago is ensconced in a chair with a wineglass in one hand.

The nurse approaches, smiles. "Welcome. Do you know your number?"

"7162," I say, the number Aiden gave me earlier. Even though my name is best kept quiet, I'm not sure I like being known by a number, not after being Slated. Not after having a Levo around my wrist with my number carved into it, classifying me as a criminal for all to see. It's gone now; there are no visible marks left behind, but the scars remain.

The nurse checks a handheld screen, smiles again. "Have a seat for a moment. Your IMET consultant will be with you very soon."

I sit, startled when the chair moves, adjusts to my body. IMET:

Image Enhancement Technology. Barely whispered about, hellishly expensive, and totally illegal. I'm here courtesy of favors owed to Aiden's organization, MIA. MIA may stand for Missing in Action, but it turns out they don't just find missing people and campaign for the truth about the Lorders to be revealed. Turns out they also sneak people out of the UK who need to disappear, and others in at the same time: IMET consultants who know a good black market opportunity when they see one.

The woman in the other chair turns toward me. She is attractive, fifty or so. If the rumors are true, she'll look twenty years younger before she leaves this place. There is an inquisitive glint to her eyes, a *What are you here for?* look. I ignore her.

A door opens, and footsteps approach. She starts to get up, but the steps continue past her, and a man stops in front of me. A doctor? But not like any doctor I've seen before. He is in scrubs, but they are a bright purple shimmery fabric. It matches his streaked hair and purple eyes to perfection, unnatural shimmer and all.

He holds out both hands, helps me up, and air-kisses my cheeks. "Hello, darling. I'm Doc de Jour, but you can call me DJ. This way." His words are a lilting drawl, an unfamiliar accent: Irish?

I follow him and suppress a smirk at the indignant look on the waiting woman's face. She must wonder who I am, why I take precedence. If she only knew.

If she knew, it'd go straight to her Lorder husband.

Doc de Jour is disappointed in me. "Are you *sure* that is all you want done? Hair. In *brown*." He says it like brown hair is the ultimate crime of mediocrity. But blending in is what I need.

"Yes: brown."

He sighs. "Such lovely hair you have, and so hard to match. Like sunshine on early daffodils 12. With highlights 9." He runs his fingers through it, a measuring look in his eyes, like he is copying it for his next patient. Then he studies my face. "How about eye color?"

"No. I like them green."

"They're distinctive; it's a risk," he says, and my eyes widen. What does he know? He winks. "They *are* an interesting shade. Almost apple-green 26, but more intense," he says, then spins the chair I'm sitting in around and looks me up and down. I squirm. "Wouldn't you like to be taller?"

I raise an eyebrow. "You can do that?"

"Of course. It'll take a while, though."

I bristle. "What is wrong with my height?"

"Nothing. If you don't mind jumping to see over things."

"Just the hair."

"Brown. You know IMET is accelerated gene-tech: It is permanent. Brown hair forever. It'll grow that way; no more blondy ever again, unless you come back to see me."

He hands me a mirror, and I look in it. So weird to think next time I do this I won't see the hair I've always had. The color is okay, I guess, but it is so fine—I always wanted thicker hair. Like Amy's gorgeous dark hair, the first thing I'd noticed about my new sister when I was assigned to live with her family as a new Slated, just months ago. "Wait a minute. I wonder if . . ."

He leans down and stares into my eyes with his purple ones. They're hard not to look at. "Yes?"

"Can you make it longer? And thicker. Maybe . . . some streaks in it. Not anything weird: natural-looking."

He claps his hands. "Consider it done."

. . .

Later I'm told to lie back on a table that is like the chairs in the waiting area: It molds and grips my body. Flutters of panic fight to keep me awake. Is this how it was when I was Slated? Then, I had no choice; I saw the file photograph. I was tied to a table like any other criminal. The Lorders and their surgery stole my memories, put a chip in my brain that could've killed me before my Levo was taken off. This isn't the same. This is just hair. And it is my choice: I don't *have* to do this.

There is faint music. Everything is misty and vague, and my eyes start to close.

Just hair . . . but it is *the* hair Ben slipped his fingers through when he kissed me.

Since the Lorders took him away and erased his memory, he doesn't know who I am anymore. But what if he fights it, fights what the Lorders have done to him, and starts to remember? Starts to understand why I'm his *dream girl*. What then? He'll never find me if I look different.

I swallow, struggle to form words, to tell them to stop, I changed my mind.

Ben . . .

Faces blur in and out and vanish.

We run. Side by side in the night, but Ben's long legs beat out a slower measure than mine. It is raining, but we don't care. Up a dark hill now, he slips ahead; the narrow path cut into rock is running with water. Soon we're soaked and covered in mud. He's laughing when he reaches the top, and raises his hands to the sky as the rain pounds harder.

"Ben!" I reach up, slip my arms around him, and pull him under a tree, then burrow into his warmth.

But something isn't right.

"Ben?" I pull away a little, look into familiar eyes: brown like melted chocolate, shot through with warm glints. Puzzled eyes. "What is it?"

He shakes his head, pushes me away. "I don't understand."

"What?"

"I thought I knew you, but I don't. Do I?"

"It's me! It's . . ." My voice trails away. I panic inside, casting about for a name, not just any name, but my name. Who am I, really?

He shakes his head, walks away. Runs up the path and is gone.

I sag against the tree. What now? Should I run after him, just so he can deny me again? Or go back the other way, alone.

The sky lights up: A blinding flash dazzles my eyes, shows the trees and pounding rain. Before darkness returns, a tremendous crash shakes into my bones.

While the rest of me whirls with pain at Ben's departure, some part of my brain processes: Standing under a tree in a thunderstorm is dangerous.

But who am I, really? Until I can answer, I don't know which way to go.

2

DAYS LATER, DJ HANDS ME A MIRROR FOR THE FIRST TIME. I stare, then reach out gingerly with my fingers. The hair—my hair— even *feels* different, foreign. I don't look like me anymore. Of course, that is kind of the point. A rich brown it may be, but shimmering with golden highlights. They bring out the green of my eyes so much that I stare at them suspiciously, wondering if DJ had been unable to resist adding some enhancement to them as well, but decide they are still the eyes I was born with. My hair is not, not in any respect: It's silky, thick, halfway down my back. I wince as I turn my head: It's heavy, so much so it hurts. It'll take some getting used to.

"Your scalp will be tender for a while." DJ holds up a small bottle. "Painkillers, no more than two a day for a week. So . . . ?"

I tear my eyes away from the mirror, and look up at him. "So?"

"Do you like what you see?"

I smile broadly. "I like."

"One final touch is needed, I think." DJ places a finger on either side of my chin, tilts my face up and stares at my eyes. He stares long enough for it to be uncomfortable if it were anyone else, but somehow it isn't with him. It is like he is measuring, and assessing—what? The skin, the bone structure supporting it, the tissues, almost as though if he stares long enough he can see the individual cells and the genes inside them. He nods to himself, then turns to a cabinet with many drawers; he opens one, then another, and draws something out, then holds it toward me. Something low-tech.

"Glasses? I don't need glasses."

"Trust me. Put them on," he says. I do, and look in the mirror. Startled, I gasp; look back at him, then again at the mirror.

The frames are a delicate silvery-gray metal and suit my face as if made for it, but that isn't what made me gasp: It's my eyes. The lenses are completely clear, yet somehow, I am changed. My eyes aren't green anymore. More a blue-gray. I turn my head side to side, take the glasses off, put them back on again. Study myself like looking at a stranger. This dark-haired girl is *other*. She looks older, too. No one would recognize her. Not just Ben; I could walk past Mum and Amy in the street, and they'd be none the wiser.

"That's amazing. You're amazing."

"Why, yes, I am." He smiles. "And this technology"—he touches the glasses—"isn't known in the UK, at least not yet. So wearing them shouldn't arouse any suspicions." He spins my chair around so we are facing each other again. "So. The green-eyed blond girl is gone, re-placed by a more sophisticated version, one who can pass for the eighteen you need for ID and travel if necessary. What is next for you?" I hesitate, and he laughs. "Keep your secrets. I hope—no, I am sure—we will cross paths again."

"Thanks for everything."

He tilts his head, something in his eyes still measuring, assessing. "What is it?"

He shakes his head. "Nothing, and everything. Time for you to go." He holds the door open. As I step through it, he adds, "Tell Aiden I need to see him."

. . .

Later that day I'm in a small room hidden in the back of a factory. A dark room where new identities are forged. New lives begin.

"Name?" an unidentified man asks.

This is the moment. I'm not Lucy, the name given when I was born. I'm not Rain, the name I eventually chose for myself after I was taken by Nico and his Antigovernment Terrorists—Free UK, as he called them—and shaped to be their weapon against the Lorders. I'm not Kyla, the name picked for me at the hospital after I was caught and Slated for being an AGT terrorist.

I am who I choose to be.

"Name?" the question is repeated.

I am none of them. I am all of them.

"Riley. Riley Kain," I answer, one name that combines them all.

Soon I clutch a forged ID card in my hand: a dark-haired, gray-eyed eighteen-year-old cleared to travel and live her own life: Riley Kain.

What life do I choose to live?

3

THE BUS RATTLES DOWN CITY, THEN COUNTRY, ROADS. NO
more hiding needed with my new ID and new look, and I'd insisted
on traveling back from London by myself. But who could have known
an AGT bomb would be found on one of the London trains today, the
entire network shut down while they were all checked? So the bus
was the only option. Every jar of the road reverberates through my
sore head, and I have to hold my hands together to stop them from
gathering my new hair up to support its weight.

Fields, farms, and villages rush past, become familiar. We're
nearing the village I lived in with Mum and Amy, the one I left the
day Nico and his remote-detonated AGT bomb nearly killed me. I
ran away to hide at Mac's. Mac is a friend, yes, and one I trust, but
he hasn't known me for long to take such a risk. He is the cousin of
Amy's boyfriend, and somehow involved with Aiden and MIA. Without knowing or insisting on knowing all that happened—what I've
done, or why—he and Aiden were there, offering help. A safe place
to hide. A chance at a new life. The old one with Mum and Amy
ended just a short time ago, but already it feels distant, another life
slipping away.

A long black car approaches from the other direction, a coffin in
the back, and traffic slows to a crawl on both sides. A second black car
follows the hearse. It has two occupants, arms linked: one young,

with dark hair and skin, one older and pale. In a flash, they are gone. My eyes widen.

That was Mum and Amy.